Snake Road

Sue Peebles

Chatto & Windus
LONDON

Published by Chatto & Windus 2013

2 4 6 8 10 9 7 5 3 1

First published in Great Britain in 2013 by
Chatto & Windus
Random House, 20 Vauxhall Bridge Road,
London SW1V 2SA
www.vintage-books.co.uk

Addresses for companies within The Random House Group Limited can be found at:
www.randomhouse.co.uk/offices.htm

The Random House Group Limited Reg. No. 954009

A CIP catalogue record for this book
is available from the British Library

ISBN 9780701187637

The Random House Group Limited supports the Forest Stewardship Council®
(FSC®), the leading international forest-certification organisation. Our books
carrying the FSC label are printed on FSC®-certified paper. FSC is the only
forest-certification scheme supported by the leading environmental organisations,
including Greenpeace. Our paper procurement policy can be found at
www.randomhouse.co.uk/environment

Typeset in Bembo by Palimpsest Book Production Limited,
Falkirk, Stirlingshire

Printed and bound in Great Britain by
CPI Group (UK) Ltd, Croydon, CR0 4YY

for Charis

A Clear Midnight

This is thy hour O Soul, thy free flight into the wordless,
Away from books, away from art, the day erased, the lesson done,
Thee fully forth emerging, silent, gazing, pondering the themes
thou lovest best,
Night, sleep, death and the stars.

Walt Whitman

So Soreen

THIS IS all I have to go on, this waxen face slipping under a July moon. I often gaze at it. Sometimes during the bright summer nights I prop myself up on one elbow and watch him sleep. He looks much older asleep than awake. Already his skin has started to sag a little and the slight slip towards the pillow creates lines he hasn't seen yet, an emerging map of cutaneous folds that suggest the older man. In particular, the flesh of his cheek slides nose-ward, giving him a hoggish look.

I wonder where he came from?

Awake, he is boyish, needs a good scrub. Mud freckles all over his clavicle and up his neck, but not on his face. His face is clear. 'Such a lovely complexion,' his mother said, in a tone that suggested his skin made up for something else, the hair perhaps, or the femurs that weren't quite long enough. 'Just an inch would make all the difference.' Diana Thackeray has a way of saying things, marking the place where a 'but' ought to be with a tiny, silent barb. She and her husband David adopted Alasdair when he was just a baby, a tabula rasa with no previous history and no other claimants. I can imagine their optimism, the joy of finding a baby so entirely theirs, but that notion of entirety was

1

where they went wrong, I think. They failed to reckon on the ghost in the machine.

I suspect Alasdair blames himself for what happened. Of course, no one's to blame; blame doesn't come into it. But if anyone *is* to blame it's me, although I probably haven't really said so, or at least, not in a very convincing way, possibly because I think he can carry the blame more easily, having had all that practice.

WE WERE in the orchard when Alasdair first warned me about his general culpability, how he had learned from a very young age that things were usually his fault. I was lying in a hammock, dangling between two old apple trees, wishing I'd never climbed in because when I did I dropped like a dead weight cut loose. With the trees too close and the hammock too old there wasn't the tautness needed to support me in the easy elegance I had envisaged, where my body settles into a wave of gentle curves, slight and careless and swaying in the summer breeze like a Fijian palm. Instead, I condensed into a great ungainly bulge, as if in a sack. There was no fighting it, my only option was to roll out sideways, but suddenly Alasdair was talking and although I couldn't see him, the source and carry of his voice told me he was lying on the grass with his face to the sun. He must have closed his eyes and it felt important to listen and not distract him. He was telling me how lucky I was to have grown up in such an extraordinary place with such a lovely family.

'Your sun is amazing,' he said. 'It's so bright, even in the trees.'

And right away I knew there was something unusual about him, or at least something unusual about his relationship to the world.

'It's your sun too.'

'No, it's not.'

In the pause I listened to the starlings blethering in exotic riffs.

'My mother—' He stopped. I heard his body stretch, a long sigh; imagined his hands clasped behind his head, his feet probably crossed.

'My mother—'

But he had no words for her, and things petered out. I sensed a beginning, though, the start of something. The jungle chatter of birds rose and fell and I knew that by the time the starlings left we would be together. I tumbled from the hammock as gracefully as I could, levering myself round on the heel of my hands and landing beside him. He was lying exactly as I had pictured him. I propped myself up on one elbow and took my first long look at his face. It was quite an audacious thing to do, I suppose, since we hadn't long met, but that's when you stare the longest, at the beginning, and again at the end – just as I am doing now.

I'M NOT sure what happened that day in the orchard, whether it was love or something else, but as we walked back to the house I felt different. I know Alasdair felt different too, having spoken for the first time about the persistent cloud of disappointment that had tainted his childhood – the sense that whatever he did, he fell short. For instance, when he told his mother that he had scored a ninety-eight in chemistry it was the missing two per cent that struck home. 'What happened?' she'd said, and explaining the consequences of mistaking an alkane for an alkene only made things worse, her patience running out when he confessed to the erroneous double bond. She was often angry with him, sometimes for reasons he didn't understand; not that she ever hit him – Diana (call-me-Di) Thackeray abhorred violence of any kind so nothing like that went on, it was all in the looks, the sudden cold that might descend at any moment. He called it the grey mist and said it was always out there, hanging about — each sunny day bringing the possibility of haar. When Alasdair told me this there wasn't a trace of self-pity or anger in his voice, but there was sadness, and I sensed something else about him, an oddness I liked, so different from anyone I had been involved with before.

'Christ, I haven't thought about that for years. It's all coming back. Saturated hydrocarbons. Oh my God.'

He spoke slowly, and there was a fondness somewhere — as if Saturated Hydrocarbons were an old friend back from the dead after twenty years. While he lay on the grass with his eyes closed and enjoying the sun I gazed at the freckles spilling out from the neck of his shirt, then slowly I worked my way down to his feet and back again, back to those beguiling marks. They were drawing me in, tempting me downwards. I wanted to lie with him, clamber on top of him there and then, and I might have, but we were positioned quite close to the house and despite the trees we were probably visible, certainly from the upstairs windows. I sat up to drink from the small bottle of water that he had carried with him all afternoon as if it were an elixir, something to mask the taste of an unpalatable life. As I unscrewed the cap I noticed how symmetrical he was, his forearms extending from his head to form a neat kite-mark; log-straight body and legs tied at the ankles. It was a strong, confident pose, but I could see he was shielding himself, his brawny limbs flexed against whatever might assail him, even here amongst the soft mosses and ancient trees. Already falling for this unexpected treasure lying in the grass, I tipped the bottle to my lips and took a long drink. The water was so delicious I scanned the label, searching for the source — a mountain spring in the Cuillins, its tumult a blend of glacier melt, warm snow running down my throat, and the temptations of idle love.

★

4

FIRST AND foremost there was pleasure. Body and brain pleasure, the taking and the giving of, each as seductive as the other. It began with brain. We met at a British Psychological Society talk entitled 'Anomalous Memory'. These university talks were open to the public and each free ticket entitled you to one glass of wine. Tickets collected beforehand were limited to two per person, and it was when we collided at the wine table for the second time that we remembered colliding the first time, fifteen minutes earlier.

'Did we just meet, before?'

'Possibly.'

Normally this would have been a straightforward recollection, but we had just listened to a Ph.D. student from Bristol explain the various theoretical perspectives of déjà vu, so we weren't sure. I was in my second year at university and had come along because my gran was losing her memory, but not in a straightforward, amusingly forgetful way, she was remembering too, talking about the strangest things, things she'd never spoken of before. Hard to describe or understand, it was as if for each forgotten thing she would conjure up another, from further back.

Clever really, but then she is.

Dad says I've got her brain and I've always been very happy about that, but less so now. I thought from the title of the talk that I might learn something new about how memory works. Alasdair had come along because he was interested in amnesia, for reasons he didn't explain to me until much later. Frankly, there was enough in that one talk to keep us braining for a lifetime. And it wasn't just neuro-chemistry, we spoke about neurophysics too; not long after that day of strange resurrections in the orchard we moved on to bodies. I was leaning towards a theory of cryptamnesia whilst Alasdair had concluded that déjà vu was nothing more than one eye catching up with the other.

'There's only one way to settle this,' he said.

'How?'

'We need to approach it more scientifically by removing as many uncontrolled variables as possible.'

Then, using no discernible method, we took off our clothes.

FOR THE rest of the summer we spent most of our free time together, neglecting friends and family yet loving them more than ever in that resurgent, generous way that sweeps over you when you yourself feel loved. I still drove back to the house every Sunday to spend time with Gran, and each time she made the same observation based simply on what she saw before her.

'You're happy!'

Mum said it too, but was more cautious.

'You seem happy today, Aggie.'

Dad didn't say anything as such, but he might hum a song as he pulled on his jacket – something schmaltzy like 'Love is a Many Splendored Thing' . . .

Which it was.

The starlings began to gather and flock over the Tay, an impossible Escher cloud cutting from light to dark. Autumn was tinder-dry and crisp, the trees petrified and the sharp splinters of grass frosting the earth, wondrous through our crystal lens. Keen-eyed and new, we delighted in all of it, even the darkness, *especially* the darkness – all that night to make love in! By January (lovely January, long and dark and piercingly cold) we were married. Alasdair wanted me to take the Thackeray name, which surprised me but didn't bother me, since it didn't matter. What mattered was our own family – the one we were now so set upon creating; less braining and more brooding, making love in a bluebell wood, our bodies sticky in the crushed stems.

Spring was a rushed affair. We didn't take it in properly

– the blossom and the birds and the smell of wild garlic. I suppose we assumed there'd be another just like it. Suddenly it was summer and still nothing had stuck; the bluebell glue hadn't worked. Mum said we should stop worrying and just take our time, we were both still young, and anyway, I had my degree to finish. 'Focus on that,' she said, sounding odd because she was holding a peg between her teeth, hanging out the washing with her face to the wind and the sheet smacking against her body. I was lying on the garden bench like a spirit level, flat out and unable to help because I'd spent the morning with Alasdair having urgent sex and was keen to let everything settle.

With the sheet tethered she carried the basket back and threw it into the porch so it wouldn't blow away.

'Budge up.'

I moved, but only slightly since she took up so little room. Letting her shoulders drop she slowly rotated her head to ease her neck.

'She's so much worse, Aggie. I don't know what's going to happen.'

She wiped the damp sting from her eyes and closed them against the warm wind. I closed mine too, joined her in the true dark, where everything is stored. We were both thinking of Gran and remembering how things were; different recollections, of course, but the feeling the same. I'd already seen Mum engage in small acts of longing – resting her hand on the back of Gran's chair, or setting then un-setting her place at the table because she prefers to eat in her room now, where things are familiar. At first this change of habit brought a kind of liberation. We no longer needed to spread out the tablecloth or fiddle about with cups and saucers – all that washing-up! And the teapot, clad in its ghastly knitted cosy and topped with a woolly rose, no longer sat in the middle of the table. Meals were eaten with less ceremony and ended more quickly once we gave up the cheeseboard, and although nobody missed the stewed tea and the Cracker Barrel cheddar that Gran swore protected her bones, we all missed her, so Mum restored some of the ritual, beginning with the table-cloth (to protect the table), then the saucers (to protect the cloth), and so on. The cosy, however, went on Gran's tray, since we felt sure that she would miss it, despite having no memory of it.

A fragrance rose from the laundry and blew over us, scenting the air. I couldn't recall the sheets ever smelling like that before, a sickly perfume that reminded me of the Silver Jubilee soap Gran had kept since 1977, not because she was a royalist but because the box might come in handy. That soap had been in the family longer than me. Lying on my back with my feet resting against Mum's thighbone, I was trying to picture her and Gran as younger women, mother and daughter sitting here on the same bench sunning them-selves, when suddenly the wind dropped and they were gone. This terrible prospect seemed to come from nowhere, imposing a momentary stillness before a slight hush in the grasses bore them both back. It was almost immediate, but nevertheless I was scalded by this small fright, pushed upright and catching my breath in the thin air.

Mum moved closer in and we both held on to the outside strut of the bench as if we were bracing ourselves, our arms locked straight and a slight lean into the wind.

I went back to the start, to what we were talking about when she first came out with the washing. I was trying to explain the urgency of things, how I felt weakened by a dogged sense of time running out, and that it was all somehow connected to Gran.

'I think that's why I'm in such a hurry to have this baby, so she can meet her great-grandmother. I want them to get to know one another.'

Mum let go of the bench and started brushing pollen from her long black sleeves. She was frowning, still picking her sleeve as she spoke.

'You shouldn't keep saying *this baby*, you know. You can't just make one up.'

WHEN AT last we did make one I knew right away. I didn't test for another two weeks because although I was sure, I wanted Alasdair to be sure too, and even then a clear blue positive wasn't enough. He insisted on coming with me to the clinic. The moment the results came through he put on one of his perversely dated albums and we danced round the room singing the first part of the baby's musical legacy. He'd been working on this for some time apparently, compiling an eclectic mix on the iPod of pretty much everything, with the exception of opera which he regarded as tainted by the sensibilities of those who owned it ('Nessun Dorma' being the epitome of self-sacrifice). After the dance he sat me down, held up one splayed hand to indicate five minutes and left the flat without even closing the front door. I swung my feet onto the sofa and lay down for my first official 'rest', opening my eyes occasionally to look about or smooth out my clothes or hair. This attempt at serenity was short-lived and boredom was soon pushing my smile into a range of pouts and grimaces, so when Alasdair got back, breathless and bearing a single Hamlet and a malt loaf, my face was exhausted.

'You look tired.'

'Do I?'

The observation pleased me. I watched him peel the waxy paper from the Soreen, a whimsical purchase he'd never made before.

'Didn't they have any Madeira cake?'

'Yes, but this is better for you,' he said, passing me a huge slice before lighting his cigar and standing up to smoke it. I waved him to the far side of the room.

'Open the window.'

'Yes! Good idea.' (Like I'd had some kind of brainwave.) With the cigar clenched between his teeth he pushed back the snib and pulled down the upper window, then he finished his smoke and sat down.

'Listen, I've been thinking. Maybe we shouldn't tell anyone just yet.'

'Why not?'

'I don't know. I just think we should wait.'

'But I have to tell Gran.'

'Right. Well, I don't suppose that matters. She won't remember, will she?'

'No. She won't remember.'

And I ate my Soreen, washing it down with a swill of strong coffee that made my heart race.

As soon as he left the flat I picked up the phone and told Fiona, just out of habit really, and to practise saying it.

'Guess what.'

'What?'

'I'm pregnant!'

I've known Fiona since primary school. I was drawn to her pencil-thin legs, the attraction of envy, I think, and empathy too, as I watched the other girls grab her and tie her tights together at the knees. I can still see her, chicken legs and hen-toed − like a wishbone; she's pulling at the knot, furious, and I think that's what I liked best about her, that fury, an indignation that suggested she knew she was worth something.

'Oh my God, that's wonderful! Does Alasdair know?'

This is typical of Fiona; only she would consider it likely that I would tell her before I told anyone else, including my husband.

'Yes, of course he knows. We've already celebrated.'

'Aw, that's lovely. Did he bring you flowers?'

'Kind of.'

I didn't tell her about the malt loaf because although Fiona understands a lot, she doesn't understand everything.

Broken Hearts

S HE WAS wearing a pair of shoes I'd never seen before, two-tone slip-ons with a side button and a small square heel. The buttons were wrong. They were on the inside of her feet instead of the outside, so that took a while to sort out. It's the kind of thing that used to make me laugh but now it upsets me – Gran wearing her shoes on the wrong feet. She was bemused by it. 'Whose done that?' she said, surrendering her feet. With the shoes sorted I told her I had some exciting news. I was pouring tea from the woolly teapot and she had already started teasing the edge of her Jaffa Cake, rooting for jelly with her dark marbled tongue. She was so intent on it I had to stop and touch her arm to get her attention.

'I've got something to tell you, Gran.'

Smacking her tangy mouth, she seemed not to hear me.

'Gran, listen, I'm going to have a baby.'

I didn't expect her to say anything so it was a surprise to hear her, never mind what she said. Whenever Gran is caught by an unexpected moment of happiness she doesn't speak, she just presses her palms together and holds her hands to her closed lips; the joy goes inwards, but you can see it in her eyes. I've watched those eyes all my life, taken them as my guide.

'A baby?'

'Yes!'

And then she said the strangest thing.

'My baby had a watery mouth.'

'What?'

'She wasn't right. Never even opened her eyes. I don't know how long, just the rain on her face and then she died.'

There was no drama to it. She sounded so matter-of-fact I thought I'd misheard her.

'What do you mean?'

But she wouldn't answer.

'What do you mean, Gran? – about the baby?'

She was drinking her tea, holding the saucer under her chin and tilting her head with a sudden gentility as she lowered her cup – a curious refinement after the noisy smacking and licking of lips, sucking on her own tongue. I wanted to hear more about the baby but there was an odd look about her that stopped me from asking again. She was concentrating on the line of gilt that edged her Japanese teacup, following it round as if checking for flaws. I felt a sudden protectiveness towards her, but I also felt disappointed at the way my baby had been so quickly usurped by another, a watery-mouthed fiction who came out of the blue, or the not-so-blue – who fell from a rainy sky.

Later that day I sensed a new darkness, as if my gran's illuminated heart were slipping away from me. I was alone in the kitchen when it happened, on my own and thinking about the baby's heart, not hers – puzzling over how a pulse begins, that very first spark of being. Suddenly a shadow cast across the room and when I turned to look out of the window there was a blue portrait of sky hanging there, strangely bright in the gloomy interior.

I didn't sleep at all that night, and now I wonder about the strange umbral shadow that swept through the house.

Was that the instrumental darkness? Or is it madness to think of it that way, the possibility of an elemental conspiracy – both hearts stealing off into the black night?

ALASDAIR WAS right, she didn't remember about the baby and I didn't mention it again. I thought it would be easier to wait until the first slight swell of belly, that lovely rise. It would give us something to focus on. Gran has an eye for detail and is a habitual chronicler of change; typically she charts the weather, but since the forgetting took hold there has been a paring back and now we could chart anything, including the baby's progress. It's something we could do together using an ordinary measuring tape; we could make a graph or something, plot a few points. We both love a good graph. Of course, there would be no lasting trace for her, it would only be those moments – but each immediate pleasure would be shared and that's what would be familiar, the two of us together, living the present just as we lived the past, and with so much more to come.

Three weeks later, on a day soaked in fog, I felt a dull pain low in my abdomen, a pain so familiar I knew immediately, recognised the tenacious claw and that awful downward pulling – and then the blood, but no relief from the deep sinewy tug. I stood like a blank wall as she was dragged out.

Alasdair had called her a moon seed because she was the size of a grape but with a single crescent heart, and although he sang to her in a crooning voice there was still a kind of guardedness, as if he knew. I'd wanted to buy her one of those little French giraffes but he said we should wait, mark each stage as it comes. Then we lost her and it was too late; buying something afterwards felt morbid. I wanted a keepsake not a memento mori.

'We should have bought something.'

'You keep saying that. Why do you keep saying that?'

We took no comfort from each other, he and I. There was a brief hour of holding, but then we got on with ordinary things, moving around in the same domestic spaces, careful of each other.

And at night, lying under the same empty sky.

I TOLD Gran anyway, said about the bleeding and that I'd lost the baby – and this time she seemed to take it in without distraction. She cried out a little with the shock of it, because it was shocking, a terrible disturbance that spread outwards and gathered strength. There had been a numbness up until then, but when I sat on the floor in her room that day and said it out loud her sorrowful eyes showed me how to feel, just as they always did when I wasn't sure.

Bird in a Tree

ALASDAIR AND I have been married for almost two years now. As soon as we got hitched we decided to have a baby, and with each as keen as the other there was no reason to delay. I couldn't help worrying, though.

Here's why—

My great-grandmother was an only child, and my grand-mother was an only child, and my mother was an only child, and I am an only child. That sounds like the start of a riddle, and in a way it *is* a riddle – a paucity that has been described as 'idiopathic'. If I draw out my maternal family tree and turn it upside down it makes a series of neat steps that climb up to me (assuming we are looking at my descendants face on, with the man always to the left of the woman, like those wee figures on a wedding cake). I don't know how far back that genetic neatness goes; perhaps my great-great-grandmother was an only child too? I've certainly never heard my gran talk about any great-aunts, or any great-uncles, and I don't think these great-offshoots would be over-looked in such a tall, linear tree. In particular, any great-uncles would certainly have been noted, since we are all girls.

'Always girls.'

When Dad (also an only child) made this sage observation he feigned disappointment, shaking his head as if to provoke us, but smiling too; it was an intriguing smile – happy enough, but with a slight camber to the mouth that suggested life was complicated, that it was possible to both accept and hope at the same time, like someone who still bets each way even though their horse always comes in second.

This proclivity, the fact of our girlie ancestry, did not escape the notice of my father's mother, who, concerned that the family name might disappear within one generation, did everything she could to stop my mother from hunting down and marrying her son (for that was how she saw it – my mother the pursuer, a predatory siren with her eyes fixed on the main prize – a hundred acres of arable land, including a house and various steadings). On the day of the registry wedding my father's side of the marriage room was almost empty, and as they took their vows, his mother was vowing elsewhere in the presence of her solicitor. That's why I grew up in a tall, skinny house with a long skinny garden full of apple trees. It's why I shared a bedroom with my gran until I was seven (when I descended to the basement and the unsought privacy of my own room – with its new partition wall and a WC equipped with extractor fan and a tiny sink). It is also why my father never bets to win.

These are things of great consequence, and sometimes I wonder which of my two grandmothers influenced my life more: the one I grew up with, or the one I never met. I think about this a lot – the way people who are missing can fill your life. They stand at the window of your house and watch you through the glass, whether you know it or not.

MY GRAN is called Peggy. She lives at the top the house, having risen through the ranks, from all those mornings spent in the basement, storing the apples and washing the clothes, then occupying the chair by the kitchen window, where she directed Mum in matters of husbandry, and next, ascending to the comfort of the first-floor living room, with its carpets and soft furnishings, the wide-screen TV, and a view of the garden. The bathroom is on the second floor, next to what is now my parents' bedroom; this part is split-level, with just four steps leading to Gran's room. The house is like a Japanese puzzle box, full of structural irregularities, yet looking, from the outside, like a straightforward terrace. Even the name is a puzzle. It is called 'North' but it doesn't face north and nor is it located in the north; the village sits in the east, just below Scotland's humpy back. From the top-floor windows you can see the river Tay, reed beds swaying on the pull of the North Sea. Perhaps that was it – the notion of tidal forces pulling us northwards. It is the only house at this end of the High Street with its own name, and even though there are other, quite similar houses, the naming sets it apart. If that was the intention, it worked, since the house seems to bulge slightly, as if it were being squeezed as well as pulled. There are bulges inside too; they groan, wanting to be touched and hugged.

Ouch, I say, resting my cheek against them and giving them a pat.

'These walls need strapping,' says Dad, regularly and to no one in particular, as he runs his hands over the various swellings, and I imagine the house all trussed and bolted like a bonsai.

Not everyone notices the name that is painted in plain blue letters above the front door – it is more often referred to as number eight, and since there is not much coming and going underneath that lintel, those who feel obliged to fill in the gaps have developed a mild curiosity about Gran, bestowing her with something I can never quite put my finger on – a kind of celebrity almost, a separateness that has suited her well. Mum was seven when they moved here, and I was born here, but it was never Gran's intention to stay. They arrived in Plum Town (that's what she calls it, on account of all the fruit trees) on a return ticket, having travelled on what turned out to be the last passenger train ever to stop here. After that it was just goods traffic – a loading point for locally grown seed potatoes going to England. Gran always maintained we didn't belong – that as soon as the trains started running again she would use that ticket to get us out. Every New Year's Eve she would close the curtains and assiduously ignore the torchlight procession that marched past the house at midnight. 'That's not for us,' she'd say, pulling me away from the window whenever she caught me looking. When she spoke about moving I could tell she had somewhere in mind, a place she missed more than anything, or a place she had yet to find, but she wouldn't be drawn on it.

During the day Gran rarely leaves her room except to reach the small bathroom, which is four steps down a narrow stairway that has banisters on both walls; she refuses to go any further, claiming she's making her way to heaven (that's what she sings, 'Four Steps to Heaven' – she doesn't realise she's overshot). She is less fond of heaven in the middle of the night and often descends all the way to the kitchen, indulging in earthly pleasures while the rest of us sleep (except Mum – who frets, but has learned to stay put). Eventually, morning comes – bringing surprises: shoes in the oven; spoons neatly wrapped in newspaper and hidden in a towel; a liberal sprinkling of couscous on the floor, like she's been feeding hens.

The forgetfulness has shifted from being a part of her to not being a part of her, it is overtaking her; it's the one thing that keeps growing while the rest of her shrinks. I think of it as her cuckoo – an invidious bird that feeds on her brain (which is as good a summary as any I have come across so far). Sometimes the invidious bird flies off and you never know how long it might be gone. It could be most of a day, or hours, or just the few seconds it takes to say something sensible. When the cuckoo goes she is herself, and when the cuckoo comes back, she is not. *She's not herself today*. Everyone knows what it means. Since Gran's cuckoo came to roost people who had not previously shown an interest have acquired an insatiable curiosity. Everywhere I go in the village I get the same thing.

'How's your gran?'

I don't mind, in fact, I enjoy talking about Gran – there is always some amusing thing to tell (a judicious tilt from the spectrum of dark to light) and I like to keep her reputation circulating. I sprinkle it about like fairy dust, and there is a general brightening, an afterglow that she never left behind in person.

My mum gets it all the time too.

'How's your mum doing, Mary?'

Conveying how Gran is doing has given us a whole new frame of reference, a means of communicating at last. Before, it was difficult to think of anything to say. I don't think we did speak, out there on the street, in the shops; but now, because of the greedy bird, we have become more interesting (in an approachable kind of way). The parlance is easy and shared, lots of brief little heartfelt encounters with women of a certain age who *squeeze* your hand rather than shake it.

'How's Peggy doing? We haven't seen her for ages. Not since that beetle drive last year.'

Everyone remembers that beetle drive and what she did

(except Gran, of course, who used her score card to create a Braille alphabet by making exact drawings of whatever face of the dice looked up at her). It was the district nurse who'd suggested we take her; she said it was important not to let Gran withdraw, that she should have a blether with folk her own age, share some memories.

'You'd be amazed,' she said.

It was ludicrous. It was always going to be ludicrous – the notion of Gran at a beetle drive being told over and over that she can't have eyes until she's got a head; then the sudden, disproportionate cry of *Beetle!* from somewhere across the room, and the inexorable descent into bedlam.

I ATTEND the local carers group in place of Mum. She wants to benefit from the group but she's too shy to go herself, or too reticent. Actually she is both these things, she is shy *and* reticent – 'near as damn it a recluse' was how Alasdair put it. I'd never really thought about her that way, but when I did, I could see he was right. Of course, Gran is near as damn it the same, but that is a different confinement, a circumstantial state, whereas Mum's seclusion is more of a trait. I hope it is, I hope that's why I've never really thought about it – because it's just so much a part of her, an aspect so familiar as to go unnoticed; that way, the surprise I felt when Alasdair said 'recluse' can be taken as a sign of acceptance rather than indifference.

'*Grey Gardens* but without the racoons,' he said. The comparison conjured up a whole new view of family life back in Plum Town, a closed-ness that I didn't recognise (and still don't, although I am beginning to notice certain barricades at points where they have begun to collapse, revealing new glimpses of old obscurities). I think Alasdair sees us Copellas as Godless monks, the possible descendants (on

Dad's side) of an errant thirteenth-century Benedictine from the nearby Abbey of Lindores; a singular family, lean to a point of reluctance, seemingly self-reliant but mutually dependent; private, quiet, all dreamers. A small quartet of illiterate poets.

I did try to persuade Mum to join the group, but not that much. She worried over the leaflet for several days, picking it up from the kitchen table to read and reread over numerous cups of tea. In that sense, there was already a benefit – a few sit-downs that would not have otherwise happened, but I knew she would never go; picturing Mum as part of a virtuous circle of carers stretched the imagination too far, a configuration as unlikely as Gran at a beetle drive. There was something about the leaflet, though, a promise within it that she couldn't quite ignore, and eventually, aided by my own persuasive arguments, she asked me to go instead.

Initially the group viewed me with suspicion. This was understandable given that I was their first proxy member – but slowly, I think because I am quiet and attend regularly, and because the first really painful experience I shared with them was nothing to do with Gran, I was accepted. It took about five or six sessions.

It was August when I started to go along – almost a year since we lost the baby (ten months and two weeks, but I don't count). The main topic of conversation during my first meeting was plums, and with just a few weeks to go before the first plum market of the season it was a natural enough subject to start with, but what I thought was an icebreaker didn't seem to be leading us anywhere; in fact, the slight honey taste of plum flesh carried us right up to the tea break, and I was beginning to think I'd wandered into the wrong group when the only man there came back to the circle and the others joined themselves up again and fell quiet. It was easy for me to slip into the silence. Then the man spoke.

'I've written something down because last week it didn't come out right. I'd like to read it out if that's OK?'

There was a murmur of assent, then quiet again.

'I'm Kenneth, by the way. I live with my father. Sorry, I used to live with my father, but he's in hospital now and he won't be coming home.'

I thought this preamble was for everyone but when I looked up I realised he was talking directly to me. I assumed he wasn't local because I'd never seen him before. I would have remembered. Definitely.

When he looked at me he didn't smile. He was holding a black notebook, one of those fancy moleskin ones with the elastic loop that keeps the thing shut (I was holding a notebook too, a spiral one – its 49p price label still sticking to the front). Kenneth's notebook had the dimensions of a small bible and fitted perfectly into his left hand; he even held it in a ministerial way, his fingers curved round the spine and his arm bent, folded in towards his shoulder, the book pressing against his collarbone. As I admired his, I fancied he was looking at mine – so I pushed my pen through the spiral loops at the top of my pad, just to show off its superior utility. He lowered his book and slipped the elastic free, then loosened his grip and tugged the tail of the cloth bookmarker sideways. The book opened at a page of cramped writing – *mercifully short*, I thought, not knowing what to expect, but bracing myself for something mawkish.

He pressed a knuckle to his mouth and cleared his throat.

It all started with a red and grey cardigan, one of those Pringle types with the diamond shapes down the front. The nurses came and put it on my father but it didn't belong to him. When

23

he protested they just laughed and said how nice it was, so much better than his old one, the one with the missing buttons and the torn pocket, and a hole in one elbow. But that hole meant something. That hole was where he always leant on the arm of his chair at home, his hand holding up his face and the other one curled right over the top of his head, until his fingers could touch the bony ridge of his left ear. Back at the house, there is a worn patch on his chair that matches that hole exactly. When he became frail (it wasn't gradual, there is nothing gradual about my father) he conducted his life from his armchair, but not in a lazy way, more in a Captain Kirk way, still exploring and gathering, pulling me into his orbit, his swivel-top table holding all his things, double-sided coins and cards that were slightly tapered. Short pencils that you needed to lick before they would write. But all that stuff was gone. And all his money was gone too. Absolutely nothing in his pocket, because he'll only lose it, they said, and anyway, he has everything here he could possibly need. He only needs to ask. And him not a sixpence to his name, searching his empty pockets again and again, over and over, wondering where on earth his money is. He's been robbed. 'I've no money,' he keeps saying, 'It's gone.' And it must have all added up to who he was more than anybody realised, because now, it's like he's gone too. His face is smaller, his look, mean. But I know he isn't mean, and I can't help thinking that if they just put him back in that chair, with his swivel-top table beside him, if they would just give him back that old cardie and let the hole find the patch, it would be like a classic docking manoeuvre, the satellite returning to the mother-ship, and he would be restored. That hole is the way in.

Dingo Baby

I HAVE never kept a journal. My week-at-a-glance diary is all the personal history I need. At the end of each year I glance through it and distil all that temporal noise into a few main events — it's an effective mnemonic, three plots on a graph and the rest just floods back.

Last year, however, there was no such flood, other than the cruel rush between my legs in September — everything else was just aftershock. By the end of that year I had dropped out of university and was working at the dentist's. I honestly can't recall much more than that, but if I were to plot these things out as Cartesian coordinates along an axis of misery they would form a kind of tick, indicting that it was all going in the right direction.

Life goes on.

So many people said it, including a GP whose name I can't recall.

'You've had a bleed,' she said, as if the remark were something explanatory rather than descriptive, or declarative — a lament, surely? Alasdair turned white, so furious I thought he might hit her. When I touched his thigh to placate him he grabbed my hand and kept it all the way through, squeezing it whenever she spoke.

'Try not to worry, Mrs Thackeray, it doesn't mean anything. It's really not that uncommon, you know.'

But she didn't know about our spindly tree, or the diagnosis of 'unexplained secondary infertility' that explained why my parents couldn't have another baby (seemingly it was always marginal – with me they were 'just lucky').

And then came the reminder.

'Life goes on,' the GP said, smiling as we stood up to leave. Alasdair turned and was looking at her as if she had lost her senses.

'I'm sorry?'

But she didn't answer. She just kept smiling, her eyes taking him on – a cautionary look that might have drawn him into all out combat had it not been for the blush that rose from the collar of her pearl-button blouse.

Even Fiona said it.

'Life goes on, honey.'

Incredible on two counts, since she'd never called me 'honey' before. I could hardly believe my ears.

GOING TO university was never in doubt. I was a bit of a swot at school and became transfixed with photosynthesis and the anomalous behaviour of water, so it was assumed by all of us that I'd either be a biology teacher or a physics teacher. Such was the certainty, I put it off for years, working in various jobs and travelling, always to northerly places because it seemed to make sense to start at the top and work my way down (and because I knew I would feel the cold more, later on). I was happy enough, but there were moments, brief disjunctions when I would cast a whimsical glance towards convention, and then, quite suddenly, during a restless night in an ice hotel in Lapland, whimsy turned to longing, and the glance locked into a prolonged stare.

When I announced my intention to study English Gran

clapped her hands together once and held them there, extending them slightly towards me in a distinctly Indian way, her shoulders rising to catch what looked like joy. She was thrilled. Mum less so. Dad bemused.

'English!'

I met Alasdair during my second year, and it was not long afterwards that I stopped sleeping, or if I did sleep I woke up gasping under a pile of coats – grey tweedy ones that leave hairs in your mouth.

'What coats?' Alasdair asked, looking puzzled.

'None. I'm speaking metaphorically.'

But Alasdair never really understood the way I felt – the sense of loss when I opened a book of poetry, straining to hear the *iamb* in an iambic pentameter – slipping into the *Tum ti tum ti tum ti tum* of *The Archers* instead of the *Ti-tum ti-tum ti-tum ti-tum ti-tum* in the lines of an unrhymed poem.

Drawing a blank.

I struggled and finally fell to my knees in the middle of the sixteenth century, having grown weary of the silver poets. Then tiredness turned to hate and it got personal; I was *glad* that Philip Sidney died of battle wounds at Arnheim, and took solace in the thought of Walter Raleigh's long imprisonment and execution (*Hurray!* was the nymph's reply). Alasdair suggested I change subjects, having himself grown weary, and when I did (to Psychology, so I could examine my hatred) the silver shone again, glinting here and there in a restored beauty that was easy on the eye, and, to my great relief, the one person I worried about – the one I thought would be the most disappointed that I'd given up English – didn't mind at all.

'The Department is full of old duffers, Gran – and anyway, I don't have the right brain for it. I *hate* studying poetry. All that criticism and deconstruction just takes the pleasure right out of it. I feel like I'm skinning an animal to try and understand what makes it beautiful.'

'Pinning the butterfly,' she said (the cuckoo briefly flown).

'Yes! That's it exactly.'

And almost immediately we began to share poetry again; we always had – ever since her moving rendition of A. A. Milne's 'Alexander Beetle' when I was four, but we stopped when I left home. By the time we got back to it all those years later Gran was struggling to read out loud, even though (as far as anyone could tell) she still spent much of her day looking at books, turning pages and marking her place. So it was mainly me reading to her, a kind of role reversal but with blissful interruptions when she would suddenly recite the occasional line or two from Tennyson, words tumbling about, then falling into place, like dots joined up – *a gleaming shape she floated by, dead-pale between the houses high.*

It was then, as we were making our way to Camelot, that she first told me she had written poems for a magazine called *The New Moon* when she was young. That was the start of it – notions of a life *before me* that I had rarely, if ever, thought about. When I pestered her to tell me more she brushed it all aside with a wave of her hand – *tch!*

It was nothing – the careless buzz of a whimsical fly, the flick of a frog's tongue.

The idea of Gran as a young poet intrigued me, as did her refusal to talk about it, but I could not persuade her to speak about it, and eventually I stopped trying.

Now, I need to know more, and it's not just the poems; I keep remembering what she said about the baby – the one who never even opened her eyes. 'Just the rain on her face and then she died' – I'm sure that's what she said. But what baby? And why would a baby be out in the rain? I want to understand Gran's story, develop a sense of continuity with the past, perhaps to compensate for the future I lost. You'd think of all people, Alasdair would understand this, but whenever we talk about it we argue. He holds a very different view about the importance of family history, accuses me of being a determinist, whereas he believes in free will (which is why he is so determined not to trace his birth mother).

'No matter how much you know about someone you can never understand another person's life.'

He looked angry when he said it, yet his voice was quiet. I didn't think his anger was anything to do with me; I wanted to touch him, but then he started going on about the way I pore over everything Gran says.

'It won't get you anywhere you know – worrying every utterance to death.'

'But if we don't talk about it now it will be gone for ever.'

'So?'

He dropped his head suddenly and started to rub his eyes, as if he were exhausted.

'Aw, Christ, Aggie – you really need to let things go.'

And I knew what he meant, but I can't let things go. It would be like letting her go, which is impossible.

Love does not permit it.

She is my gran. We shared a room until I was seven. She taught me to read, and how to draw a leaf so it curled up from the page. She taught me how to create magic – catching invisible pennies in a paper bag, wrapping my bus ticket with invisible thread and pulling it this way and that; all you needed was some paper and a little imagination. She taught me to swim, we worked a system with the coloured time-bands so we could stay in the pool as long as we liked, floating till our thumbs turned white. She wore a nose-clip, I remember that, the only person I knew who wore a nose-clip – she had a whole box of them. I have no idea where they came from. Gran didn't say much about her past, never ever spoke about the war, for instance, but occasionally she did speak about Pennyland, the farm where she grew up, and she told me about the time she saw a black puma on the hill, how nobody would believe her.

Everybody thought she was crazy.

'They'll take a baby,' she said, and as if to support her story she told me that on the day I was born a baby in Australia was taken by a dingo. It happened near Ayers Rock and even though the mother saw the dingo they didn't believe her either; they put her in jail for cutting the baby's throat.

Gran and I used to go walking every Sunday and we were halfway up Ormiston Hill when she told me about the puma, and then about little Azaria. I was generally watching out for eagles and snakes, and – in that moment – big cats. The world was such a strange place; for instance, below us the river was bulging with cucumber fish that were so full of eggs they could hardly swim. I knew this to be true, so it seemed to follow that there might be pumas roaming the Scottish hills. It was possible.

I wasn't frightened, though – when I was with my gran I was fearless. Once, she and I put on yellow clothes and let a plague of ladybirds crawl all over us. We sat in the garden and we never moved.

WHEN I left university Alasdair used his connections in the dentistry business to find me a job. He said it would help me take my mind off things, although I'd already taken my mind off 'things' and put it onto other things, namely, my attempt to save Gran's identity from disappearing under a pile of wrong shoes and discarded clothes. She had started to fuss about certain items and often refused to dress in clothes that she insisted did not belong to her.

'That's not mine.'

'Of course it is.'

'It's not.'

'Whose is it, then?'

'I don't know. Try the other department.'

She quite often refers to the other department, but as far as we know she's never worked in a 'department'. I really puzzle over that one, or as Alasdair might say – I worry it to death.

I enjoy working at the dentist's, that's how I describe it – *working at*. I need to be careful when I talk about what I do because I'm not qualified, I'm just there to muck in. The team is described as a meritocracy and I've moved up the order of merit quicker than anyone expected. The dentist is called Florence McKendrick, but we know her as Flossie. She doesn't believe in talking over the patient's head so much of my working day is conducted without conversation, and although Radio 2 is always playing in the background, it is turned down very low. This quietude came as an unexpected bonus; a kind of *home from home*. When I started this job I thought of it as a stop-gap between dropping out of my course and dropping in again, but over time a kind of natural ossification has occurred and the gap has been bridged. I find that I like looking into people's eyes while the dentist excavates their mouths; I like watching the irises dilate – inkblots, sudden on a paper face; and I like the relief when it's all over. I can feel it and see it. The patients carry it carefully as they leave the surgery, like a gift.

The dentist is a friend of Alasdair's and at first I assumed they had met through the tooth business (he works on the technical side and they both have links with the Dental School) but it turns out he's known Flossie since secondary. They used to study together. He called it 'mutual coaching' and I had to suppress a laugh because he seemed quite serious about it – I recognised the look. Alasdair has a very expressive face; life plays across it in a kind of cerebral puppetry, his facial nerves twanging like harp strings. Despite the spontaneity

(I don't think those capering eyebrows are in any sense composed) there is something stagy and disingenuous about these looks – as if the expressions have been learned, or perhaps, more profoundly, the feelings themselves (a mask masking a mask, I sometimes think, in my worst nightmare). It is only when his face stops that his eyes come alive.

Taking my cue from his assembled features, I didn't laugh about the teenage mutual coaching – all that urgent revision in the back bedroom of the Thackeray bungalow, interrupted only by a round of Di's carefully cut sandwiches and a plate of Fox's Favourites (Alasdair's dad was a biscuit salesman, so where love may have been lacking there were always lots of double chocolate-chip cookies). Ignoring all my childish thoughts about Alasdair and Flossie and those suggestive biscuits, I didn't question his assertion that he just happened to bump into her one lunchtime, and that she just happened to mention that the surgery was in a bit of a flux because the receptionist – someone called Sylvia who was not long married – had run off with another man.

It's a heart-breaking tale.

Apparently Sylvia fell in love with the man who came to fix her gutters. They became lovers, and things came to a head when they were sighted down in South Queensferry sharing a fish supper. They were leaning on the bonnet of her blue Nissan Micra, which had very distinctive markings – a thread of daisy transfers arching over the rear right-side panel, just above the wheel. It was the daisies that did it. They were spotted by one of Sylvia's neighbours – a clear, leisurely sighting from the Edinburgh train as it crossed the rail bridge above them. Within days Sylvia had gone, leaving her husband and almost all of her belongings behind, including the Nissan Micra, even though she'd saved up and paid for it with her own money and put the daisies on herself; in fact, before she went, she filled out the Registration Certificate, put her husband down as the New Keeper, and left it on the kitchen table with a note. He just needed to sign it and send it off and the car was his.

But he couldn't do it. Seemingly, it's still sitting in the driveway exactly where she left it. Alasdair says he probably doesn't want to drive around in a car covered in daisies (they're a bugger to get off, apparently – it was clearly a car for life), but I have a different take on it; I think it is a declaration of his enduring love. Signing that certificate would be like signing her off.

The more I hear about the missing receptionist (Sylvia is rarely referred to by name) the more I like her; she has become a kind of divining rod, a revelatory device that sources compassion.

'What do you think of the dentist's receptionist, the one that ran off?'

Mad / Sad / Bad *(tick one).*

We had quite a big argument about her, Alasdair and me; we ended up shouting, him with his back to me, looking out – and when he left the room I could see spit on the window. I told Fiona about it and she said he was probably just feeling insecure.

'Husbands don't like to hear that kind of thing. He's probably worried that you might leave him one day.'

'No. I don't think that's it.'

I was lying on her sofa, chewing my nails and eating her marshmallows, getting away with it because she was pregnant and therefore, in the circumstances, I could get away with anything. Poised on a low stool and very straight-backed, she was rubbing her huge bump in a circular motion, the way she always did, and I was thinking, *If that was me in there I'd find that really annoying.*

'He gets angry so easily these days, and he never talks about the miscarriage.'

(That's the word I use, whereas Mum doesn't, because, she says, it wasn't really a baby yet. She is oddly adamant about it.)
'And do you?'
I popped the last marshmallow into my mouth.
'No.'
'Well, there you go then. One's as bad as the other.'
Fiona pressed both hands into the small of her back and rotated her head – her neck long and her hair tumbling about. She was wearing baggy velveteen trousers and a long open cardigan, with a stretchy top pulled down over her bump and hips; on her feet she wore socks and rubber clogs that she called Crocs (like that made a difference). Her legs looked too thin to support her.
'Oh!'
'What is it?'
'He's kicking. Do you want to feel?'
She offered me her stomach.
No. Of course I don't.
I put my hand where she guided it.
'Wow,' I said, feeling nothing.

FLOSSIE IS a very laid-back dentist. She smiles a lot and although some people are put off by her over-bite and scatty demeanour, generally her patients are loyal and grateful. She was happy to give me a go and didn't even request any references. Alasdair's word was enough. I expected her to ask me why I'd left university but she never mentioned it. After a while I suspected I was being given special treatment, like someone *in recovery*; something about the way she put her hand on my shoulder as she passed. *Well done!* she kept saying.
'Well done, Aggie!'
So well done that I started doubling up in the treatment room, interspersing reception duties with a few easy 'patient care' tasks while Louise (the real nurse) had a coffee/popped

out/grabbed a sandwich. As a true professional Louise was secure, and didn't seem to mind what I did.

'Stick that on, would you?' she said one day, handing me a nurse's tunic as she pulled on her coat.

'It's dead easy. You'll be fine – and anyway, I won't be long.'

I took to it quickly; just tidying at first, refreshing the mouthwash, that kind of thing, no contact as such, but then – because I had social skills just 'going to waste' – I started settling the patients in, passing the goggles and tying bibs.

There was one incident, when I accidentally stood on the foot switch and the patient's head sank below her knees, but she didn't mind; she thought it was a dream – the dentist floating off like a disembodied spirit. It happened in the middle of a Radio 2 phone-in about non-viable pregnancies; someone was explaining how it felt to hear her lost baby being described as a 'blighted ovum' and this set me swaying a bit. As I corrected my stance, the patient – open-mouthed and silent, began her slow descent, drifting from the recline setting to the supine and beyond.

Flossie immediately threw me a sympathetic look.

'You all right there, Aggie?'

And that's when I knew she knew, and I realised I was wrong when I said to Fiona that Alasdair never talks about the miscarriage.

What I should have said was he never talks about it with me.

Puzzles

W E EAT breakfast in our yellow kitchen, bright clammy walls that are always breaking out in a sweat. The floor is checked – Alasdair's black slippers merging with a black tile, and my white slippers merging with a white one. I haven't ever noticed this before but I notice it today, the way we sit – much the same as each other – with our knees pressed together and our feet neat on the floor. We probably always rest our feet on those particular squares in a kind of postural echoing that we find attractive at an unconscious level (but it must be at a *very* unconscious level, since now, at the conscious level, I can see that we look ridiculous).

Footless and fancy free, we share the paper in an amiable way. I'm reading about a man on Capitol Hill who has found a flaw in the free market ideology that has guided US monetary policy for decades; he's not sure how significant or permanent the flaw is, but it is enough to place him in a state of shocked disbelief. Alasdair is stuck on the front page of the sports section; he can't get beyond it. He leans forward and back and forward again, uneasy in his chair because Rangers are closing the gap on Celtic. I look at him and see that despite his anxiety his feet have remained in the square. I wish his feet were bigger. I want him to sit like a man, his feet wide apart – black spilling on white, or legs stretched out with two big feet resting one on top of the other, getting in everyone's way.

'Feet!' I want to say, like Fiona does, sending her tall husband into an automatic apology as he re-arranges himself, placing his limbs elsewhere.

Fiona's baby was born in early summer. He's called Thomas but I call him Tufty because he looks like a squirrel (although she can't see it). He wears huge nappies – three layers of fabric of varying properties (absorbent, washable, organic, fair); they seem to grow disproportionately to his tiny frame, as do the rest of his clothes, and it's surprising to see how small he is out of the packet (a bit like an Easter egg, but without the disappointment). Tufty is always being carted about here, there and everywhere, together with his huge BAG. I believe that, later, Tufty and I will be friends; we share a sideways look sometimes as his mother zips him into his spacesuit and transfers him, stiff as a dead starfish, into his transport system, and I'm sure we're both thinking the same thing: *Is all this really necessary?*

Me and Tufty lost in the same puzzle.

But that's later – for now, I am unreliable. I love his spaceman ears and his little po face, but sometimes I just can't look at him.

I STACK the plates and prepare to leave, then come back into the kitchen and touch Alasdair on the shoulder. He raises his head and I kiss him on the cheek.

'Slater,' he says.

It is so difficult to catch his eye. Before, I might straddle him and kiss him on the mouth, but now I can't. He's never said anything, I don't even think he's noticed. I get the distinct impression his thoughts are elsewhere.

I drive a few miles down the A9 then off again, back to Plum Town to visit Gran. I always visit on Sundays, unless

Alasdair has been dubbing my boots, in which case we go walking, but we haven't been walking together for months. He tends to go out on his bike, and I *go back to my village* (that's how he puts it – he says it in a funny voice and waggles his fingers, I don't know why).

When I walk into the house Mum always greets me the same way: 'Alasdair not with you?'

I have various answers to this, excuses that protect Alasdair's excellent reputation within the family (they all like him, and seem to want him to like them).

'No. He has to help his dad move some slabs or something. Sends his love.'

Which is straight-talking Copella speak for, *He doesn't want to be with me. I can't catch his eye or kiss him on the mouth, and he doesn't notice, even though he loves to kiss. Kissing is his best thing. I thought I knew what a kiss was but then I met Alasdair.*

I never say he's out on his bike. I wouldn't want them to know that he prefers cycling to spending time with us.

I MISS my gran. When I think of her I feel homesick, but being with her doesn't necessarily help; it's not that simple.

For example, this morning I woke to the smell of bonfire and when I looked out the window I pictured her standing at the foot of the orchard, tending a damp pile of smoking leaves. She was wearing an ivory mackintosh with large brown buttons, her hair in a French twist – scarf and wellingtons, no gloves. I could just make out a glimpse of nightie hanging below the hem of her coat. Her hands and chin were perfectly balanced on the end of a rake, and she was swaying, heady with smoke and the smell of lichen – stealing pleasures while the rest of us slept.

Never to look out and see her alone in a garden, bare legs in wellingtons, even then – these are the things that hollow me out; my heart aching as if she has already gone.

Today I don't want to see her; I don't want to touch those papery hands. They flit about like a pair of trapped birds, stopping in thin air when they should drop. She's often like that, stuck somewhere, stranded in mid-sequence – and I try to imagine where she is at that precise moment, but her eyes turn black and I can't go any further; I can't go with her when she's like that.

Dog eyes in their bony sockets.

Mum is chopping root vegetables into rustic chunks and sliding them into the stockpot. I'm sitting at the table, playing with Dad's sugar cubes (he insists on them, taking three in a cup; he says it's the only sure way to achieve consistency).

'Aren't you going up?'

I slump and let my shoulders go round. Gran's tray is ready, the pot warming, the Jaffa Cakes sitting on a doily (she saves doilies now – folds them, flattens them, places them between the pages of a book, like scraps).

'Aw, I don't think I can today.'

'Why not?'

'I don't know. Just not in the mood. Do you mind?'

'No – *I* don't mind.'

Mum is a woman of few words; she uses them sparingly, utilising the *stress* wherever possible. Her eloquence lies in the accent. This reticence runs in the family, following a womanly seam in a rather unwomanly way. Dad rejoices in it (quietly), and it is more often the house that speaks and is heard – the floorboards or the clocks; or the slow replenishment of the above-head cistern. More recently it is the constant noise of the washing machine on spin that fills the house – the noise frenzied and high-pitched, as if a train is passing through the kitchen, whipping up storms in our teacups.

I had not fully appreciated quite how taciturn we were (singly, and as a group) until I started to make friends and go to their houses, and even then – although I wondered at the noise and chatter and the casual way that words were thrown about, spilling and scattering and no matter if most of them were missed – I didn't really think about the difference, but when friends came to my house I could see they felt uncomfortable. They rarely came back.

'Come to tea.'

'I can't.'

'But you don't know when I'm going to say yet!'

Fiona was the only exception. She was one of seven. Seven! She loved the quiet orderliness of my house and I loved the din and discord of hers. We attracted a lot of attention in each other's environments, me, fussed over because I was so quiet, Mrs Cook whacking seven grubby hands away from the stack of bread like she was swatting flies. *Wait! For goodness' sake, give Aggie a chance*, then everyone watching in a moment of uncustomary silence as I delicately picked from the top of the pile, feigning diffidence; and Fiona, astonishing us with her boldness and speed at the dinner table, my parents struck dumb by her loquacity.

When I was ten Fiona asked me who I'd most like to be and I said my gran (that was my second choice – my first was Fiona, but I didn't want to tell her that because she puffs up very easily). Even then I knew my answer was a bit unusual. I wouldn't have said it to anyone else.

'Your gran!'

'Yes.'

'But she's so old!'

'I mean my gran when she was young.'

'You're mad.'

But Fiona hadn't seen the picture of Gran looking like Vivien Leigh – sitting bareback on a horse with nothing on her feet, scowling and still lovely.

'I'd like to be Diane Fozzy.'

'Who's Diane Fozzy?'

'She's that woman who lived with the gorillas.'

'Oh! I've seen that film!'

'But it's a twelve – how come you've seen it?'

'My gran took me when it was on in Perth.'

'Did she?'

I could tell she was impressed.

'I've not seen it yet but it's out on video. I saw a trailer when we were at *Driving Miss Daisy* last week. It looks brilliant.'

'Yeah, it's a great film.'

'It's a true story.'

'I know, but once you've seen it I don't think you'll want to be her.'

'Why not?'

'Well—'

'No!'

Fiona jumped off the wall and put her hands over her ears.

'Don't tell me! I don't want to know what happens, we're gonna get it out next weekend. Have you seen the poster?'

'Aye.'

She tried to tuck her hair behind her ears but there was too much of it so she flicked it all loose again.

'My sister says I look like her.'

'Which sister?'

'Elsie.'

'Elsie! You don't look anything like Elsie.'

'Naw – I don't mean that, I mean Elsie thinks I look like Diane Fozzy. What do you think?'

I looked at her standing there, posing.

'Oooh yeah – so you do.'

And I wasn't just saying it, she did look like the woman in the poster, which meant she looked more like a movie star than an anthropologist – ten years old and already the high cheekbones and that thick wavy hair that did actually seem to tumble over itself and move in a wavy way (she knew this – and was forever running her fingers through it, making it ripple). She was pleased, suffused in a self-love that should have been intensely irritating but wasn't. *Fiona going dreamy, wishing she could be somebody who looks just like her.*

We walked back down the street, heading for the church hall, where we spent an hour every week hating being in the Brownies but not quite managing to dispel our desire for approval and another badge; Snowy Owl smiling, round and squidgy – her soft hands bringing us to silence when she pressed a finger to her lips.

I promise that I will do my best to love Mike Odd, to serve the bean and my country, to hell bother people, and, to keep the Brownie Law.

And we did keep it – a quick spin round on one foot before we entered the hall. 'That's my good turn,' we'd say, at first giggling, but eventually more mature, executing it quietly and without fuss – like two Catholic girls making the sign of a cross.

I'd like to look at that photograph of Gran on the horse again and figure out where it was taken – and when. Was she writing poetry then? I want to know more about the magazine she mentioned – *The New Moon* – and why she came to Plum Town, and about the baby who fell from a rainy sky.

It's all I think about.

Socratic Questions

WE SMILE and rest our gaze on him. *Lovely Kenneth.* He is sitting in a low-slung chair, an item Ikea called a *Boing* (or something like that – 'a deckchair by any other name would smell as sweet' he whispered to me when Noreen first urged him into it).

'Take the *Boing*, Kenneth!'

Trapped, with his legs crossed and his knee higher than his shoulder, there is something arresting about the way his feet are set and the way he has to reach *up* to his knee (I am trapped too, captivated by those feet and the thought of them messing up my floor tiles).

With some difficulty, he lifts his tea, puts it down again, gives the milk a lazy stir.

'Sugar?'

'No thanks, Gladys.'

'Oh – sweet enough, are we?'

'Aye, that's it.'

A tray of condiments is carried round the group then placed on the coffee table next to me.

'Sugar, dear?'

'No thanks.'

'Oh! Here's another one. We're in good company the day.'

'And no milk thanks.'

'No milk!'

Gladys puts the jug down and shakes her head – a brief lament for sweet milky tea. She's not sure about the custard creams now, offers them with a stern look. I take two to make up for the black tea. Kenneth takes one but I notice he doesn't eat it straight away; in fact, I keep an eye on that biscuit for the rest of the session and he doesn't eat it at all.

'It's the young folk that don't take the sugar,' Mima says, as a matter of fact and with no hint of judgement; soon they're talking fondly of sugar on buttered bread, jam pieces, condensed milk spread over a loaf-end, which leads to half loafs and toasted door-steps, plain and pan. Lovely wee bread and butter squares. In the sweet nostalgic lull, Jessie leans towards Kenneth, who is still protruding from the *Boing* like an insect caught in the jaws of a carnivorous flower.

'Confabulation is a very big word. Can you spell it, Kenneth?'

'Probably not.'

'Have a go.'

'C O N F A B—'

'No.'

'Um – C O N P H—'

'No.'

'I give up.'

'I T.'

'Ha! You got me. I should have confabulated my way out of that one.'

Kenneth laughs and shakes his head, then looks at Jessie and gives her several appreciative nods. Jessie is the joker in the pack, despite having the least to laugh about. Her husband Stan has Pick's disease, which makes good old-fashioned Alzheimer's look like a walk in the park. He's not even sixty. Apparently Stan 'always liked a drink' (as did Jessie), and his first diagnosis was Korsakoff's – which, according to Derek (the CPN), is not a 'true' dementia, but never mind.

Turns out it is a disease called Pick's, cause unknown, named, we assume, after a Mr Pick.

'Or perhaps a Mrs Pick,' piped up Noreen (and quite right too).

'Luckily it's very rare, but its effects are particularly devastating,' Derek said when he came to give us a talk. 'The damage is mainly to the frontal lobes, which leads to a deterioration in the personality rather than the intellect. Sufferers think they are acting normally when in fact they are causing social havoc.'

Derek paused here to give us time to look at his slide of a lurid, crayon brain – all coloured lobes and criss-cross cortices. The term *social havoc* hung in the air, a useful summary for what came next – everything we needed to know about dementia laid out in a very un-dementia way (as if to compensate) – neat rows and columns, with numbers and scores and the proper words for things: *emotional lability, diurnal variation, neurological disinhibition, perseveration of action*. And because Derek was sorting out his slides we all had the chance to ponder over what Jessie had previously found unspeakable, but what she referred to thereafter as *Stan's Social Havoc*.

You could have heard a pin drop.

Just the soft tick of Jessie's tiny wristwatch (an anniversary present from Stan), and the group, when they reached the end of the list, examining their own and each other's shoes, and thinking what I was thinking – that this was Stan's list; recalling all those times we barely smiled, because with the best will in the world, Jessie's jokes begin to sap your strength.

The only one who always laughs is Kenneth.

Today, as we gather our coats and tidy up, I notice Kenneth slipping his biscuit back in the box. He must have taken it just to be polite.

Outside, he catches up with me.

'Needing a lift?'

'Oh, no thanks. I'm going back to my mum's. She likes to hear about what we did in the group.'

He nods, and we both hesitate. He's looking about, hands in the pockets of his heavy coat and pulling his shoulders up. He looks behind him then swings back round again, springing on his toes.

'It's cold.'

'Yes.'

'I'll walk you back.'

'That's OK. We're only just up the road.'

More little bounces.

'Right. See you next week then.'

He says this without looking at me; instead he's peering into the distance, like he's tracking something, his eyes holding their blue against the dark. He pulls out a hand and raises it to just below his shoulder, palm facing out, then he turns – head first, followed by body – and walks towards the bowling green, where he'll pick up his car and drive back to his dad's empty house.

I watch him for a while, knowing he won't look round again, that it wouldn't matter if he did. Expecting him to slowly evaporate into the night, like an angel.

THE NEXT time I climb the stairway to heaven Gran starts to cry. I've no idea why, and when I ask her she doesn't know either – something just seems to come over her when she sees me standing there clutching a box of After Eights. We hug and I dab her eyes, then I shake the box a little and we laugh.

'What was that all about?' I ask.

'What was that? Silly fool. Go on, you open them.'

'No, they're for you.'

'They're for you. Open them.'

She watches me as I struggle with the cellophane, all bunched up in her lilac cardigan and with her blouse buttoned up wrong across her flat chest; there are folds of fabric spilling out from her necklines and cuffs. Sumptuous. With her bony asymmetric wrists resting on her lap, she is motionless, stilled by a complete preoccupation with my face.

'You're very pretty,' she says.

'So are you.'

'Is it your birthday?'

'No, Gran, this is a present for you.'

'For me?'

'Yes. Take one.'

She looks at the open box, then looks back up to me. I nod, encouraging her.

'Go on − take one.'

Her hands stay in her lap and I realise it is probably quite a challenge to take just one, the paper casings will be too slippy.

'Take a few.'

She pulls one out, remembering how. I discovered After Eight mints about two months ago, or rather, I developed an appreciation of all the things a box of After Eights can offer; a sensory delight on every dimension − dark yielding chocolate and minty goo that melts (making it impossible to choke), the smell and rustle of all those exquisite little packets stacked so precisely in the box − and just the uncertainty of it all, the never really knowing how many are in there. A box of After Eights can occupy Gran for hours; the eating is the least of it.

She sucks at the chocolate, her jaw flexing as she spreads the fondant across the roof of her mouth. She is examining the wrapper in her hand, looking about for the place to put it. The table at the side of her chair is stacked with books and magazines, a mess of sundries – pens and pencils, elastic bands, a tiny screwdriver and a comb. There is a rubber with *TATE* written on it (my present from London) – it is a smooth white pebble, still wrapped in cellophane and there to be discovered each day, the red letters slightly out of focus, like a slurred word.

'Have another, Gran.'

'You'll put me off my tea.'

'What are you having tonight?'

'Tonight?'

'For tea – what will you have for your tea?'

'Mince and tatties. We always have that on Mondays.'

(It's Sunday – but I've learned to let that kind of stuff go.)

'We pick the carrots ourselves and take them to the kitchens. You've to thin them out very carefully – those go to the pigs, everything in a bucket and take it down to the pigs. Curly is the pet one. He's got curly white hair on his head, all springy on his wee legs. He's a clever wee thing. Doesn't miss a trick.'

She taps the side of her nose.

'He goes straight to the carrot beds if you don't watch. You've got to shut the gate properly or he'll just push it open again with his snout. He's so smart that one, makes you wonder.'

I am about to ask Gran about those carrot beds – we only grow apples and plums, potatoes and onions, the rest is flowers – when I remember something Ruth said, something about how to ask questions that don't 'invalidate'. Ruth (surname Pinsky) is a Validation Instructor who gave a talk to the group not long after I joined. Her visit was, in the words of the group chairman, quite a *coup de bonheur*. She came from the New York School of Social Work at Columbia University and was over here to visit her Scottish ancestors, who were all dead except for her great-aunt

Bunty (since deceased). Bunty lived in Plum Town, in what is known affectionately as the Secure Unit, a quadrangle of very sheltered flats that have been built on the site of the old cottage hospital. These flats are *SMART* – they have things like soft foam corners and floor-mats that can detect movement, or, more importantly, can detect no movement. Some of them have STOP signs on the inside of their front doors.

When word got out about Ruth's visit to Bunty she was quickly tracked down by Noreen and agreed to come to a meeting. Things were never quite the same after that. *According to Ruth* became a popular – some would say over-used – prefix amongst those who knew. She was very clever, and so enthusiastic. She even appeared in my dreams, or at least, her thoughts did – the glow from her hippocampus lighting her brain.

'Who's Ruth?' asked Alasdair.

'What?'

'You've been talking in your sleep about someone called Ruth.'

As soon as I started to explain he switched off. He'd been doing that for a while, glazing over whenever I spoke about Gran's cuckoo (Alasdair was bored with it, Dad was scared of it, and Mum distrusted it).

Ruth explained that *who/what/where/when/how* questions were OK for a 'Stage One Mal-orientated Person', so, for example, I could ask Gran a *who/what/where/when/how* question about the carrots and the pig, but I shouldn't ask her a *why* question, because, according to Ruth, 'mal-oriented people don't know *why*, and you're asking for an intellectual answer, which they can't give'.

The trouble is, all those other exploratory questions (I call them *WHOW* questions) leave me preoccupied with the *why*, so now we're both confused, and even though I'm curious about Curly, and wonder why she refers to the kitchen(s) in the plural, I change the subject.

'I can't sleep, Gran.'

'Why?' she asks, stroking my hair, her eyes clear as she waits for my intellectual answer, wanting to understand.

Je ne reviens pas

S HE LOOKS very comfortable sitting there, very at ease. She is wearing two skirts, one pulled over the other, each with a heathery fleck to it. I count her hemlines, one cream rayon petticoat then the two wavering seams of muted colours. There might be another one, a shorter one that doesn't show – three skirts, the layers bulking out her hips and waist, so she looks, perversely, even smaller than the small woman she has become. I'd say those skirts are her comfort – a shelter that she carries with her. This is the sort of thing I'm figuring out – the meaning of all those skirts. Alasdair says they don't mean anything. He says I am obsessed with Gran's illness, that it has become a distraction, a means of avoiding what's important. What's important, he says, is this: I need to move on, get over what has happened.

But he doesn't know.

It's the other baby I think about most, the one Gran spoke of the day I told her I was pregnant. I used to picture my own baby, her chalky face round as a clock, but now there's this other one. When I stand down at the river she rises to the surface like a dead fish.

Today there is no baby; there is James, my grandfather,

who suddenly appeared out of the blue and dazzled us with his fancy card shuffle, prompted perhaps by the rhythm of turn-taking as Gran and I play 3D dominos (where pieces needn't stay flat, they can be stacked upwards, or stood on their sides), and now here's someone else – Edward emerging from a talcum cloud.

I'm dusting Gran's hands with *Je Reviens* using her best Coty powder puff. It's air-spun, which is essential since anything else would feel too harsh against her thinning skin. Talcum powder has become a bit of a polemic; Mum is very much against it, but Gran has always used it, and given the years we spent sharing a room I've probably ingested quite a lot of the stuff. A victim of passive powdering, I imagine my once clean and tender lungs are now laced in the fragrant particles of *Je Reviens* (imagine, at best, flouring a piece of liver). The container is a distinctive blue, very Farrow & Ball; I can picture it on the chart – *Je Reviens (1932) a French blue, dense but light. Very like the colour of the paper used for lining drawers in the late eighteenth century at the palace of Versailles.* Gran told me that from the age of two I was able to twist the golden top and wink open the little eyes; I'd hand it to her with great care, then we'd both enjoy the smell of oranges and roses, each taking a turn to press our noses against her velvety hands.

Too late, Mum became convinced there were health risks associated with talcum powder. I tried to reassure her (and myself) by looking into it a bit more and pointing out that all that stuff about cancer was based on very dodgy evidence.

'But your lungs, Aggie – why take the risk?'

'Mum! I keep telling you if there is any risk, which there isn't, it only applies to excessive exposure to industrial talc. *Je Reviens* is not industrial. It's cheap, but it's not that cheap.'

'All I'm saying is why take the chance? Why risk it when it's easy not to?'

But maybe it isn't easy not to – because the truth is Mum has no idea about that talc and what it means to Gran; she doesn't know that the aquamarine colour of the box reminds her of Vincent van Gogh's painting of almond blossom – that so much stems from that.

When Gran first saw the orchard and looked at the fruit trees against the darkening blue sky it was like looking with van Gogh's eyes, she could see what he saw – blossom trapping light that had already gone. That's what she told me, years ago. She said that it started to rain and the land-lord let her shelter in the empty house and by the time the clouds had passed she'd decided to stay and 'live in the painting'.

'But where did you see the painting?'

'In a book.'

'Do you still have it?'

'No. But we can get it from the library if you like.'

And when we did, and found the page, she looked at the picture for a very long time, and I looked too, but not so long, and although I could see a darkening like distant rain, I knew I was missing something.

As if following a demonstration, she watches the airy puff flitting across the back of her hands. These hands don't belong to her, and when I catch her eye I wonder if, in that moment, she thinks I'm someone else, or just doesn't know who I am. I smile and she smiles back. 'Yes,' she says, very softly.

'That's you – done and dusted.'

I sit back and grin but I've said it too abruptly; she starts – then searches about for something.

'Where's my . . .?'

'Your bag?'

'No, where's my little . . . my wee . . .?'

She's looking at the strange room. The dog eyes flash briefly but go when she puts a hand over her mouth and smells the musk on her fingers.

'How long have you been using *Je Reviens*, Gran?'

'Pardon?'

'Has this always been your favourite talc?'

I pick up the bottle and pass it to her. She looks at it, rubbing the lettering with her thumb.

'This?'

Checking with me, I nod – then she presses a finger to her lips and whispers.

'It's a present.'

'From who, an admirer?'

She laughs.

'*Tch.*'

Holding onto the bottle, it takes her.

'He's a doctor from the other department. He plays cricket.'

'What's his name?'

'Edward. He is a *Second Assistant Physician.*'

She enunciates *Second Assistant Physician* in a very syllabic way, reciting what she has taken the trouble to learn.

'He has a very important appointment in Perth.'

'Did Edward give you the talc?'

'Yes. Wrapped up in yellow.'

'And did he do what it says on the tin?'

I've confused her again (colloquialisms were one of the first things the cuckoo gobbled up).

'He did very much, just as he does. Everything that was necessary.'

Her chin was determined now. She was looking straight at me.

'But did he come back?'

'No.'

I guide her attention back to her hands and she is surprised to find the talc. She loosens her grip when I touch the lettering.

'*Je Reviens* – it means "I will return".'

'Does it?'

'I think so. Did you not know that?'

'No.'

'So, he didn't come back, then?'

'Who?'

'Edward.'

'No.'

Opening her mouth to speak, nothing comes. She gapes at me, her stare flat, like pennies on the eyes of the dead. I have taken her somewhere she doesn't want to be, and rightly she has stopped and will go no further. She picks up a notebook and turns the pages over and back.

'Do you remember something?' I ask.

'Do *you* remember something?' She smiles at me, a wicked grin that suggests she already knows the answer but is daring me to say it.

'I remember our walks up Ormiston Hill. I miss those walks, do you?'

She laughs, then with clear purpose she lifts the book and checks underneath. The cat stirs on his cushion. He's called Jack and since he moved into the house twelve years ago he has always migrated to the warmth of Gran's room for winter; we can set the seasons by him. He licks a paw and starts to pull it across his face, then immediately falls back to sleep.

'Just look at that,' she says, shaking her head.

Jack is lying on his side, his back legs straight and parallel, and his paw is resting over his eyes, like he has a headache.

'Incredible, quite incredible.'

'That's Jack,' I say.

'Up the bean stalk – lost his boots.'

'Yeah, he's some boy.'

'Hopeless. He won't catch much that way. Left his mother too soon I think, eh, puss?'

She stirs, rustling as she moves towards him, her voice high and ageless.

'Pussy – pussy pussy.'

Jack drops his paw and opens one eye; he's learned to be vigilant when she's on the move, never knowing when he's going to be unceremoniously thrown out.

FIONA AND I are sitting in the Christian café, where we regularly worship the lemon drizzle cake. I'm telling her about Gran's skin and how hesitant I am to touch it because it looks like it might tear, when she interjects – cutting across like she's wielding a scalping knife.

'How's Alasdair?' she asks.

I'm slightly thrown by this non sequitur but I go with it since the subject of Alasdair rarely comes up.

'You'd have to ask him. He barely speaks.'

'Oh, God – what's his problem?'

Her sardonic tone is another surprise since she's the one who's asking after him; perhaps she just wanted to change the subject? Fiona is not very interested in old people – they're not one of her categories.

'He says all I talk about is Gran.'

'Mmmm.'

'What do you mean – mmm?'

'Well – he's right, isn't he, Bug?'

Bug is what she calls me when she is either hurting me or loving me. I acquired the name at school, and there is a kind of entomological link, I suppose, since I earned it by excelling at biology (my class presentation on spiders included a terrifying list of diseases that plagued me for weeks). Initially

56

it was a pejorative jibe, but Fiona managed to turn it into a term of endearment.

I am about to tell her that Gran's been talking about a dead baby when something stops me.

'She's mentioned someone called Edward, a doctor that I think she had a relationship with. I just can't make sense of it.'

'That's because it isn't sense, is it? She's confused. Look, I know how much you love her but you need to accept what's happening.'

Her sombre tone unsettles me in so many ways. I am wary of it, too close to giving in. How to speak here, in this café – to express the terrible fear of losing Gran, of not being able to penetrate her loneliness? Already I regret mentioning Edward.

'You're right. You're right, Alasdair's right, everyone's right.'

'That's not what I meant. We're not saying—'

We?

'No. It's fine. I understand. Not everyone's interested in an old woman's testimony, but it's not all nonsense, you know.'

And to tip the day towards rationality I stick to what's plausible, the part of Gran's history for which there is proof: the blossom; the starry nights; the way Vincent van Gogh led them to Fife – and I am lamenting the fact that Mum doesn't seem to know anything about this part of Gran's story when Fiona interjects again.

'Bug—'

'What?'

'Don't you think that's a bit harsh?'

'No.'

'You're always so hard on your mum.'

'Am I?'

'Yes. Maybe she knows more than you think but just doesn't want to talk about it?'

'No, I don't think so. I get the impression she's just never bothered to ask.'

'See – there you go again!'

'What?'

'Why do you say never *bothered* to ask? Why not just say "never asked"? You're always judging her.'

'No I'm not!'

'Oh come on, of course you're judging her.'

'I'm not.'

I pull a broad smile to throw her off, and because I don't know what to say. I don't want to talk about Mum any more, the way she makes me feel; we have been discordant for some time. I think briefly of Fiona's mum, sturdy and prunish. I can't recall Fiona ever talking about her much. I finish my coffee, pressing cake crumbs with my finger and licking them off. Fiona looks at her watch.

'Oh shit! I told Donald I'd be back before two.'

She's making moves to go, gathering up her things.

'I'm going to stay here for a bit. Flossie's having a late lunch so I don't need to be back till half past.'

'OK. You all right?'

'Yeah, I'm fine.'

She zips up her coat, picks up her bag and guides the strap over her head and across her shoulder.

'By the way, Aggie, I keep meaning to ask you – when your parents got married did they know that your dad's mother was going to cut him off from the farm?'

'I don't know. Why d'you ask?'

'Just wondering – it feels like an important part of your history. I'm surprised you haven't ever bothered to ask.'

And she smiles that way she does, like she genuinely likes me.

When she's gone I pay the bill and walk back to work, moving slowly because I'm thinking about my last conversation with Mum. When I reach the surgery I pause at the door to lick the sugar from my teeth. I'm still thinking about Mum, but it's not the words I remember, it's the non-words – the characteristic reluctance that scrunches her mouth inwards, like a rag doll sewn too tight.

The Pulling Power of Dentists

THE MOMENT is very precise – a thought forms like a tiny dendrite, then it crystallises, growing in a fractal pattern across the inside of your skull. That's what happened this morning – the sudden formation of a suspicious mind.

We don't usually talk in the mornings. Usually I follow in his wake, but today, because I skipped my shower, I caught up with him. It wasn't intentional but I could tell he thought it was. His face winced in the bedroom, and then again in the kitchen, the eyebrows stalling in quiet alarm. He was already unsettled by my presence and the difference it made, and I realised it was probably a mistake to talk to him, but that's how we learn.

'I rang you yesterday to see if you'd bring home some Post-its but you weren't in.'

He didn't raise his head from the paper but his eyes left the page and looked into middle space.

'Oh? What time?'

'Quarter to three. Nobody knew where you were.'

'I had a late lunch.'

'So, where were you?'

'At lunch.'

'But where?'

He jumped up.

'Shit! My porridge is burning.'

'You shouldn't have the gas so high. It cooks better on a low heat.'

'I know how to cook porridge!'

He said it with *huge* indignation, the words spurting out in dry bubbles (like boiling porridge, it has to be said – *puh!*); you'd think I was insinuating something. I apologised for the tacit affront, whatever it was, and he dropped to a simmer. The porridge clung to the spoon and he was banging the whole tacky mess against the side of the bowl, trying to shift it.

'You could lay a brick on that.'

He turned and raised his spoon but I got in first.

'Sorry! I'm just saying—'

'Don't.' *(Puh!)* 'Don't say anything.' *(Puh! Puh! Puh!)*

I gave him the silence he wanted and we both pretended we'd fallen out over culinary differences. And that was the very moment – the fixed boiling point of porridge – when all the tiny facets, the looks and the looking away, the late lunches and the unexplained outbursts, when all those micro-moments suddenly increased in magnitude and I knew that he was seeing someone.

I realised it was fanciful but that didn't lessen the power of it; a shock crystal snapping in my head, its brittle symmetry came as a relief, like a diagnosis that explained all my ailments.

It's not unusual for me to call Alasdair at work, although I don't always know why I'm doing it – it's not like he has a nice voice or says nice things to me; he obviously has to share a phone because sometimes another person answers and I can hear him saying 'that's someone for you' and when Alasdair says 'who?' he just says 'a woman'. I've tried asking if I can speak to *my husband*, but right after I say 'speak to' I swallow a fishbone. It happens every time.

Alasdair is a Dental Technician, or rather he's a Registered Dental Technologist (an RDT). RDTs are the most unsung of all dental professionals; they design and construct teeth – and not just dentures, he makes all toothy paraphernalia (crowns and bridges, veneers, that kind of thing). When we first met and he told me about his work I was gripped by a series of *Walrus and the Carpenter* dreams where Alasdair and the fanged walrus drag themselves along the shoreline in an Alasdair universe full of weeping and sulking. I believed I had somehow entered his sub-conscious; it was a bleak, protean place – deeply coded, and delivering Alasdair from it became very important. I tried everything to cheer him up – humour, philosophy, various forms of love (except tough love, I can see the idea but it feels confusing) – and although nothing seemed to work and the only consistent aspect of the whole thing was his misery, I enjoyed it. It gave me something to do.

When I told Alasdair about my dreams he discouraged me. He didn't like being the carpenter, and discouraged my night-time walks along the briny beach. He pointed out that it was not his universe, it was mine – and they were not fangs, they were tusks (he is master of the spurious, in the form of both observation and interrogation – it is the only thing about him that reminds me of my dad). Eventually, the walrus and the carpenter grew tired of each other and went their separate ways. I learned to listen sensibly and to appreciate the distinctions between fangs and tusks, and why these things matter; I understood the frustrations of being viewed as a prosthodontist (falsers) when really he wanted to be a conservationist (bridges and other bits). I was sympathetic, but it was his friend the dentist who encouraged him.

'Flossie reckons if I just play the game I could be in line for Chief Technician.'

His face was still when he said it, his eyes ardent.

'What does she mean *play the game?*'

'Well, you know, toe the line, do a bit of teaching, that kinda stuff.'

And I remember thinking how sensible this friend of his sounded, and how kind.

YESTERDAY, FLOSSIE had a late lunch too. She didn't get back to the surgery until after three, which is why I'd had time to call Alasdair – and why today, seeing him cloyed with porridge, his mouth clamped shut with the stuff (eating it anyway to mortify the flesh), I decided not to push the conversation any further.

The kitchen fills with the smell of heaven. I make perfect almost toast – almost soft, butter almost melted, best served almost cold. And it *is* perfect, but something is bothering me. With Alasdair gone and a little time to spare I transfer my heavenly bread onto a plate and sit at the table to eat. I have even made tea in a pot, and, because I sense that just ahead there will be the need for comfort, I have laid out some marmalade and a silver-plated jam spoon, my only one.

I am re-configuring, thinking about the concurrence of late lunches, and the way Flossie always insists she has a terribly sweet tooth, like it's something she's proud of. She's forever bringing in confectionery that no one buys any more – fruit jellies and strawberry bonbons, those posh travel sweets that come in a tin. We only eat them to be polite. This odd lack of taste suggests to me that she doesn't really understand or appreciate confection, she's just pretending in an effort to seem like the rest of us. It isn't sweet, it's patronising.

Suddenly there is a brief, sulphurous flash, and there they are – Flossie and Alasdair hand in hand and with their arms raised to shield their eyes from my terrible glare. I know it is a strange morphology, a discontinuous jump – but that is the nature of dynamic revelation, and at last there is someone to blame.

I have always known they were close but I've never felt jealous – not a single pang, not even when they spent two days together at some dreary conference in Durham last February (come to think of it, 'dreary' was the word they both used – independently and on different occasions – to describe it, suggesting rehearsal). I did not suspect. We are so different, Flossie and me – she is pale and translucent whereas I'm more ruddy, a kind of russet Bramley to her Pink Lady. Further, Alasdair is not easily swayed; he has clearly defined tastes and knows what he likes and what he doesn't like, I think because he has constructed a life from nothing – a self-creation of self. I assumed his sureties and preferences applied as equally to women as to everything else. So I thought nothing of it.

But now, with all the power of the subliminal, they are entwined in my head, and I just know they are sleeping together. They probably do it every Sunday when I'm away visiting Gran, right after *Songs of Shagging Praise*. It would explain a lot, but I don't understand it. Alasdair always said he loved my stamina, but Flossie is quite delicate, feeble almost. She is thin and has weak wrists, can barely manage molar extractions, which require a lot of strength (I've seen many a splintered attempt – shards and crumbs clogging up the suction pump, and the patient, eyes like gobstoppers, staring wildly at Flossie or the amusing *Where's Wally?* poster that has been stuck to the surgery ceiling for as long as anyone can remember, our own little Sistine Chapel). With extractions, she might have a tendency to leave in the roots (more of a hoe than a dig), but her work with veneers is an art; she has a good eye and a gentle touch, and approaches each tooth as if it were a rare and tiny thing, a small Venus from the Palaeolithic age. I have many reasons to like her

– not least she is my employer and my dentist, and she's NHS (the uneven practice notwithstanding, her lists are full). She has been kind and generous – but I have misunderstood, and I wonder, given the choices she must have, what she sees in my stocky husband. He has such a peppery temperament, and his opinion of dentists is very low.

Deceit is the worst betrayal – it was Flossie who said it. We were all talking about the errant receptionist's daisy car and I remember she was quite hard on Sylvia in an uncharacteristic way.

'Deceit is the worst betrayal,' she said.

'I don't think it's that straightforward,' I said.

And everybody looked at me. We were sitting up close, squashed into the tiny staff room, drinking coffee and eating Spanish nougat.

'Mmmm – who brought this in?'

'Oh God! I think it was Sylvia! Did they no go to Majorca for a holiday?'

'That's right! – they did! They weren't long back when she left.'

We each unwrapped another piece and lodged it in our mouths.

'Tewwible—'

Slurp.

'Aye.'

Shloop.

Eating marmalade with my silver spoon – *my only one, my constant* – I think of that daisy car still sitting in the drive up Blackness Road, and I wonder, is it a wee silver beacon of forgiveness, something bright to guide Sylvia home? Or is it hopelessness that keeps it there? Whatever it is, there is an unashamed candour to it, a bravery that draws me away from the craven. The car has been catching my attention for some time and I have pondered over its meaning so often I

65

can hardly believe I've never actually seen it. I'd like to see it. I feel that I ought to see it, having thought about it so much. As I flick through the paper I am thinking about it again when a photograph of the night sky reconnects my eyes to my brain. It is a very beautiful photograph. Taken earlier this month it shows a crescent moon tilting above a dark silhouette of trees, with Venus and Jupiter in close conjunction, and with the headline – 'Was Jupiter The Star of Bethlehem?' I read the article and try to follow the argument, but as always when it comes to astronomy, too many celestial bodies spin across too many constellations and soon my mind explodes in starry confusion and the whole thing collapses, an earthly crash that comes as a relief. Staring at the stars is a kind of surrender – that's the whole point. It is incomprehensible, a state of unknowing that erases everything.

I clear up the breakfast things, fill Alasdair's porridge pot with hot water and set it aside to soak. It looks irredeemable. I'm about to leave for work when I decide not to.

Let her get on with it. I'm not going back.

Everyone will understand. I certainly don't expect to be challenged by Flossie. In fact, I could probably get away with murder. Minute by minute things feel different, tiny mixed-up surges of something, a power shift maybe; definitely a shift of some sort.

Sod it – I'm not going in.

But I'm worried about how they'll get through the appointments – there's a molar erupting in a strange direction, and a root canal booked in for ten. The molar is terrified; he's six years old and already traumatised (a Ribena baby who had eight extractions before he was three), and that root canal will gush saliva – there could be a drowning without Louise's help, so someone needs to cover reception. I know Flossie is off in the afternoon – if I can just get through the morning, then the day should ease. I need hardly see her.

Taking in the view from the moral high ground, and already sensing an odd but pleasant distance from the whole tawdry mess, I pop some Panadol, undecided except for this – tonight, when it gets dark, I'm going to walk up to the observatory and stare at the night sky. With no sacred space to comfort me I will gaze at the unfathomable and forget all earthly conjunctions. I might see Jupiter rising, or merging with Venus – they might overlap and become indistinguishable, two halves of the same star.

And I will understand none of it.

THE TEN o'clock root canal didn't turn up. This isn't unusual. Patients will endure anything to be rid of an abscess. They will floss after every savoury morsel and swear that they will never, *never* again use their molars to grind added sugar into syrup; Irn Bru no more; Pepsi no more. They'll splash out £4.99 on a bottle of Listerine and stand upside-down head first in a bucket all day if they have to – but, once the antibiotic kicks in, they change their mind. They become deluded by the sweetness of a pain-free sleep. Heady on comfort, they make peace with the tooth and the sagging gum, and decide to 'give it another go'. At first they start sucking on confections that don't require teeth – some dark chocolate perhaps, or a soft mint, then it's the odd wee toffee, and soon they're cavorting with Mr Kipling again, light as a French fancy and swooning into his arms after too many Viennese whirls. Dizzy with it. Then, perhaps in a few months, or less, they're on the phone to Flossie, contrite and desperate – and she always forgives them; when it comes to teeth she is completely non-judgemental, and her compassion is genuine, you can tell. There's no one you'd rather turn to.

Flossie took over the practice from her mother, Hester

McKendrick, who retired quite a few years ago after a very long career in dentistry. Hester was a feminist; she subscribed to *Time and Tide* and in the late 1970s patients could still find old copies of it in the waiting room, along with the *Reader's Digest* and *National Geographic*. On the back wall of reception there is a framed copy of an alphabet poem (where D is for Dentist, naturally) taken from that magazine; when I commented on it Flossie told me about her mother, how she rallied against prejudice and blew gaskets at any suggestion of her as a 'petticoat practitioner'. This honourable legacy is just another set of contrary facts that get in the way of my attempts to nurture a dislike of Flossie, whose gentle nature (which probably grew tentatively, in a quiet nursery filled with absent love and the faint smell of ether) is not relevant. I don't need to know anything about it.

In fact, it only makes things worse.

TODAY IT is my turn to pick the Lottery numbers. Usually I put down someone's birthday; I close my eyes and whoever comes into my head I put down their birthday or something else about them, their age or house number, whatever I can hang on them. This time when I shut my eyes no one appears, all I see is a brown sky pressing down on a yellow field. The field is bright, but there is no light in the sky; rain starts to fall from somewhere at the back of my head, and when it hits the sky, brown bleeds into yellow and the horizon is lost.

It's mesmerising. I could stay here all day.

'Aggie?'

Ah – someone's coming at last.

'Aggie.'

Someone emerging from the yellow field.

'That's your mum on the phone for you.'

'Oh – sorry.'

I open my eyes and Louise hands me the phone. (The

nurse often mans the phones – we all move up and down here, depending on who's in. Flossie says we move from side to side, not up and down, which I suppose is true, since the only hierarchy here is monetary. Everything else is equal.)

'Hi, Mum, how are you?'

'I'm fine. What are you doing? Are you busy?'

'No. I'm just doing the Lottery.'

'Good. Listen – your gran's come downstairs. She's going through all the drawers taking everything out and sifting through it all over and over again. The kitchen's in complete chaos but she won't tell me what she's looking for.'

Immediately I think, Not won't, can't – she *can't* tell you what she's looking for, but I have the sense not to say it.

'She hasn't got anything on her feet and she keeps calling me Sally.'

'Is she upset?'

'Well, a bit. She's getting upset. The thing is, she won't do anything for me.'

'What do you want her to do?'

'What?'

'What do you want her to do?'

There's a pause, then a sigh.

'I want her to sit down and put her slippers on.'

'Can't you just give her something? Maybe search with her for a bit and then say "here it is" or something like that, like you've found what she's looking for?'

'Do you think that would work?'

'Yes – or maybe just distract her onto something else, that's the best thing. What about getting her to lay the table? She likes doing that.'

'She can't do that any more. She's forgotten where everything goes.'

'Well, it doesn't really matter, just leave her to put things where she wants.'

'But why's she suddenly come downstairs?'

'I don't know. Maybe she got bored.'

'She's got about three coats on. I'm terrified she's going to try to go out. I just can't persuade her to sit down.'

'But why do you want her to sit down if she doesn't want to? She's got to move.'

I can hear Mum sigh again, louder this time, and longer, more air drawn from a deeper place. She's frustrated with me now; when she answers her voice is raised and the words are sharp, clipped clean one from the other.

'Because – I – want – her – to – put – her – slippers – on.'

'But it doesn't *really* matter, does it?'

'Of course it matters! Her feet must be freezing. Oh, never mind, Aggie. You get on with your own things. I just wanted to see if you had any ideas.'

'Well, try what we said.'

'Yes, well, thanks for the help.'

She must have turned away from the phone because her voice sounds more distant. 'No, not that, Mum – you're going to—'

There's a crash. She lets go of the phone and the mouthpiece swings from the cable like a roving antenna, so their voices come and go. 'Right – come on, Mum.'

I can hear them moving about, and still a slight undulation that distorts the room and all that happens within it.

'We need to take these back, Sally.'

'I'm not Sally.'

'Sally.'

'I am not Sally, I'm Mary.'

'Who?'

'Mary. I'm your daughter.'

'My daughter died.'

There is no answer.

'How old are you now, Sally?'

'I'm fifty-eight.'

'Are you?'

'Yes.'

Silence. I picture them both, caught in a still frame – they are exhausted, and look as if they have been dropped from the sky and have no idea where they landed. Then Mum crosses the room and hangs up the phone.

I'M WALKING up Blackness Road, heading for the woods beyond the cemetery and the road that leads up to the observatory. It's a steep climb – a hill you'd think twice about if it were covered in grass rather than tarmac. Having had less than twenty-four hours to accommodate the inchoative fact (or intuitive certainty) that my husband is sleeping with my boss, I don't feel like pushing myself.

There – suddenly and at last, he has become *my husband*. I'll probably call him that from now on. I have dislodged the bone in my throat and given it a name. Alasdair. Deceptive as a kipper bone, soft and podgy in a Philip Seymour Hoffman kind of way, except he's smaller, and he isn't acting – those really are his thighs. I can tell from old photographs that he's had them all his life. They have clamped rocking horses and straddled push-along cars, and (reluctantly by the look of it) the odd trekking pony.

Now those perfidious thighs are straddling Flossie.

I stop every few yards on the pretext of admiring the Christmas trees. This late November flourish has caught me by surprise; perhaps Christmas is closer than I thought. The trees wink and blink, not quite in every window but almost; there are only one or two exceptions (each with a story to tell). The lights are getting smaller every year, pin-prick tiny like lunar dust motes; soon they will disappear up their own plugs. My husband wanted us to go LCD last year but I said no, and because he didn't bring anything to the Christmas box, he doesn't have a say. Anyway, I reckon our Christmas lights – large plastic lanterns that don't blink – won't be naff for much longer. Soon they'll be cutting edge, just like our standard lamp with the fringe shade, and our ton-weight cut-glass vase (perfect for big-headed flowers – like hydrangeas).

My walk up Blackness is not just about following the stars; there is something else, an added purpose. I move past the darkened rooms, looking up every driveway because I know that the legendary Nissan Micra is somewhere nearby. I realised this the moment I set out. The possibility shifted the whole prospect, for although the moons of Jupiter excite me, Sylvia's daisies excite me more.

I'm nearly at the top of the hill when I see him. I'd recognise him anywhere now, a partial view from a great distance would be enough, or no view – just a gesture would do, the way he moves.

I'd see him in a blink of an eye.

About ten yards ahead Kenneth is un-strapping a Christmas tree from the roof of his car. He's wearing a strange leather hat with ear-flaps, but gets away with it. In fact, he more than gets away with it, he looks fantastic, like a gorgeous bear. His coat stops just below his knees, and his trousers are pushed into his wellies. He has gloves, but no scarf, and I'm thinking, *Put a scarf on*, when he stops what he's doing and looks down the street towards me. I give a feeble, insouciant wave as I puff towards him, head down and smiling.

'Hiya.'

On reaching him I straighten up, hands on hips and surveying the surrounds like I've just arrived at base camp.

'Phew! It's quite a climb.'

'Hello.'

He gives me a look I can only describe as understated

astonishment – incomprehension with a wry smile. It feels very warm, that smile – thaws me out.

'How are you?'

'I'm fine.'

'I'm just on my way up to the observatory.'

'Are you?'

'Yes – searching for Jupiter.'

We both look at the crowded sky.

'I wish I'd known,' he said, still looking up.

We pause in a moment of contentment, pleasure of some sort.

'Do you live here?'

He lowers his head.

'Yes.'

He's still smiling. *Does he think that's a fake question?*

'Which one? This one?'

'Yes.'

We are standing in front of a semi-detached terraced house with a small front garden. It's one of those Victorian houses that are always bigger inside than you expect. There is a black wrought-iron gate and a low wall with metal stumps protruding from the stone where the railings used to be; I know about those stumps and see a chance to show off.

'Did your bit during the war, I see.'

I nod towards the wall.

'Well, they weren't much use, in fact.'

'No?'

'No. Most of the railings are lying at the bottom of the North Sea.'

'Oh. I thought they built planes with them or something?'

'No.'

We scrutinise a metal stump.

'How's your dad?'

Kenneth's dad is in ward 22. Were he in ward 18, there

might have been some hope; under the guise of 'assessment' a stay in ward 18 means the family can take a break and make a few adjustments, get things ready for the return home, but nobody ever comes home from ward 22. Kenneth scratches his chin, exploring the slight cleft like it has just appeared. He considers the question carefully.

'He's all right, I think. He's found a girlfriend.'

'Really?'

'Yes. Miss Deborah Kerr.'

'Didn't she die?'

'She did, actually – last year. I checked, just in case.'

'Only last year – she must have been ancient! So why Deborah Kerr?'

'I've no idea. The woman's real name is Charlotte.'

He looks up at the sky again and I follow him.

'You've picked a good night.'

'Yes. You seem very organised.'

I nod towards the tree and he shakes his head.

'That tree – you wouldn't believe what I—'

A light comes on and he stops. Kenneth's front door opens and a woman dressed in bright colours peers out.

'Is that you, darling?'

Shit!

'Yes, just coming.'

'I'll come out and help you. Hang on.'

She disappears from the doorway, leaving us caught in the light. I want to dive into the darkness and disappear.

'Right. I'll press on. See you at the group?'

'Yes—'

He stands in the light and I hesitate because I think he is going to say something else but he doesn't.

'OK. See ya!'

Too much alacrity! And to make matters worse I take a few jaunty steps before settling into a brisk stride. I can still hear them as I make my rapid ascent up the hill – her voice rising with delight, excited, I assume, by the lovely tree.

He probably thinks I engineered that whole encounter. I'm so distracted by this awful thought that I miss the main gates that lead to the observatory and have to stop and get my bearings. Turning to look back I find what I have been looking for. The car is on the opposite side of the road, sitting in the narrow drive just as I'd pictured it. Fairy-lights have been strung across the house and along the garden path, and there, floating dimly in the soft light like Galilean moons, are the daisies.

I cross the road to take a closer look. The car is clean, inside and out, and it's the cleanness that gets to me – the clear glass and the pristine hubcaps, mirrors shining under a night sky. I have made my pilgrimage to the shrine of lasting love. *Proud of my broken heart since thou didst break it . . .*

I reach towards the daisies and when I touch the car there is a loud mechanical click, and then another, and I'm immediately flooded in a white light that extinguishes the fairy-lights and turns the car hot; bright grass rushes up to meet me as I stumble over my own feet and bolt from the scene. Swerving to avoid an open gate, something snaps in my ankle – the sudden sharp pain of ligament ripped from bone – and each time my foot touches the ground I yell. I can't help it. Yelping, I descend the hill, lurching from gate to gate, from tree to twinkly tree. I fancy I hear someone (a man's voice) call out – *Wait!* But I don't. There's a knife in my ankle that twists each time my foot touches the ground, so I'm moving quite slowly now. When I reach the shops beside the traffic lights I sit down at a bus stop and rest. The low metal bench is the most comfortable seat I have ever sat on and for a few moments I forget about my ankle and wonder at the ergonomic genius of it. I raise my foot and find a tiny, precise locus that's free of pain. I don't want to take off my shoe in case I can't get it back on again, but I think my ankle is possibly broken, certainly strained; when I move my foot, even slightly, the pain is terrible. I can barely walk. I won't be able to drive. I probably won't be able to go to work until after Christmas because of my injury.

My visible hurt.

At last something's going my way.

Where Pumas Prowl

THE DOCTOR said it was only a sprain; she doubled up my painkillers and told me to rest. I suggested to Alasdair that it would probably be easier to rest at Mum's for a few days and this idea overtook the medication and brought immediate palpable relief to both of us.

Under the circumstances, I couldn't stay.

I didn't have the will or the stamina to bring up Flossie, or the evidence – even I could see that (although there was the acrid sting of all those little lies, and that moment when I saw their molten sin – *flagrante delicto* in the green sulphurous light). And anyway, Alasdair was fed up with hearing about Gran's narrative. He doesn't even like the term, pronounces it with a sceptical *g*.

'Gnarrative.'

'Story, then.'

'Story is right. You're making it up as you go along. And what's with all the Post-its above the fireplace?'

I'd started to write down some key words to capture the things Gran was coming out with, memories peeling off like old paint, taking her back to the bone. Sticking them up on the living-room wall was perfect; I could sit on the sofa and stare at each one individually, but I was also seeing them as part of a whole – a line of semaphore flags that were telling me something, and since she no longer tracked time like the rest of us (because it didn't matter) I could move the Post-its around, change the order to impose that very thing, an order of some kind.

If I stare long enough, eventually something will emerge.

'I'm trying to make sense of what she's saying. Just leave them.'

With too much haste Alasdair pulled out a rucksack and helped me pack, zipping me up with a few chattels and finally appearing in the hall with my toothbrush.

'You'll need this. Are you taking the Post-its?'

'No. Don't touch them please.'

He pulled a stupid face and raised his hands like I was pointing a gun at him.

'OK. Don't worry.'

We drove past inert fields, lay-bys and ditches and dull verges, the old ruins on the outskirts of Plum Town evoking the future rather than the past, and higher up, when I could be bothered to raise my eyes – a scattering of miserable gorse, cast out and clinging to the side of a hill. There was no talk, not much. When he did speak I didn't answer, there was no requirement.

'Do you remember that film *The Usual Suspects* with Kevin Spacey? He was the one with the limp who sat in the office. You remind me of him.'

I did remember it, and I knew what he was referring to. As we pulled up outside the house I asked him not to mention the Post-its, especially not to Mum.

'Why not?'

'Because I don't want you to.'

'But why? I'm sure she'd be really interested.'

'I don't want to speak about it.'

I might have said more. I might have said something about my theory that Gran is drawing from a deep Jungian well of universal feelings, the kind we find at the heart of fairy tales, but I already know what he thinks about that. I might have said that I'm not searching for narrative, I'm searching for her; that I don't want her to be alone.

That she mentioned a baby again, only this time she gave her a name – Eleanor.

There is so much I might have said, but I couldn't – and anyway, all he could muster was a loud sigh, then he sucked on his teeth and shook his head, like it was me that was beyond the pale.

'*Speak* about it. Honestly, Aggie, the way you talk.'

Mum was so bloody pleased to see him she barely noticed my injury.

'Eh, excuse me, Mum. Crutches? Bandage? Bag full of painkillers?' (I didn't actually need the walking aids, they were just kicking about the flat, relics of an old bike injury incurred during the very early stages of our marriage when crutches were fun, sexy even – all that hilarious falling about.) I shook my wee rucksack and it obliged with a loud medicinal rattle, bringing me the attention I craved. Alasdair stayed long enough for a cup of tea but declined a slice of Mum's Ecclefechan tart, patting his tummy like it was something special – not to be sullied by Mrs Copella's delicious pastry. *Bastard! Just take a bit. If it's good enough for Thomas Carlyle it's good enough for you.* When he left I watched him from upstairs; he looked through the car window and waved. *Don't. Don't bother.* I composed my best 'wronged' look (based on a performance by Imelda Staunton, I can't remember what it was but she was wearing a bonnet). I planned to turn away first but he was moving faster than I thought.

And like that, he was gone.

STAYING HERE gives me the chance to spend more time with Gran. I like the mornings best – waking to the sounds of

Mum moving about in the kitchen, putting back whatever has moved in the night. She has already spent time with Gran, massaging her feet and, if she is in an agreeable mood, rolling down her socks and stockings, changing her clothes, enticing her to undress by enthusing about a pretty vest she pulls from some tissue paper, as if it were new. This is a trick, one of many techniques she has learned – the way Gran responds to something wrapped. She uses the promise and excitement of presents a lot, and has even wrapped up soap, so she might wash; food, so she might eat; silver nail-clippers and fancy emery boards, so she might enjoy a manicure. Boxes work too, especially shoe boxes containing shoes; and light-bulb boxes are good for holding things in bottles, like cod liver oil, or almond oil to soak her toes in, a possible precursor to cutting her nails. 'So clever,' I said, and of course, Mum said it was nothing to do with clever, it was necessity.

But Gran is not always in the mood for presents, and Mum is not always inclined to give them. There are days when the house – our quiet sanctuary of apple-scented rooms – is assaulted by noise and acrimony and the slamming of doors, the loud anguish of misunderstandings that go back fifty years. From my narrow bed I can hear Mum running down the stairs and it frightens me. I lie there, practically buried in the basement, unable to move.

IN RESPONSE to the news about my injury Fiona visits, filling the house with chatter and baby paraphernalia. She unbuttons the huge bulging coat that swings and swells around her and pulls out her little brown Michelin man.

'Here he is!' she says, and we all peer in at his hot face, like a firmament of Gods.

'*Awww.*'

When Tufty has been fed and changed Fiona passes him to Mum and we leave them to it.

'There's something about a room that doesn't have a baby in it that's absolutely bloody marvellous,' she says, sinking into the best chair in the living room and nabbing the pouffe that I've been using to rest my foot on. I stare at her.

'What?'

'Nothing. You're looking good.'

'So are you.'

'Am I? I feel crap.'

'Is your foot still sore?'

'Yes.'

She raises her head slightly from the back of the chair and looks at my foot for a moment, then collapses back and closes her eyes.

'Oh, this is bliss. Thomas had us up four times last night.'

I know that 'us' means Donald – it doesn't include her. The deal is that when he's home Fiona rests (I'm not sure when Donald rests, or where – at work I presume).

'I can't wait till he's going right through. It'll make such a difference. I'll never ask for anything else, just ten hours of unbroken sleep.'

Just *ten*?

This is a good way to talk – with our eyes closed.

'I'm not sleeping either. I lie down on my bed and worry that the house is going to collapse on top of me. I can hear the bulges in the walls shifting and groaning, just one more inch in the wrong direction and the whole place is going to fold in on itself and I'll be buried alive. I'll lie there for about twenty hours, then just before they reach me, I'll die.'

There are noises outside, a gusting wind and rain skittering against the window. Something is banging, a door or a gate; the noise heightens the interior quiet. When I open my eyes Fiona is staring at me. She looks worried, or irritated.

'What?'

'Your lip's bleeding.'

She pulls a blue polka-dot hanky from her pocket and dabs my chin with a gentleness I didn't expect. So tender, this foreign touch fills me with a sense of terrible deprivation.

'Don't cry, Bug – you'll set me off.'

'Sorry!'

And we laugh, sharing the hanky to dry our wet faces.

'Fancy you having a hanky,' I say.

'It's motherhood. Does the weirdest things.'

Resting back again, Fiona finds a comfortable position and immediately returns to her exhausted state; her eyelids drop intermittently but she resists, like someone fighting an anaesthetic. When her lazy gaze falls on the sideboard and the small display of family photographs there is a brief focusing before her eyes close.

'Your mum's so good-looking, isn't she?'

'Do you think so?'

'Yeah. She's reached that fading-beauty age that makes you look twice.'

I think about what she's saying, think about Mum and how she has achieved invisibility (almost – it's only the beautiful people who can see her now, they always recognise their own kind). She makes it look easy – a chameleon in her kitchen habitat, blending effortlessly behind aprons and tea towels until the room is all there is – pots hanging on hooks in a pleasing way, their copper bottoms shining like new pennies.

'I don't really see it.'

'No?'

'No.'

But I do. I don't know why I said that. *Fading beauty* – Mum is one; Gran was one; I'll never be one. Naturally I blame Dad.

'When are you going home?'

'I don't know. When I'm missed, I suppose.'

That opens her eyes; to cast out self-pity she needs to see what she's doing.

'Meaning?'

I hesitate, close to telling her about Alasdair and Flossie, but I can't because I know she'll ask for evidence – put me through it.

'Meaning, maybe never.'

She looks at me, smiling slightly (since Tufty was born she has become much more tolerant).

'Aww – hasn't he called?'

'Yes – he calls every day.'

'Well then, come on, Bug, chin up. I'm taking Thomas to his first Christmas fayre on Saturday. Why don't you come with us?'

'Christmas fayre! It's not even December.'

'I know, but it was the only day they could get the hall. Oh, please come – you can bring your little crutches.'

'Will Santa be there?'

'Of course he will, darling. He's coming specially, just to see you.'

'Don't beat – fold.'

In the sweet spicy heat of the kitchen I am more of a hindrance than a help. I can tell that she doesn't really want me in the kitchen at all; it would be best if I stayed upstairs with Gran, maybe try to 'sort her hair out' because for now she won't let Mum brush it – she prefers to brush. I sit at her feet, down amongst the hems and the socks that never come off (until they have to, forcibly and most cruelly, roughly about once a fortnight) and she lightly pulls the bristles across the top of my head and round the sides, gathering my hair with her other hand. I don't like the feel of it; her nails are too long (requiring further acts of sporadic cruelty) and they catch in my ears.

'Ouch!'

'Ouch!'

She sends it back to me in an *ET* moment, more than an echo, I think. I believe feelings are not yet alien to her, unlike other, more relative things – words that connect or describe.

Back in the kitchen I'm asking Mum questions.

'Did Gran brush your hair when you were a girl?'

'No.'

'Never?'

'Never. Mind out.'

She's stepping over the foot, which has rather outplayed itself; nobody bothers with it any more except me – and even I forget. I keep losing my crutches without realising they're lost, then I see them propped against a wall or leaning on a chair, abandoned at the site of a miracle.

'That's a shame.'

Mum wipes her brow, hot with steam or sweat.

'It didn't need much brushing. It was always kept short.'

'Didn't you ever want to grow it?'

'No.'

'What, never?'

She pulls a jar of crushed walnuts from the cupboard and tries to unscrew the lid.

'Maybe, I don't know – I can't remember. It doesn't matter whether I wanted to or not, I wasn't allowed to and that was that.'

The lid won't budge so she bangs it against the side of the table.

'Aw – poor you. That doesn't seem fair.'

I see her, small and dazzling, her short hair completely unadorned. She's wearing a long box-pleat skirt with button straps; her jumper is tucked into her waistband and the straps go over the top; her beauty goes uncelebrated, and there's no one else there to say, *Go on, Peggy . . . let the child have her way.* Suddenly I can hear my own sympathy, we both can. She is working herself into a state over that jar, and with a final twist the lid comes off and the walnuts fly everywhere.

'Oh, buggery – now look!'

'It's all right, Mum. They'll be fine.'

And they will be, because Mum's floor is always clean (something Dad appreciates having grown up in a large house full of middle-class dirt). She sighs and sits down, rubbing her forehead then tugging at her hair, feathering it behind her ears with her fingers.

'Don't you like it short?' she asks, catching the ends and pressing them against her bare neck.

'Of course I do. You look lovely. Fiona was just saying how lovely you look.'

'Huh!'

'It's true.'

She watches me picking up the nuts, calm now, and still teasing out her hair.

'Your gran was the beauty.'

She's all smoothed out, smiling at something she doesn't put words to. I slow up, taking the time to gather the last crumbs of walnut in the hope that she'll say a bit more.

'She had a lot of suitors, you know. Some of them seemed really nice, but the nicer they were the more distant she was. She'd keep them all dangling on a string and when they tried to get too close she'd just flick them away without any regard for their feelings.'

She pings her middle finger against her thumb, like she's flicking a dead fly from a window sill.

'The two of you must have caused quite a stir when you arrived here. It must have been like that film, *Chocolat*.'

'Oh, God – I wish! Your gran wasn't the nurturing type. She didn't believe in presents and all that giving and receiving stuff, and she never accepted gifts. She would never take anything from anyone.'

'She did once. Have you heard of someone called Edward?'

'Edward who?'

'I don't know his second name. She says he was a doctor. He was the one that gave her the *Je Reviens* talc.'

'No, I've never heard of him, but as far back as I can remember she's always used that awful talc. Maybe she knew him before I was born.'

We both sit at the table for a while, forgetting the walnuts. I share what little I know about Edward the physician, soon to be *Second Assistant Physician*, but I don't share the fact that last night I actually saw him struggling to wrap the talc in the thick yellow paper. When he'd finished it looked like a dog's dinner, a big lumpy bone of a thing. Mum not knowing this doesn't feel right because I think it's important. I was hoping that she had dreamt about it too, witnessed the wrapping and unwrapping – and later, just the scent of fragrant greens and orange-flower. Nothing else.

'So she's never mentioned him to you?'

'No.'

'I get the feeling there's a lot she's not telling us.'

I watch her when I speak, feeling duplicitous because I'm looking for a sign that tells me she knows a story, maybe the same story; maybe we're both keeping the story of Eleanor to ourselves, hiding the baby just as Gran has; an act of protection perhaps, or respect, or is it a kind of shame? (I do not yet understand my own silence.)

She sweeps the table with her hand, gathering up the last of the walnut pieces. She's about to drop them into the compost bucket, then she changes her mind and puts them in the bin, wiping her hands on the long black apron I bought her for her birthday about two years ago. It's a very trendy apron, just like the ones they wear in delicatessens; she looks good in it and I assume she likes it since she wears it every day. The apron was the perfect gift for Mum, practical and about the right price. Anything extravagant or expensive causes her great discomfort and now I can see how far that uneasiness goes; there is a thrift emerging, a careful economy of emotion. Even curiosity requires stemming, as if enquiry itself is somehow frivolous.

'Well, she's never mentioned anyone called Edward to me.'

'Do you know if she was ever in hospital?'

'I don't think so, but then I wouldn't know. She never really talks about her past.'

Neither do you, I want to say, but without it sounding like a charge. I have never sensed suppression in the house before, but I sense it now, the weight of things unsaid.

'Your gran is a very private person. She talks more to you than she ever did to me. All I know is she worked on the family farm and when she got married she moved to William's Lea. Before that she lived with her parents at Pennyland. I went there once.'

I look in astonishment, I think because she is touching the other world, where pumas prowl. I've never pictured Mum anywhere but here.

'It was only about a mile from where we used to live. I was out with the dog and he seemed to know where he was going. I remember him sniffing his way across the fields like he was tracking something so I decided just to follow him and we ended up at Pennyland farm. The farmer caught us crossing the yard and he told me to tie Bobby up and take him home or he'd be shot for worrying the sheep.'

She's scooping up the cake mixture and dropping it into a tin lined with brown paper, great dollops falling like cowpats. The greaseproof lining puckers along the edge and Mum teases it out so the cake can settle into a perfect round.

'Do you want to lick the bowl?'

I shake my head.

'Sure?'

'Well, OK – go on then.'

Butter melting in my mouth but my heart's not in it.

'It's funny, you know – when Bobby and me got back and I told your gran where we'd been she went daft.'

'Did she?'

'Oh yeah, really angry. She yanked Bobby by the collar and sent him to his bed. She sent me to bed too – middle of the afternoon, no explanation, just said not to go there again.'

I see her, downcast and compliant, a wee girl doing as she was told.

'Were you upset?'

She doesn't answer until the cake is in the oven and she's checked the clock.

'I was actually,' she says, surprising herself. 'I'd never seen her that angry before. I just thought it was about Bobby worrying sheep, but it might have been something else. We all have things we don't talk about. Finished?'

Her hand is already on the rim of the mixing bowl and before I can answer she's on her way to the sink.

An Unexpected Recovery

M Y MUM'S father died during childbirth. He was
sluicing out the byre, because the world doesn't stop
every time someone decides to have a baby; that's how
Gran put it, and it's just the sort of thing you'd expect her
to say – but of course, she may have been quoting him,
I'm not sure. I don't know who's the pragmatist in this,
her or my dead grandfather. The fact that he slipped and
cracked his head open doing something he did every day
suggests that, despite his apparent lack of interest, he was
distracted, or excited, or somehow altered by the birth that
was taking place in the south-facing upstairs bedroom back
at the house.

It was the birth of Mary, my mother, and it happened
on a flock mattress under the supervision of the local vet,
who had arrived just twenty minutes before the baby was
born, having been sent for the previous day to put down
the dog. Half on, half off – and hanging onto one of the
large brass knobs at the foot of the bed, Gran said it was
the sight of Mr Bryson's veterinary gloves that gave her
the strength for that last almighty push. She also said
(because I asked, thinking there must be some kind of
indirect association) that the presence of the vet – who

was considered to be the best lambing expert in the whole of Nithsdale – had nothing to do with the decision to name my mother Mary; that had been decided earlier by my grandfather, simply because it was a very popular name in its day and he was a very conventional man. Had it been a boy it would have been called George. I always thought that when someone unexpected delivers the baby you have to name it after them, in which case Mum would have been Cyrilina, which has a lovely ring to it – much nicer than my own name, which carries the timbre of a stubbed toe. *Ag-ath-a.*

My full name is Agatha Brody Copella, and my initials are my only solace.

I know Mum feels responsible (indirectly, she concedes) for her father's death. She has been dogged with a vague sense of guilt all her life, and I suppose that when a parent dies during the birth of their child it is natural to believe the two events are connected in some way; for them not to be stretches the notion of randomness too far, even for an existentialist like me. Mum believes that she was the source of his fatal lapse in concentration, and I wouldn't argue the point, but the more I hear about James Alexander Brody (which isn't much) the more I wonder. For example, my gran's waters broke while she was helping him with the milking. Now there's a lot I could say about that, but I am told I need to put it in context, so my only comment is restrained, and charitable, and it is this: *he could have gone for help then.* And I can't help wondering if his distraction was more to do with the fact that Queen of the South had just reached the semi-finals of the Scottish Cup (for the first time ever, or certainly in my grandfather's lifetime); his thoughts might have been on Hampden, or he might have been worrying about the size of the vet's bill; he may also have been preoccupied with the inconvenience of having to find another dog. What I'm saying is, it might not have been down to any concern for his wife and baby's well-being – there were other possibilities.

As it turned out, in all the excitement everyone forgot about the dog that lay dying in the back kitchen, and following the sudden death of his master he experienced a miraculous recovery and enjoyed a new lease of life. His name was Bobby, and he lived for at least another seven years. Bobby was a big part of Mum's early childhood; she remembers dressing him in a paisley frock and pulling him round the farm in a bogie, and whenever I hear those tales of his late flowering I can't help but muse on the contrast between his grief, or lack of it, and that of his more famous namesake – Greyfriars Bobby, whose loyalty is immortalised in the form of a fine granite fountain in Edinburgh. It's a contrast that says more about my grandfather than the dog, but I want to take something good out of the whole story, so I dwell on the following deduction.

At least he couldn't shoot his own dog.

References to the late James Alexander Brody are rare. A whole year can pass between mentions, but never more than a year, since there is always a toast on the morning of my mother's birthday – a respectful raising of glasses to my grandfather, who was spared not only the shock of the vet's bill, but also the cruel dashing of hope that swept through Dumfries and its surrounds when Rangers knocked out Queens 3–0 in the semis.

This apocryphal tale is a rare nugget, and doubtless I am prone to over polishing (that's certainly Alasdair's view), but when it comes to family history I want to make the most of what we have, there is so little of it.

'To James, may he rest in peace.'

A Sigh is Just a Sigh

I HAVE gone through her things, drawers and cupboards and under the bed like a sneak. Something unexpected – a slant of winter light perhaps, hazy with cloud – drew her downstairs in the daytime. This noontide descent was too rare to squander; a chance for Mum to blitz clean, turn the mattress and generally sort things out; and for me a chance to rummage, looking for anything that might help in my quest for clarity.

It must have been an unedifying sight, Mum and I in a frenetic scramble and with no need to cover our tracks, since she'd never notice.

Up until recently, Gran's room was a wild place full of unfettered things. She would pick something up and cast about, then scrutinise whatever she held – a pen, a spectacle case, scissors – then cast about again, trying to match the particular thing to a particular place, but with nothing to guide her. Her expressions were wild too, untamed looks of bewilderment, disgust, joy. Whatever the feeling inside her, there it was on her monkey face, baring its yellow teeth.

My gran is a woman of immense discretion, and it broke my heart to see her nakedness, to see her searching for something, an unnamed thing that left her speechless, such was the strangeness of it.

Heartbreaking.

Her lovely face turned monkey.

The squall passed. She began to look outwards again, to where the horizon was more reliable; trees turning and the fruit picked; the earth feeding on windfall apples, fattening up for winter. It was comforting to see her less agitated, even though we knew it came at a cost (progress always does), and in that period of relative calm I did not feel so compelled to make sense of the things she said.

But now that I am here − resting my ligaments and numbing the pain because at last I have an injury − I can see that when we stop trying to understand it is the beginning of a new malignancy.

What happens is this: *You can say what you like, nobody believes you.*

We have talked about it in the group, the way we invalidate the unbelievable by seeing it as 'confusion' rather than 'confused' − that way, it makes some kind of sense.

'But delusions are part of the illness, and anyway, it's just easier not to argue,' someone said.

'I don't mean we should argue, I mean we should listen,' I replied, bringing a silence. 'What? That's not what I meant, I know you listen, of course you do, I just think there's always something in it, no matter how daft it sounds.'

And someone tried to help by urging me to give an example, so I made another one of those light, judicious choices − something about realising that when Gran won't eat because the food is 'too shaky' it's not an hallucination, it's salt; she's talking about salt. Too much of it hurts her mouth.

It wasn't a very good example but I didn't want to

share the one clearest in my mind, which happened on a cloudy Easter Sunday: playing cards with Gran and in comes Dad carrying a jug of water. He's singing 'I left my heart in San Francisco' when she looks towards the window and says, 'I buried the baby. She wasn't right.' She appears worried, so wretched that Dad kneels in front of her, takes her hands and just keeps singing the same song, humming the lines so she can join in, and she does, swaying and looking at him like she's in love.

We sang to Gran quite a lot after that; it calms her down – 'Fly Me to the Moon' or 'Tennessee Waltz'. Her favourite is 'Bye Bye Blackbird' – she knows that one all the way through, says it's her funeral song.

We sang and sang. What we didn't do was pay proper attention to what she said about the baby; we didn't ignore it exactly, we just assumed it was a kind of fiction, the baby as part of a fable. It wasn't the words, it was the feelings, and we did comfort her, soothing away the things that made no sense – like symptoms that would eventually pass.

But the story of Eleanor is not a fable, and now we're eight months on and I'm trying to understand, fighting fire with fire by going through her things.

I've only done it once, and when I found what I was looking for I stopped. I would have stopped anyway because no matter how honourable my motive, ferreting through Gran's belongings made me sick to the stomach. It was everything I swore I'd never do, but when I found the map and an ordered stack of magazines called *The New Moon* on the top shelf of the press I couldn't put them back, they were too important – the only tangible things that might help us find a way back to Eleanor.

So I took them, and I hid them in the basement, under my bed.

★

94

MY LITTLE closet sink is, in a sense, bespoke. The colour is a kind of pale jade, nothing like the stone – and although it was not specifically designed for me, it was specifically installed for me, piped in at just the right height for a seven-year-old.

When I stoop down to splash my face I feel like Alice in Wonderland; the feeling is not of a small room, but of a giant body, a clumsy body that belongs to someone else. I'm late – but I expect Fiona and Tufty will be late too; they're coming round to take me to the Christmas fayre, an outing that will involve the disproportionate packing of everything that is required to meet Tufty's basic needs (never mind the rest – rattles, mirrors, bells, biscuits like calcified bone).

I step back into the room and am surprised to see Mum lying on my little bed with her feet pointing upwards. She is wearing her black apron and her eyes are open, her face still. She looks like Mrs Woodentop and for a moment I long for a brother and a baby and a spotty dog. It would all be so much easier if we were made of wood. I try to climb onto the bed but there is not enough space for both of us; I can only stay on if I lie on my side dead straight, which is hard to do. When I bend my knees my bum slips off the bed. I haul myself on again, more on my front now, and Mum shuffles herself closer to the wall. She's all squeezed up, her arms resting on her body like she's been packed away, pinned down by my right arm, which I've had to throw across her chest so I can hold onto the edge of the mattress to keep myself on. We manage to stay like this until the noise of the extractor fan in the toilet cuts out. In the sudden quiet, we can hear ourselves breathing and I say, 'This is nice.'

But I'm not sure if it is. I don't know why she has come in here, or why she is lying on my bed. I wait for her to speak, but she doesn't say anything.

'Mum?'

I open my eyes and look at her, wishing I was seven again and so lovable that rooms are built for me – tiny palaces with painted furniture and curtains that match the bedspread. She bends her right elbow and rests her hand on my arm, turning her face to the wall. I breathe out; it sounds like an impatient sigh and right away I want to retract it. I want to stay like this, clinging on to Mum, and I want her to know she can stare at the wall for as long as she likes, that it wasn't that kind of sigh. But she stirs now, wriggling down and freeing herself, slipping from the room as if dismissed, and when I look at the space she occupied I can see it is too small, an implausibly narrow strip of candlewick, its raised furrows holding their geometry as if it has just been pulled taut – like she was never there.

'KNOCK KNOCK – only us.'

I'm still on the bed when Fiona breezes in. I can't see the 'us' at first, then she turns to close the door and Tufty swings into view, strapped to his mother's sheep-skinned back like a young koala.

'First outing for the Bushbaby – thought I'd better go hands-free for the Christmas scrum. You all right?'

All I've managed to do is turn my head towards her, my body has stayed put, pining in the meagre gap Mum has left behind.

'I'm fine. Just resting my foot.'

'Ah well – you'll need it. I've heard there's going to be loads of lovely stuff at the fayre. I think it's going to be really busy.'

She's brimming over. I sit up and look at her, wondering at her happiness. She doesn't make sense to me, and yet she is so completely familiar. This happens sometimes; déjà vu

96

in reverse, or as Alasdair might put it – *jamais vu*, one eye seeing as the other eye, the lazy one, falls behind.

'Mouth,' she says, letting hers hang open then pushing it shut with the back of her hand. I close mine and stretch my legs out. Fiona is like a cat without whiskers, unable to judge the girth of her hump; the baby is banging about the room like a pin-ball.

'D'you want your crutches?'

She smells like a Christmas tree and is threatening to grow bigger and taller and move further into my pine-clad chamber, my land of giants.

'It's OK, I'll get them. I just need a minute to get ready. Why don't you wait in the kitchen?'

'Should I go and show Thomas to your gran?'

'No, she'll be asleep. She's been up half the night.'

'Really? How do you know? Does she wander about?'

Wander about. It sounds rather lovely. I see her, trailing her fingers across the backs of chairs, twiddling with her hair, which is loose, yet high – like spun sugar, and humming 'Come into the Garden, Maud'. Her skirts have multiplied and are approaching crinoline proportions. She is a ghost ship that rises from the gloaming, sailing through the house until dawn.

'Aggie?'

'What?'

'I'm saying, how do you know when she's awake? Does she get up?'

'Yes. Mum can hear her moving around. You need to watch because she can do some strange things, like she'll scrub the kitchen floor with whatever she can get her hands on. Last week she mixed up some oats in a bucket and tried to wash it with that. She must have thought it was a box of soap powder.'

'My God – that's amazing.'

Fiona shivers; the door to her future has suddenly swung open and the cold air is blowing through. She shuts it quickly.

'Right! Come on. Hurry up or we'll miss all the bargains.'

It's not like that – Gran wandering about, dreamy and luminescent; a night-time story with a white moon and a rhyming broom that sweeps heavenly dust from the rooftops.

My mother gently guiding her mother back to bed just by resting a fingertip on her shoulder – like changing the course of a paper boat.

It's not like that at all.

Gran doesn't want to go. Her skirts and pants are wet and she doesn't know who this woman is who appears in the doorway, this irritated woman in a nightdress who interrupts her work, sending her off to bed without saying what she's done.

What is it that she's done?

WE ARE drawn in by the hilarity of the condemned; gales of laughter shaking the high-set window frames in the church hall, mirth bouncing across the smooth wood floor, great whoops of it slapping the walls. At its source we find several boxes of mistletoe, gathered from the soft bark of old apple trees, and from the forest of larch that grows behind the ruins of the abbey. A women in a navy blue gilet is holding up a sprig behind the minister's back; she is intent on mischief and her antics cause another outburst, the notes too high – a squeal almost, a short scream. Onlookers cover their mouths to hide their smiles, some blush, excited just to see him, and others appear grateful – as if their prayers have been answered.

Mistletoe. Smooth stems, like bones – and the creamy ripe berries clinging at the tips and forks of the shiny boughs, winged leaves ready to fly. I dwell on that mistletoe, unable to resist the pull of its creaminess and greeniness, the way it retains its sap, succulent in a winter desert of spent passions; a dry kiss – the brief scrape of chapped lips against an unyielding cheek.

Merry Christmas!

There is a snap frost and another chilly dendrite forms in my mind – Alasdair and Flossie smooching. She has just rung our doorbell and he has just opened the door and their lips are clamped together in a magnetic field of lust that could go on for ever; the only thing stopping them is their need for air, and when they do break he stares at her Cupid's bow, then they each eat the other. *Peach squishing against juicy plum. Drinking each other's honey spit . . .*

'Are you all right?'

I have stumbled into a small clearing in the middle of the hall. It's just big enough to accommodate me and my splayed crutches; people are keeping their distance, careful not to step on my shadow. They're sticking to one side of an invisible line that I feel sure will move with me when I move. The minister, uncloaked and friendly in a cable-knit jumper, is stretching his hand out towards me and if it wasn't for the crutches I'd probably take it, just to see where it led.

'Do you need a chair?'

I look into his eyes and see two little tripods, miniatures of me.

'Why don't you come and sit down?' he urges, his voice so soft I want to fall into it. I could just lean towards him and his words would cushion me, save me, wrap me up and tuck me in. He has stepped into the clearing and is curving his arm round my shoulder – a virtual touch that guides me past the trestle tables piled with mistletoe and holly and great bunches of honesty, flat translucent pods that look like they'd melt on the tongue, dissolving all sin. He conjures up a chair and I sit, expertly releasing the crutches so they relax against my arms. Somebody says, 'I'll get her some tea,' and now we do touch; he stands to the side of me like a sentry and places his hand on my shoulder. We both wait for the tea, and when it comes I smile and sense that feeling again, as if I am recovering from much more than an injured foot.

'Christ, it's chaos in here! Trust you to find the one seat in the whole place. Where did you get the tea?'

Fiona has sauntered over like a camel arriving at the oasis as the last drop is drunk.

'God, I'm parched — it's so bloody hot in here. Does Thomas look all right?'

Tufty is perched in his baby-carrier, cheeks red as Christmas berries. When she turns to the side to proffer her hump there is a pungent waft of baby excreta. The mustard-yellow stink overpowers everything else — the cinnamon and cloves, the vanilla candles, the pot-pourri, those timeless gingham bags of dried lavender — every last scented trace gone. Tufty has just spotted Santa Claus and is petrified, his face white and neat-lipped. When Santa waves Fiona spots him too and waves back, swinging Tufty away from the festive scene, and hence to a safer world of cooing, bug-eyed women who wiggle their fingers at him and shape their mouths into a round, issuing soundless exclamations.

The minister checks my well-being with a look. His raised brows and slight smile tell me he thinks he can probably leave me now, but he wants my permission. I grant it with a sober nod, and as he moves through the throng I watch and wonder. *Maybe I can talk to him, tell him everything? Ask him what to do?*

'Christ, was that the minister? I didn't recognise him with his clothes on. Do you think he heard me?'

'Of course he heard you. Why do you think he left?'

'Oh my God. What were you two talking about?'

'We weren't talking. We were communing.'

'Holy or unholy?'

She's looking at him. He's carrying a tombola machine towards the stage, his flock clucking and moving about him, and I notice that not only is his dog collar almost completely but not quite (in a very considered, not-quite way) obscured by his jumper, but he's also wearing jeans. His congregation have no trouble embracing this sexy *Sirdar* look; I can see they like him very much, and as an ex-Sunday school helper who knows something of the parish and its parishioners, I suspect for some it won't just be lust, it will be love.

Every time Fiona moves I gag.

'What a smell – can't you see to him?'

I am pleading with a high voice, pinching my nostrils. She stares right at me.

'You're just so sure it's Thomas, aren't you? Well, take a look around. I think there's a few other candidates.'

She treats me to her Cherie Blair look – clenching her molars and squaring off her mouth in an impossible way, her eyes still fixed on me, disconnected from whatever else is going on in the face; she can do that – isolate muscle groups, both bilaterally and unilaterally – up and down as well as across. The Cherie Blair is one of my favourites, so I reply by doing the blind woman out of *Don't Look Now*, because even though Fiona can manipulate her muscles along any axis, she can't roll her eyes; her extra-oculars let her down every time. I close my right eye and half close my left, rolling it up and over, so just the white is showing. I'm looking through my aching eyelids, tilting my head up like a sleep-eyed doll. She laughs, exactly the way she always has, from a place further down than her throat – a rogue laugh that chugs like a cold engine, sometimes dying after just a few kicks, sometimes bursting into life. It's not something you can learn or acquire – it's a genetic laugh, the vocalisation of a rat-tailed piece of DNA. Somewhere there's another exactly like it, turning heads.

'Ageist,' I say.

'Babyist,' she says, still squared up, and me still blind, but not completely, because when I open my mouth wider and let my left eye drop I can see Kenneth looking straight at me. I gather in my crutches and close up, retracting like a small salt-water creature that's been poked with a stick. When my eyes open, he's still there, still looking. He's wearing that leather hat again; it's been pushed back a bit, probably because of the heat, which has suddenly started to climb and is approaching a rolling boil. We're being steam-cooked, glistening and soft and jostling about in a spirit of goodwill. A child – hip height – is tugging at Kenneth's heavy tweed sleeve. He frowns at me, a stern, honest expression that breaks through a resistance. A rod-straight shaft of light hits me, warming my face, and his eyes hold still as the sleeve-tugging pulls his head round. I scowl back, learning the language – focusing on his face because it is the only way to stem my embarrassment, which, if I move, will ignite and burn me up.

Kenneth is listening to the child, who takes his hand and pulls him towards a diminishing stack of home-made Christmas fudge. The crowd flows in behind him and carries him off. I catch glimpses of him, his hat high – bobbing on the waves like a yuletide log. I want to tug his sleeve too; I want to see if my arms will stretch all the way round him in that coat, the rough wool pressing against my cheek, my hands locking together so that I can't be dislodged.

'Hello again.'

Inevitably, he's here, arms dangling below those sleeves, feeding my desire to tug.

'Hi, how are you?'

'Better than you, by the looks of it. What happened?'

'I hurt my ankle. I just kind of went over it when I was running.'

'Oh, I didn't know you ran.'

'Oh, well, you know, not much.'

My forehead has the word *LIAR* written across it in large capital letters but he's too polite to mention it, just as I am too polite to mention that leaving his hat perching high on his head like that makes him look like Elmer Fudd. What we can't ignore is the smell.

'Have you met my friend, Fiona?'

'No, I don't think so.'

Now he takes off the hat and Elmer Fudd is gone, there's not a trace of him left. Fiona shakes her mane a little and grins, giving him a circular, flapper wave.

'Hi!'

'Hello.'

I don't think he's noticed her hump yet and I'm watching for the 'Fiona effect' when, from out of the throng, the small girl reappears and takes Kenneth's hand, her cheeks plump with chocolate fudge. She stares at my crutches.

'My daddy'sh got those. He losht hish foot in the war.'

'Did he?'

'Yesh,' she says. She lets go of Kenneth's hand so she can take out another piece of fudge from the cellophane pouch in her pocket. As soon as there's room she pushes the sweet into her mouth, then twists the bag shut and takes his hand again.

'Ish that your baby?'

Fiona raises her shoulders in a small sudden movement.

'Yes! This is Thomas.'

She bends down and swings round a bit to show him off and this time there is no doubt about the source of the smell. The girl screws up her face and throws herself into the folds of Kenneth's coat, swinging from side to side and muffling, 'Yuk! Stinky poo.'

'Yes, you really do stink, Tufty, tell your mum you need to freshen up for Santa.'

When they leave, Kenneth touches the girl's head.

'You can come out now.'

But she's buried deep and getting deeper.

'This is Morag, my favourite niece. She's a very good dancer.'

He raises his voice on the *very good dancer* and I feel a sudden surge of love for this little girl because I think she must be the daughter of the woman who appeared in his doorway that day, the woman who called him darling, which means she must be his sister, or his sister-in-law.

Either will do.

'Wow, that's great. What kind of dancing do you do?'

She's still in the coat and I don't know what to say next; she's moving her feet around, jumping from one to the other.

'That's an excellent dance. You're very clever.'

'Actually, I think she just needs the toilet. We'd better go.'

'Oh, right.'

I'm left, superfluous in a world of urgent needs. I'm thinking about the missing foot, wondering which war — suddenly depressed by the foot, and the war, and the which. Fiona's laugh explodes from the back of the hall and everyone turns to look; she's holding the baby, sharing something funny with Kenneth. He's smiling, and soon everyone else is too, like they're witnessing a scene from *It's a Wonderful Life*. I look, trying not to mind, trying to be like Capra's angel but feeling more like Kafka's cockroach. Then, finding strange comfort in the knowledge that Fiona can't roll her eyes, I stand up, tuck my crutches under my arms, and make a miraculous exit.

Great Big Crazy Moon

T HE HOUSE is no longer on the point of collapse; it feels stronger, the swellings less tender – I don't know why. Having hidden the map and the magazines under the bed there was no rush, but now I am ready to look at them. *The New Moon* trembles in my hands, so I rest my wrist on my pillow and the shaking stops. It is easier to read from a static page, although I am still nervous; there is an ambiguous, unpleasant feeling in my stomach that I can't quell.

I'm reading the first, the earliest of the magazines. She has kept them in date order, a small private archive of monthly pamphlets all printed in 1937, and each with the same sub-heading written underneath the title: 'Crichton Royal Institution Literary Register'.

Only two lines in and already I have to stop. I've heard of the Crichton Royal before; there is an association between the place and my brief academic foray into psychology. I put down the magazine and squeeze my temples, as if this might help me remember. And it does. It's amazing what I can extract from my studies – strange correlations and paradigm shifts, anomaly and paradox, poles that invert. I didn't realise I was paying that much attention. When I dropped English to switch courses I was glad to discover that Psychology could be seen as a storytelling discipline. As an eager student I was intrigued by the essays of the famous American psychologist George Kelly, and, on this side of the Atlantic, by the work of Miller Mair, a clinical psychologist based in the Crichton Royal Hospital in Dumfries. I remember the discovery well, the sense of connection between art and science; it looked as if the little I had already learned about language and metaphor would help me understand other things, including the ideas of these radical thinkers. Of course, this coming together was short-lived. I soon realised that life was incoherent and easily fractured – but at the time it felt very exciting.

Picking up the magazine, I begin again, this time with less sense of foreboding. *The New Moon* is a charming chronicle of life in the hospital. Written (as far as I can tell) by patients, there are poems, articles and round-ups of the marvellous activities of various clubs: tennis, bowling, football, badminton, gymnastics, dancing, music, drama – the list seems endless. One article, entitled 'A Day's Joy', describes a trip to Glen Trool, where at 12.45 the party rested on a grassy crag and took in the view –

```
The tiny islets dotted about the loch, the crags at
either side, with the mountains beyond - all in that
glorious light - created a sylvan beauty, which held
one spellbound.
```

Was she there? I wonder. Spellbound in the glorious light? Did she drink the lemon squash and soda, enjoy the repast before trudging on to a silvery waterfall, and beyond – to a cottage in the dim distance, gathering wild orchids on the way?

The more I read the more connections I can make; I can

see the origins of things. For instance, Gran records the weather much as it is reported here, setting out her notes and numbers in a similar way to the summaries printed in each monthly issue (albeit her numbers made up, but the precision the same). Looking at the detail in these reports I recognise some of her idiosyncratic turns of phrase, such as 'fog days' and 'unusual phenomena' – her own voice quizzing me after school.

'Any unusual phenomena today, Aggie?'

'Nothing to report, Gran.'

It is a shock to see it written here. We never gave it much thought, although we did wonder at it, the particular way she described the weather, the way she marked things down. The most she said about it was that someone taught her how to do it a long time ago and it 'just stuck'. On blue-sky blue-river days she would look upwards and shake her head, as if she were trying to make sense of something implausible.

'So much sunshine! Like living in California.'

Not that she ever did live in California; she lived at Pennyland, and at William's Lea, and I believe she lived here too, in this asylum, where the weather was much more unsettled, and where, it occurs to me, she met Edward, the Second Assistant Physician.

I catch my breath, sucking air because my mouth has unexpectedly filled with ice – a brief, gushing assault that leaves me with a sudden sorrow and an urge to cry. I'm holding myself in, probably because I'm not supposed to know any of this, and almost immediately the sorrow goes, passing through me like a bullet. There is shock, but also a kind of bafflement.

Why didn't she tell me?

I know this sense of disappointment is somehow ignoble, that I should be thinking of her – but allowing for everything: for grief, for shame, for recovery; even allowing for the love of me, there is still a base sense of umbrage that springs from the fact that she has never told me anything about this.

Why didn't she tell me?

Like it's the main thing.

THE ROOM is hollow and too small. I curl up on the bed and cradle the magazines. They smell like old cabbages. I let myself wallow for a while. Then, at last, I think of her.

We all know that many roads led to the asylum in the 1930s, particularly for young women who liked to ride bareback with nothing on their feet. These magazines suggest she was taken there, possibly in January 1937 – a month described in the February edition as 'dull, wet, muggy, and sunless. It rained on twenty-three days and on the thirtieth the temperature did not rise above freezing point (32°F).' She is young, a farm girl aged seventeen – educated, strong willed and looking like Vivien Leigh. It must have been terrible, but having arrived there, which she undoubtedly did, it seems that in this mansion of despair the story changed and parts of her found their place; her love of poetry and song, her passion for weather – the way the sky entrances her (when she wakes it is the first thing she looks at, even at night).

Chilled by the wet January air, I read my way out of the cold, moving through every copy of *The New Moon* until, in June, a poem catches my eye. When I read it aloud my voice sounds strange and overly dramatic, yet the room fills with something familiar.

> *Night came,*
> *And then a pregnant silence fell,*
> *That left us in the deep sweet well*
> *Of beauty:*
> *We watched the great big crazy moon*

Come climbing up into the sky; and soon
We said good-bye.

                        P.

I stare at the *P* and immediately feel wretched because I
have no right to read this; I have no right to read any of it.
These are Gran's private papers, they contain secrets she has
guarded all her life, and although I reconstrued the act of
finding them as venial – a technical transgression in a world
of good intentions – I have, in truth, stolen them.

I sit on the edge of the mattress, smooth out the magazines
and push them back under the bed. But the knowing cannot
be undone. My head aches with it, and my heart too. As if
unable to believe, I pull out the same magazine and look
again at the page. A bower of leaves has been drawn in pencil
above the verse and I recognise her style, the light hand and
the way she shades with her fingertips.

These were her leaves, her imaginary green.

But the life; the life was real.

LAST NIGHT the moon hung low over the river, contemplating
a dip. When I woke my feet had been pulled from the bed
and were straining towards the water. They grew cold and
waxy in the moonlight, and my blood – a dark Copella
sludge – settled round my ankles, unable to make the chilly
ascent to my toes. It was the cold that woke me. I could feel
crystals in my veins and worried that something irreversible
had happened – lunar frostbite.

The moon is not always my friend.

I sat in the kitchen, warming myself at the range having
fed it with applewood and larch. The room was neat, the
draining board clear; cutlery in drawers and plates in
cupboards, tea towels clean and dry and folded in a neat pile.
There was a note on the fridge, two days old – *Pay Papers*

/ *Chiropodist* / *Maurice's letter* / *Chemist* − and beside it, the letter *P.* How odd to see it − another capital *P* in such pronounced isolation. I pondered over what it might stand for: pads, pessaries, poultice, painkillers? Paper pants maybe? (Lately there is a distinct rustle when Gran moves that makes me wonder what's under all those skirts.) It seems Mum's discretion extends to fridge-notes and beyond. She's talking less and less these days, and when she does talk she sounds irritated, or tired, or, worst of all, disappointed; relief only comes when she sits down to watch *Little Dorrit*, which she loves beyond reason and replays every week. I don't have the heart for it − it's too soapy and scrubbed up, all that gleam makes my hackles rise. I prefer to read the book and have a smug little leather-bound version dated 1913 that gathers dust in my room.

But last night, sitting under the low moon and staring at the discrete letter *P*, I found I *did* have the heart for it. I wanted the cosiness of the Marshalsea prison to wash over me and not let it spoil a good yarn; I wanted Mum and I to sit down and watch it together, with me seeing it the way she does.

How hard could it be?

WHEN DAD first saw Mum he thought she was a vision. Her face was lit from below by morning sunlight bouncing off the river water. She looked like Botticelli's Venus, only 'without the hair' he always added, and in the telling of it, he would mistakenly refer to *Venus Rising from the Sea* − but we knew what he meant because there she was right in front of us, clad in Marks & Spencer jeans and sensible shoes, and still without the hair, but Venus nevertheless.

Even as a young man in love, Maurice Copella was known for his stability, not only in the emotional sense (although his even temper is pure Tiger Balm), but in the physical sense too. His balance is excellent, his stomach strong, so he was perfect for working the sheep boat that transported the livestock across the river to Mugdrum Island, where they would graze on estuary grasses that sweeten the meat, giving the lamb its distinctive flavour. These sailings stopped decades ago, but on one of the last – as he stood on the flat-bottomed boat, swaying easily along his own remarkable axis and peering through a pair of binoculars so heavy his centre of gravity had shifted to somewhere behind his knees – he saw Aphrodite standing on the shore (that's how he told it anyway, and only once, but I've kept every word). She was gazing back towards him and he fancied their eyes met through the lens, a glancing blow, strong and powerful, like he'd been struck (she can still do that – her eyes flash). The blow caused the binoculars to fly from his hands and land heavily on the crown of one of their best sheep; it was an unfortunate accident, the only one ever recorded during Dad's careful watch. The sheep appeared to recover but began to behave in a very unsheeply way, rejecting the flock and constantly wandering off on her own, until one day, inevitably, she wandered to the site of her own slaughter.

Weeks later, as Dad and his family (the widowed mother and various cousins) enjoyed spoonfuls of sweet, succulent mutton that had been well hung and cooked for five hours, Maurice still couldn't shake off the vision that had so thrown him. Her shocking eyes followed him everywhere, even when his own were closed, disturbing his sleep and distorting his sense of time and space; he changed, became clumsy and forgetful. His mother suggested he pull himself together, his cousins smiled, and the dogs watched his every move – as if he were a sheep in man's clothing.

I've come down to the riverbank, to the place where

Mum stood shimmering in the morning light. I'm thinking about that first day, the day Dad painted for me so vividly; it must have been very early, the sun still low, skimming across the water and catching her under the chin. I wonder what brought her down here at that time? She says she was there to watch the boat crossing, but it would have been nothing new; she must have seen it before – the flotilla of sheep no longer strange (except to the deer that watched from the island's interior, unable to adjust or learn from the events of the day before, or the day before that, never quite getting used to the day-trippers that crowded onto Mugdrum throughout the summer months). Maybe she'd heard it was soon to end.

A skylark calls. The dawn rises but the frost remains still in the grass. I'm wearing Mum's scarf and Dad's jacket, which smells of bark and fungus. I re-tie the scarf then push my hands deep into the pockets and cross them, wrapping myself in my parents' winter clothes.

She would not know, as she followed the progress of the boat, what life she was going to lead – its shape and circumstance; she would just be watching, probably just killing time, and because it is lovely here.

Perhaps, like me in this moment, she just wanted to be – no past and no future: the constant river in perpetual flow, as if the land were slowly moving west, and a bird wheeling across the sky, announcing the shift.

My family are the only people I know who have a hot meal in the middle of the day, usually involving potatoes. It's a farming thing – something to do with rising at dawn to tend sheep and the effect that has on the appetite; the farm and the sheep have long gone, but the hot lunch stayed. The food is not served until we are all at the table. There is usually a pudding too, although occasionally not, which, if it happens without warning, is disappointing (even though Dad and I protest whenever a pudding appears).

Today there is none because Mum has spent most of the morning trying to get Gran washed and dressed – or rather, undressed then redressed; she is happy to put clothes on, but reluctant to take them off. As little as six months ago she was still wearing Eastex trousers – always the same wool mix, then one day she started to wear skirts and she has refused to put on trousers ever since; it's awkward, since neither she nor Mum can get her into a pair of tights any more, although once or twice they had great fun trying. Stockings are out of the question – too many straps criss-crossing where they shouldn't and rogue garments hooking onto her suspender belt, and her legs are too thin for stay-ups, which only leaves socks (not a good look with an A-line or a box-pleat).

Mum looks washed out; she looks now the way she'll look in ten years' time, or twenty. She seems closer to 'being old' than I have ever seen her, and I wonder if Dad sees it too – or does he see the young woman who stood in the bulrushes, still as a grey heron?

The quiet of the house has taken on a sombre note, the pipes sighing at the relentless task ahead – December, and all that it brings.

Dad gets up from the table and puts on his jacket.

'I'm going to collect Gran's gauge. That was lovely, Mary –' And he pauses until his shorn Venus looks at him. 'It was lovely.'

He nods once, pushing out his chin to stem her teary look, and she raises her chin too, then they both get on with it, Mum clearing up while I sit at the table drinking cold tea.

Something about what Dad just said has got me thinking.

'I think we should all call Gran Peggy.'

'Why?' she asks, prepared to listen as long as she can stack and clean and put away at the same time.

'Because I think it must be really confusing for her the way you and Dad sometimes call her Gran, then sometimes call her Mum.'

'Mmmm.'

'Do you see what I mean? When I'm here she's Gran to everyone and then when I'm not she's Mum. I think it muddles her up. She probably can't work out where she fits in. It's like we all keep shifting about – whereas if we all just called her Peggy that's who she'd be.'

'But I've never called her Peggy. I don't think I could.'

'Course you could. It would feel a bit strange at the start but you'd soon get used to it.'

She's slowing up a bit, wiping the same spot she's just wiped.

'Is this something that that Ruth said?'

'No, not specifically. I'm just trying to see things from Gran's point of view.'

'So you and Dad would call her Peggy as well?'

'Ah, now that's another point. Maybe we should call Dad Maurice because Gran knows him as Maurice.'

'But I do call him Maurice.'

'Yes, but when I'm here you call him Dad.'

We ponder our roles and try to step into Gran's world (just the who's who part – not the dark interior).

'What do you think?'

She fills the kettle and switches it on.

'I'm not sure. Calling her Peggy feels disrespectful. She might get more confused and forget who we are. At least when I say Mum she knows I'm her daughter. Anyway, it's only a problem when we're all together, and we never are. I only call her Gran when I'm speaking to you.'

'But I'm not sure she is Gran any more, or Mum. I think she's Peggy.'

'What do you mean?'

'Well, imagine if someone you knew – not me, obviously, someone else – if they started calling you Mum, what would you do?'

'I'd tell them I wasn't their mum.'

'But if they insisted, would you think you were going mad?'

'No. I'd think they were going mad.'

'So – there you go then.'

'What's your point, Aggie? Don't you think I know all this? Do you think I don't understand what's going on? How many times do you think she tells me she's not my mum, or that her daughter is dead?'

The porch door closes and we both jump. Dad is holding a plastic measuring jug; it looks empty but when he tilts it a small amount of water gathers at the bottom.

'Who's dead?'

'I am. Didn't *Peggy* tell you?'

She spits on the *P* like she's blowing out a candle, then she throws the tea towel into the sink and leaves the room.

Dad gives me a look that I'm grateful for – one that lets me off; it would never occur to him to allocate blame. His response to a labile woman is pastoral, in a rural rather than churchy way. He gives her lots of space, behaving as if he is with a sheep that's about to lamb. There is a kind of James Hogg air about him, an eloquent stillness, but he's more shepherd than poet. It is not what Dad says, it is what he does that comforts me. (Like the time he brought me a flask of clear soup after the miscarriage. He came to the flat, alone, in the daylight, bearing the best offering he could think of – a sweet chicken consommé that he'd made himself.)

He's looking at the water in the jug, holding it up to the light and squinting through it like he's expecting to find

116

something swimming there – a rare aquatic creature that has never been seen before.

'She'll need her magnifying glass to measure this lot. Less than half a millimetre I'd say.'

Gran measures the rainfall daily; she used to take readings once a week, but lately she wants to do it several times a day, fretting over the pages in her book, the blanks where there ought to be numbers. Dad empties the rain gauge and takes the jug to her – she measures and re-measures, records the data carefully, pressing out each digit as if in gold leaf. These records have piled up over the years, each following the same format – monthly narratives and annual charts that systematically record the rainfall (in both inches and millimetres), including notes on the number of rain days, and the number of days of sleet, hail or snow. We assumed it was a farming thing, a way of combining her shepherding with all her other skills (some bookish, some not), but now that I have read *The New Moon* magazines I know where that discipline comes from.

She used to have an old copper rain gauge; it was a lovely thing. The gauge was always positioned at the end of the garden in an open spot, well away from any overhanging branches, but last summer it disappeared – probably stolen by someone who recognised a good thing when they saw it. Dad decided not to tell her it had gone. He made another by slicing off the top of an old plastic bottle and turning it upside down, then securing it into the bottom half with a few paper clips to create a funnel. He put the makeshift gauge in a container that was set into a bucket of builder's sand and positioned it in exactly the same spot at the bottom of the orchard. It was a lot of work. I wanted him to tell Gran about the old gauge going missing, but Mum said what's the point in upsetting her? She said he had wasted his time making another one, that he should just feed the jug from the tap and give her that. It's not like she'd know.

'You wouldn't even need to leave the kitchen.'

I watch as he wipes the outside of the jug. Dad has an enviable capacity to lose himself in the doing of things, much as a painter might lose herself in painting, or a writer in writing. As he passes I touch his arm.

'Tell Gran I'll be up in ten minutes to read to her.'

'Will do.'

And when he says to her, 'Aggie will be up in ten minutes to read to you', she'll not know who he means, or where 'up' is, or the name of the man who's telling her; she'll puzzle over it the way you puzzle over a key you find in your bag that you don't recognise.

Then she'll forget.

The trick is to find the up-side, and here it is − *I don't need to read any more Agatha Christie books.*

They became Gran's favourite about two years ago, and I can think of worse things to read aloud, but having got through several Poirot tales (however many, it feels like more) − all well executed and well expressed − I'm ready to kill. Thankfully plot, even when it follows a formula, holds no interest for Gran any more, what she likes is poetry, and not just the romantic stuff, she enjoys horror too − rhythmic renditions of *Straw Peter* read out to her while she eats (not that she eats much, but these visceral verses sharpen her appetite).

Reading is not what we always do. There are days when words written on a page remain just that; they are not welcome, they clutter and obscure, losing us in a thickening linguistic fog, a cloud of *blah blah blah.*

Today I am reading to myself. It relaxes us both, me being here and being somewhere else at the same time. When I look up she raises her brows and asks 'Good?' − as if I have just tasted a dish she has carefully prepared for me. Jack has crept onto my foot cushion, which is still warm, and in the silence we can hear him breathing, wheezing like an old squeezebox with a hole in it. Gran stares at him.

'Someone's missing a cat,' she says, waving her finger. She shakes her head, then tucks her hand into the folds of her bountiful skirts and turns back to her trees.

Bitter Chocolate

I HAVE been here for just over a week but it seems longer, much longer. Such a slow passing, as if I am waiting for something to happen that should have happened already; every minute another minute late. We are all keeping our distance: Mum achieves it through laundry – immersing herself in the warm steam of incessant boil washes, loading and unloading hot sheets from the Bendix; Dad works outside, pruning the trees and building small fires – he's rekindled an early love for Jap Desserts and sucks on them constantly; I intellectualise, drive everyone mad with theory and conjecture, knowing my fervent search for meaning appears absurd.

I have to go home – not because I want to, but because it's odd not to. The swelling in my ankle has gone and my crutches have been tidied away. Dad has stopped putting out those special little cereals he bought after my accident. I need to search the cupboard and find my own now, non-brand cornflakes that are kept in a huge plastic container to stop them going stale. Only this morning Mum was telling me how things keep going off 'now that it's just the two of us plus your gran. What she eats wouldn't keep a sparrow.'

I'm not sure when this permutation happened, when my family of three became my family of two plus Gran, but marooned in their bulbous house, I suppose this slow drift was inevitable. It's a matter of survival. I would like to talk about it but I know I'm already on borrowed time; there's something about the way Mum looks up when I walk into the kitchen each morning with no evidence of a limp, my rude good health exposing me as lazy and vague and lacking in purpose – and I know what she's thinking.

Why are you not at work?

Why are you not with your husband?

Alasdair has stopped calling and the curiosity I feel about this has been fanning something up that I thought might be dead. There's nothing quite as dead as dead love. The fire was definitely out, but now there is this fanning up, a few glowing embers amongst the ash that was my trust. My suspicion that Alasdair is sleeping with Flossie has forced me to reassess them both, not in terms of their deficits, but in terms of their capacities – the way they can feel and conceal and just *be bothered* when each seemed so fully stretched already. When I think about it I get caught up in the practicalities – the how and the where. And just the brazenry! I can't seem to get beyond it.

HUNCHED OVER the table with her face in typical proximity to the surface (almost touching), she is writing something down. She leans back to survey each tiny mark before she adds to it, then another mark, then another. Despite her best efforts, these marks are losing their curves. Sometimes, they make her laugh (it is not all darkness – there are moments of pure joy, as if she is emerging from a prolonged purdah). She smiles when I sit down, then she rests her head in the crook of her left arm and begins to tap her pencil on the paper, listening to the sound it makes, the evocation. She accepts my presence completely, and it is this grace that moves me the most.

Raising her head again she gets back to the task, taking on the posture of a schoolgirl who is keen and determined to get things right. I know from her own accounts that she enjoyed her schooling (that's what she calls it – in those days it was a 'doing' word) and I surmise she was good at it, though she never said so. Occasionally, when she helped me with my homework, she would talk about her own school days, her descriptions so vivid I could almost smell the chalk – a cold room with metal-frame windows set too high for distractions; if you owned a coat you kept it on all through winter. The holidays were long, too long for Gran – just a few weeks of school every so often throughout the year, the dates designed to fit round whatever might need doing at home or on the farms, but those weeks added up to more than many daughters received, and she was grateful for them. In school she would spend most mornings studying English literature (memorising poems and reading from books, and writing too – précis and an essay every fortnight). Arithmetic included decimals and the metric system, even then, and there were courses on citizenship and colonial history, with the afternoons devoted to practical housewifery – cooking, laundry and needlework – and an occasional hour of music and movement. (I picture her, swirling and twirling like Isadora Duncan – turned fanciful by a curriculum intent on 'stopping the supply of ignorant motherhood' but providing instead a realisation that heaven dwells on earth, thanks to her teacher's willingness to share her own personal collection of poetry, and Tennyson in particular.)

'Busy, Gran?'

She looks puzzled; I'm two words short and she can't make sense of my rising inflexions.

'Are you busy?'

And out pops a simile.

'Busy as a bee.'

(How come she can say that and I can't?)

'I've just come to say cheerio. I'm going back home for a bit but I'll be back soon.'

'Will you find it?'

'Yes'

'Good. I've nearly finished anyway. Just four to go.'

Four what, I wonder, buttons maybe – or coats? When they first moved here Gran was a button sewer at the local oilskin factory where they made waterproofs for the government: trench coats and raincoats; coats for the bobbies; lovely gabardines with buckle belts that they sold in the Co-op. In those days there was more to Plum Town than fruit. Then along came the button-machine and that was that.

'Good. Would you like me to make you some tea?'

'Is it time already?'

And here, on this shifting temporal plain, something happens – a slight tipping of things that makes her head and her hands tremble. Dog eyes beckoning, I put my hand on her arm.

'Gran, there's lots of time. It's fine.'

She's still frowning, but the vibration stops. She chews her right thumbnail then rubs it, buffing it up against the side of her other hand then turning it towards the light to examine the shine. It has a dent in it – a dip that has passed through the generations like a watermark (I have it too). She scrapes across the bump, over and over, pivoting the surface in the light again.

'Damaged,' she says. 'How did that happen?'

If she could, she'd throw it away and pick another one, a perfect horn button, smooth as a toffee penny.

Today I was going to ask her about Eleanor, but I haven't the heart. I kiss her thumb and tell her I love her, then I leave her to ponder the mystery of the damaged nail that has suddenly acquired a bump.

★

SOMEHOW, BETWEEN there and here, snow has fallen – a light, implausibly dry dust that softens my arrival back at the flat. It doesn't feel cold enough for snow, inside or out. Despite this, I find it impossible to take off my coat. Maintaining a tight locus I let my rucksack slide from my shoulder and bunch up at my feet. From where I stand in the hall (unable to spread out) I can see into every room: the bedroom is relatively unchanged, the wicker chair embracing a huge pile of clothes with open arms, still happy for more; I can see the lacy knickers Alasdair tore not that long ago in a joint grapple to get them off as quickly as possible (it still happens – sporadic sex to meet a need, not to realise a desire). In the living room a few things are strewn about – socks stuffed down the sofa, plates smeared with tomato sauce, an assortment of Alasdair's humorous mugs, which say things like –

This is my cubicle.

or

There are many like it but this one is mine.

or

My mug is white because I am serious.

I should have taken more notice of those mugs; they were there all the time – trying to tell me something. In the bathroom I can see Alasdair's cycling shorts hanging over the shower rail and when I take the trouble to breathe through my nose instead of my mouth I can detect the characteristic smell of home: the faint but pungent whiff of hot loin clinging to un-rinsed Lycra; there's probably some drizzle-piss in there too – what would Flossie make of that? (Maybe it turns her on after all the antiseptic?) The smell is still keen, he must have been out this morning, working those blazing thighs like pistons on a steam engine. The flying Scotsman would have sought the toughest route, maybe the Blackness Hill, right past Kenneth's house, teetering onto the summit at a snail's pace, legs thrashing just to stay upright and, most importantly of all, still in his seat.

Whereas me.

'Keep your bum down, Aggie!'

I've always taken great delight in overtaking Alasdair, standing on my pedals and swinging the bike from side to side – whistling 'Yankee Doodle' if I still have the puff. He never laughs. 'It's a joke!' I say, but the sense of humour he shows in his choice of mugs doesn't seem to generalise; it's non-transferable, unlike his choice of sexual partner.

I manage to push away my clingy rucksack and walk to the kitchen. The pillow I was resting my foot on is still where I left it and this confirms Alasdair's slobbishness. I'm keen to develop these kind of thoughts but am impeded by evidence that he's watered the Busy Lizzie we both dislike so much (but can't quite throw in the bin because it is, after all, a living thing), and there is a neat stack of empty bean tins in the corner of the worktop that are clearly on their way to the recycling box; the filthy tea towel hanging from the door hook is rancid but nevertheless hanging exactly where it should; and on the memory board he has written: *EGGS*.

I can see a modicum of effort here, and, more importantly, an enduring capacity to manage that suddenly makes me feel discarded. Evidently life carries on without me. I open the fridge and see eight brown eggs sitting in the special plastic tray that we never use; these eggs are so big they make me wince; they're almost falling out – too big to fit the very thing designed to hold them. We don't keep eggs in the fridge, never have. Why has he done that?

I call him.

'It's me. Why have you put the eggs in the fridge?'

'What?'

'Why have you put the eggs in the fridge?'

'So they'll keep longer.'

'They keep for at least a week out of the fridge.'

'I need them to keep longer than that. I bought two dozen.'

'Why did you buy that many?'

'It was a special offer.'

'So where's the rest?'

'I've eaten them.'

'On your own?'

'Of course on my own. How's the foot?'

'It's a lot better, thank you.'

'You sound very formal.'

'Do I?'

'Yes. Is this you back now?'

'Yes.'

'Good.'

WE HAD been married for just a few hours when the knot, so recently tied, tightened into a small panicky nodule that clung to the wall of my heart. As a single woman I was confident; I knew who I was without having to ask, and I knew what I thought about things; I had a position, points of view drawn from a store of something inside me – a bank of stuff that just seemed to stick as I went along (a personality theorist might phrase that differently, but this is what's great about dropping out of a psychology degree – you can say this kind of thing and get away with it). I wasn't even aware I had a 'bank of stuff' – it was just there, friendly and reliable, like the old-fashioned savings account I had as a child, with a passbook and a cumulating balance that grew in a linear rather than exponential way. But then, after the wedding ceremony, a few small things happened that on their own wouldn't amount to much, but together seemed to acquire enough substance to give me something to think about.

It began with this.

When Alasdair and I sat down and ordered our first meal together as husband and wife, he asked me what I wanted, then queried my choice. 'You don't want fish followed by fish,' he said, with such distinct incredulity that my instinct was to reassure him, shore up his constructs about 'dining out' (which, in those days, I had no desire to disassemble – seeing them as useful and right). We had booked in under his name, a fantastic 'two-for-one' hotel offer that seemed prescient and delivered me from Alasdair's notion of an alternative but romantic wedding involving fish suppers and a tent (I loved him *for* it, but I didn't actually want to *do* it).

When I agreed to marry Alasdair it was literal, and on one condition; literal because he'd said we should get married and did I agree? – and on condition that I would not be expected to 'be a bride', since all things bridal (with the single exception of the cake) fill me with horror. I could no more walk up an aisle as fly in the air. When we shared our plans – a registry wedding and an overnight followed by a party later on – with the Thackerays and the Copellas, we did so with due apology, conscious of the investments made in us as only children (and Alasdair barely even that). The resulting protest was so muted I was tempted to change my mind (the bride's prerogative) and demand the full works, right down to the ivory satin slippers and the honeymoon in the Bahaaamas, or a gated community in Mexico, or some such place.

'We're going to honeymoon in the Pyjaaamas.'

'Wow!'

Honeymoon. The word itself is something to fall in love with. I was besotted with it, even though Alasdair – my intended – preferred to use the German term, *Flitterwochen*, because it sounded dirty, and was more honest.

'It means fondling weeks,' he said, squeezing my breasts.

'I don't think it's referring to that kind of *fond*, is it?'

'Yes – let's *Flitterwochen* right now.'

And we did *Flitterwochen*. We *Flitterwochened* for days and days – and pyjamas or no pyjamas, it was wonderful. A dream. A honey moon that never waned. Yet, bitter sweet, since during our wedding dinner I thought I wanted fish then fish, but it turned out I didn't – I wanted fish then fowl, which Alasdair ordered for me, together with a red wine that I would acquire a taste for, over time.

'You don't want fish then fish,' he said, again.

That was the first moment of doubt, the beginning of mistrust when it came to my friendly and reliable 'bank of stuff'. The next moment came when I got out the shower that evening and found that he'd eaten the complimentary chocolates. I think there were four, each handmade and with its own beautiful motif; their scent laced the room with roses and cherries and lavender, making me all frothy mouthed and happy. They were from Plaisir du Chocolat, and as I showered I contemplated our delicious nuptial treats, drenching myself in deferred pleasure and intent upon the Addis Ababa – a creamy milk chocolate flavoured with cardamon, cardamon tea and pineapple. But when I came out they had all gone. The empty dish threw a small shadow over our marriage – despite all the *Flitterwochening*. I couldn't bring it up, not then, but I have since, and every time I do Alasdair can't believe we're arguing about a few chocolates.

In the morning, having converted the 'two for one' breakfast into a 'four for one' I had to lie down, bloated and slightly shamed by the wanton waste of sausages and black pudding, dipping a pinkie into a tiny sachet of honey that I had no intention of eating – just to sweeten the tongue. The excitement of free toast! Crusts lying on our plates like a disastrous pile of bones (some not even picked clean). Bang on check-out time we left the room, my last look round resting for a moment on the empty dish where my Addis

Ababa had sat in all its creamy milkiness. The gap was insistent, and drew a sigh from a place I had never been to before. It was the middle of January (hence the fantastic 'two for one'), every day cold and dripping wet; a pale sun might rise, not really trying, but mainly it was darkness. We sat in the borrowed car (a 1998 Ford Fiesta), rubbing our thighs to thaw them out, then Alasdair smacked his gloved hands together and turned the key. The motor started on the third kick. 'Yes!' He put the gear in reverse and released the hand-brake, hooking his left arm over his seat and looking through the back window as he eased off. I kissed his right ear lobe, twice, thrice, four times over before he brushed me away. The car wouldn't move. 'Come on, girly,' I said to the car, patting her dashboard, and after more throttle, less clutch, a few stalls, he said 'Fuck it!' and switched off the engine.

'What now?'

He didn't answer; he just stared through the windscreen at a harled wall, his shoulders slumped under a sudden weight. I got out of the car and looked underneath.

'I think maybe the wheels are frozen.'

Despite my tapping on the window Alasdair didn't move.

'I'll go and ask for some hot water, or maybe we just need to knock them with something. Alasdair?'

All he did was fold his arms and sink further down the seat. His face was completely inscrutable – a face that must know it's being looked at, but still it doesn't move; a hope-less face. A face that is surely thinking of something more grave than a frozen camshaft.

I have seen it since, but that day – the day after we got married – was the first.

It was very disturbing.

I have been home for two days but we haven't really talked, other than to cover the necessities. One is waiting for the other to start. We are like two crabs hiding in a tiny pool. Once, when he suddenly said 'Listen,' I thought he was about to say something, but when I looked at him his lobster eyes didn't move. It was as if he had seized up completely, shocked perhaps by how very near we were to lifting the salty rock of our marriage, how unwittingly close to exposing the dark scuttling beneath – a panic of spineless truths worming into the sediment.

But we are not quite ready.

Powerless and disbelieving, we are stuck.

In the evenings we read (thank God), pages and pages of printed words building up between us in great sound-proof blocks, walling us in. He's reading the latest Murakami and I'm still reading *The New Moons*, poring over every word, finger to page like I'm just learning, stopped only by thirst.

Here's how closely I'm reading – 'On the 9th of January 1937, a gale blew through Dumfries.'

I pause and let the page drop, listening to the wind. I cannot picture the town, but on its easterly edge, out of sight behind a thick belt of frantic trees, I can see the asylum. It looks like any other, a dark Victorian monolith in extensive grounds. The wind is banging against the grand doors and threatens to rip the external stairways from the walls and toss them into the river Nith, a furious world storming the windows, beating everyone back to inner rooms and corridors – under tables and under beds – with the exception of seventeen-year-old Peggy Kirkpatrick, who stares out from a top-floor window, amazed.

'What's this for?'

Alasdair has picked up the Ordnance Survey map I took from Gran's room. Always reverential towards maps, he's looking mildly interested, and is clearly impressed.

'It's not for anything. It belongs to Gran.'

'Really? Great condition. It's still got the sign card. What year is it?'

'I'm not sure. The fifties, I think. Please be careful.'

He ignores this, justifiably; Alasdair handles maps as if each one has been drawn by hand, and this one almost could have been, there's a delicacy to it, a milky iridescence that lightens the touch, the colours of the rivers and forests so muted I can find no names for them. He fully extends the map and rests it on the coffee table, then he traps his hands between his pressed knees and leans over it, as if it were an exhibit under glass. There are so many things I want to ask him about this map and the impenetrable language of it, the strangely futuristic keys –

Projection : Transverse Mercator	True Origin : Lat 49° N Long 2°W	
Spheroid : Airy	False Origin : 400 Kms West 100 Kms North	

What's an airy spheroid? I'm tilting on the edge of my chair, close to joining him on the sofa. I stay and watch our virtual reconciliation, watch myself rise and sit with him, side by side after so long. Just a few steps towards him, a brief moment, and we are together. It's that easy.

Alasdair once said every map holds an epic journey for someone, a journey of hope, or escape, or a journey home. Perhaps this is our map, here to guide us back? I am drawn by the powerful irony of it, the notion that Gran will bring us together rather than tear us apart. And I'm drawn, too, by his care and his searching eye, the way he sees beauty in the detail, and the way his square shoulders bolster him against the weight of a disinterested world where boys without mothers are, in essence, unlovable.

'What does this mark mean?'

His voice pulls me back to our walled room of tortuous pathways. I watch him and wait, but he doesn't look; despite his question he is incurious, has habituated to the silence.

'Someone's put a cross just above Pennyland farm.'

He straightens up and looks at the wall.

'Pennyland. That's on one of your Post-its, isn't it? What's that about?'

And still I cannot sense curiosity. There is only irritation, and an uncharacteristic tone of authority that sounds contrived and vaguely Victorian, like he's putting his foot down. I smile, because it is silly, that foot – the hint of bluster; it doesn't suit him.

'What does that look mean?'

'Nothing.'

'Why do you keep shutting me out?'

'Because you're not really interested.'

He turns his head away and pulls on his ear, scratching behind the lobe until it is red. I think he is about to speak again but then his look sets. I can't read his expression, and he can't read mine; we don't know any more. Our words and faces have become foreign. There are only pronouncements, exit signs that shine bright as neon in these dark rooms.

'I'm going to bed.'

He leaves me to fold up the map. I spread out on the sofa and the heat from his body warms my back. In a moment of contrition I mark his book and take it into the bedroom, but he is already asleep. Curled up on his side, he is snoring quietly, his mouth puckering like the lips of an old balloon. When I bend down to turn off the light I can smell his cidery breath.

Sweet Jesus

UPERY. IT seems we can all practise it. Today I practise by bringing the map and presenting it to Gran. I could have brought any map as long as it had latitudes and longitudes, a true North and non-metric feet. What she does is scrutinise and measure; she loves to peer through her magnifying glass, place her ruler along an axis, copy something down with her pencil – preferably a number. These essential pleasures or skills are more important now and need to be nurtured; she needs to play to her strengths. The task (which life has become) is one of preservation rather than restoration. Once we understood this things got a bit easier for all of us; a love for measuring and copying is quite an easy thing to nurture.

So any map would do, but this is not any map – this is her map of Lower Nithsdale, the place where she grew up. The cover is in her favourite blue – like the blue parts of the not-blue sky in that painting she loves so much – and inside, at the foot of a hill that shelters Pennyland from the moors beyond, a place has been marked with a tiny cross. When I give her the map she tries to open it from the side as if it's a birthday card.

'It's a map,' I say.

'It's a map,' she says.

She does this when she doesn't know what you mean; it's called echolalia – and she's very good at it. Instead of looking on it as disguised confusion, I see it as something clever, a preserved skill drawn from her essential self (she has always loved words, and hears them well).

The room is a bit cold. She watches as I unfold the map and from her expression I know she is neither waiting nor anticipating (the meaning of that impassive look came to me quite recently in a sudden, terrible moment). When she sees the map spread out on the table she bends forward, leaning in from the safe anchorage of her skirts. She looks and smiles, humming to fill in the gaps. At first there is no recollection of place, just the pleasure of recognition, markings she still understands, moor and marsh and coniferous wood – but when I read out some of the names and trace my finger across the ford and up to Fern Hill she brushes my hand away and follows her own route back to Pennyland. Then she speaks.

'Where did I leave her?'

And there is something about the word 'leave' – a significance that shifts my focus away from the map and onto her.

'Who?'

'The baby.'

'Eleanor?'

'Yes.'

She leans in even closer, keen eyed and chin practically touching the table as she traverses the low slope of the hill. I am drawn by her intensity and begin to scan with her; we are in cahoots, two heads better than one and both looking (I assume) for Eleanor. I am still struck by her question and the odd particular of that word 'leave' when suddenly she stops and taps the map twice with the tip of her bloodless finger.

'There.'

That's all she says – then a silence that feels dangerous, like we are looking too long at something terrible.

I do not know an Eleanor, none of us do; this lost baby makes no sense to anyone; she is a dark star that began to appear in Gran's firmament a few months ago, more like a meteor, dazzling and short-lived. Only now, looking at the map, she is suddenly earthbound, connected to a fixed point, with an exact grid reference and a bearing north-west of Pennyland farm. I stare at the place, expectant, as if she might emerge from the page just to prove herself; and then something else occurs to me, something less ghostly – *it is a true location*. Were I ever moved to go there, here it is on the map. A destination.

As the prospect rises I can think of nothing else, just this one true thing, a place at the foot of a true hill – that, and the gathering salience of the word 'leave'.

Gran has forgotten the map and is watching a cat that is lying on the bed, his body limp and implausibly long. She doesn't remember Jack and is nonplussed by his appearance and the way he swans about like he owns the place. Sometimes we play an amended version of The Minister's Cat (where I go first and she follows, echoing my mood and my adjectives). This would be a good time to play, while some cat is lying on the bed – Audacious and Black and many other things, we might even get as far as Furry (she loves a furry cat); but I am too preoccupied to play. I am bolted to this sudden hill a hundred miles away, and no matter what Alasdair says, I know what I need to do next.

So FAR I have stuck to convention and arranged my Post-its in a linear way; I might change the order, but the line remains. With the heat from the fire drawing them out from the wall they are beginning to look like arctic poppies. Tonight the group is going to talk about lifelines and I will need to be careful; I mustn't say anything about these biographical fragments because Gran wouldn't want me to. This growing reticence makes me wonder if I should still be going to the group at all. I've had doubts like this before; about two months after joining I felt like an impostor. To suggest I was even a proximate carer seemed fraudulent, but by then the bonds had set. *Everyone welcome* − that was the maxim, and true to their principles they encouraged me to stay. It was very affecting. Whilst I sometimes lost sight of my role as Mum's representative, they never did, and everyone hoped that one day she would feel able to join them.

'I don't think that will ever happen.'

'Then this is the best you can do for her, Aggie.'

But I suspect we all knew that wasn't quite it.

I used to be capable of asinine comments such as 'I couldn't ever be a carer' − like there was a choice. It's not something I have shared with the group, but I know if I did they would understand; they would look at me − a young pretender upon whom no one relies − and they would remember when they felt like that. Days when they thought they could never do it.

For me there is an internal struggle with this since I also don't want to be the kind of person who doesn't want to be a carer. Perhaps I just don't want 'being a carer' to be all there is? (But that's wrong too! That's care-ism at it's worst.)

Take Noreen − she has been so entrenched she doesn't know what she likes; she only knows what her mother used to like.

'Would you like an Oreo, Noreen?'

'I don't know!'

Everything is new to her. She is in a state of almost continual surprise, life as a series of startled peaks − such as the one experienced at her mother's funeral when several mourners told her how well she looked in black, the compliments shifting quickly from mother to daughter, from Mrs Bryden to Miss Bryden, who, twenty years earlier, was about to marry Gerry O'Rourke when her mother suddenly collapsed. It was the first of many. These woozy spins happened whenever the wedding was mentioned, so Noreen and Gerry decided to adopt a Fabian policy until the time was right, but eventually Gerry tired of waiting and turned his devotions to God.

Now, two years after old Mrs Bryden entered the first furnace of what some referred to as a 'double oven', Noreen's excitability is understandable. I see it as a kind of resumption, a bit like one of those Oliver Sacks awakenings. She has come through – a survivor of 'encardiac frenetica' – and the world is not what she expects. The more she sees the more confounded she becomes.

We are listless, our raft floating on a flat sea. Even Noreen is lethargic, looking dejected because Kenneth isn't here. I think he reminds her of her Catholic boy.

'There's been nothing in the paper,' she says, and we all know what she means. As group secretary Noreen checks the death columns everyday. She keeps a list of all the people 'living with' dementia (which is, we are told, better than 'suffering from'). Before, Noreen would draw a line through the person's name when they died, but it always made her feel uncomfortable, so now she just marks them on the list with a wee pink dot using a fluorescent pen, and because she puts the pink dot at the end of the person's name rather than at the beginning, they don't fall in a straight line, but snake down the page, petering out at the tail.

With no listing for Kenneth's dad, and no apologies noted in the group minutes, Kenneth's absence is a mystery.

'Someone should ring him.'

'Why? We don't usually.'

'That's because we usually know what's happening.'

'Any volunteers?'

Eyes dart about. I look to Noreen.

'Noreen? You are the secretary.'

'Oh no! I wouldn't know what to say. Really, I wouldn't know—'

'Right, I'll do it. What's his number?'

And without checking the book, Noreen reels it off.

I DON'T want to go to Mum's yet. The meeting did not go well but trying to explain to her what I mean by that won't be easy, probably because I don't know; I just know a lot of biscuits were consumed and we talked about Christmas, then we finished a bit early, switched off, locked up, and stepped out into the cold without the benefit of putting on our coats because we'd never taken them off. Folk are calling out to one another, their voices carrying in all directions – up the street and over the hill, down to the river and through the marsh grasses, crossing the water to the Carse of Gowrie.

'Cheerio.'

'Bye!'

'Bye!'

Noreen is clutching her collar with both hands, as if concealing something under her coat. She overtakes me as I dither and turn back, away from the direction of the house. We almost collide.

'Oh! Sorry, Aggie, must rush – *tempus fugit.*'

But why must she rush? What could possibly be waiting for her back in the post-war bungalow she has lived in all her life? She disappears round the corner with such speed and sense of purpose that she's created a tail wind; I want to catch it and let it carry me back to her door; I would like to see what she does when she's in her house and there's no one else there, when she's on her own.

I can't quite surrender to the starry night. Something physical – the slight pain in my ankle perhaps, or the way I'm shifting my weight onto the ball of my foot – is keeping me earthed. I sit at the bus shelter for a while, a resting post that draws no suspicion, then a bus comes along and stops. The doors open with a long, nasal intake of breath, like the bus is inflating, filling its lungs; the inside is bright and warm and if I get on it will take me into town. I could go and look through Kenneth's window like a love-struck teenager. But I'm not a teenager any more.

'I'm nearly thirty,' I tell the bus, and it exhales, exasperated, closing its doors with a shudder and driving off.

THE PARK is busy with people and dogs. The women in the longest coats have the dogs with the shortest legs – hems meeting the tops of their ankle boots; they are hatted and gloved, and the flap and swing of their coats bulk them out, as if to emphasise their very being. These women eschew Gortex for wool and know who they are; they look substantial and give the park a city feel. This could be one of the smaller London parks, the kind you only notice from the top of a bus – secret places that people hold close to their hearts. I often dream of London and the life I might have had.

'Could still have!' Fiona said when we talked about it that one time. I hadn't mentioned my other life to anyone, but a few years ago I told her. We were on our way to Glasgow's first ever film festival when we got stuck on the M8. 'The Ballad of Lucy Jordan' came warbling over the radio and it all just came tumbling out – my tiny attic flat in Shoreditch, my job in the theatre, the little park I frequented with my mongrel dog.

I often dream of London—

'Aggie! How are you?'

In her leather Carnaby Street hat she completes the cosmo-politan picture so fittingly that at first I don't recognise her. Perhaps I *am* in London, transported to my other life? The woman hugs herself and laughs, then things fall into place.

'Hello, Flossie.'

(I don't want to call her that any more but know I would stumble over Florence.)

Her arms are crossed, hands almost touching her shoulders.

'It's so cold! Should you be out?'

The concern is genuine; there is an expression she has, a kind of rearrangement of the features where everything on the face moves slightly upwards (we each have our unique physiognomic signature and this is hers – the complete upward tilt).

'Oh yes, I'm fine. A lot better, thanks. Nearly there, in fact.'

'Good. It sounded really painful.'

'Yes, it was – but it's fine now. I just need to rest it a bit more. This is the first walk I've had. Couldn't resist the sun.'

'Carrie! Come here, Carrie!'

I'm conforming – following the rules for this sort of encounter because what else can I do? We both watch as my dog (the one in my dreams) bounds towards us.

'You have a dog.'

'Yes, for my sins. She's a rescue dog. Mad as a brush, but happy mad. She was found wandering along the riverbank, out by your way, actually, so we don't have any background, but nothing bad seems to have happened to her.'

'She's lovely.'

'She is. You are, aren't you? Yes you are!'

Flossie is scratching my dog's ears, roughing her wiry coat, which is black and white – the same colours as our kitchen floor. Alasdair and I chose that floor together; it was one of those shared choices that we were both so sure about it felt like a validation. We used to joke about when we found our perfect black and white dog and how it would look lying on the kitchen floor – sometimes whole, sometimes half, sometimes not there at all (or maybe just a black disembodied head on a white tile – like a warning). Carrie is that dog, and the day she was found on the riverbank and taken to the pound she wasn't wandering, she was looking for me.

I watch Flossie as she clips the lead back onto Carrie's collar, all the time speaking in the only manner possible when faced with a dog as cute as this. (Yes! Yes! I know – yes! Oh yes, I know!) She is red cheeked, a mixture of love and the slap of a cold December wind, with, I would like to think, the tell-tale rise of guilt. My dog is clearly besotted with her, how could she not be? – fed on this love juice, lapping it up.

I can't undo these things. Love is love. I can't sneak through a dark fog and steal back what is mine.

Flossie straightens up and brushes down her coat, a midi to match the dog's medium proportions. There is a sudden stop and Carrie settles down with a casual ease that only comes with security.

'I'd better get this one back. I've a busy afternoon ahead.'

'Oh, I'm sorry—'

'No! Don't be daft. We're managing fine. There's absolutely no rush, Aggie. You just take as long as you need.'

The upward tilt again, and she may have finished, I don't know, but at this point Carrie pulls on the lead then spins round and sits, raising her back leg to scratch her right shoulder, but the leg catches up in the lead, strapped in mid-air, where it scratches anyway, fast enough to create a frieze of paws (or so it seems to me) – then she throws herself down, hips and bum aloft, and pushes her shoulder along the ground, the lead twisting across and between the four leg joints like a knitting Nancy, rolling on her back now, then a contorted twist up that leaves her three-legged, docked, and still itchy.

Our goodbyes are pleasant, almost warm; I can't speak for her but the warmth does feel circular, a cosy funnel of air that you have to actually step out of. Flossie has located my dog's missing leg and has untied it. It's hard to let Carrie just walk away with her, so I don't look, even though we are all heading in the same direction. I veer off towards the trees, cold and dog-less but feeling not very much at all other than mild puzzlement about the cosy funnel.

Obviously, having just met my husband's lover, who has stolen my dog, neither the funnel nor my feelings are to be trusted. I am unhinged, in freefall, perhaps having inhaled some of the residual ether that has hovered round Flossie since those nursery days. She is imbued with it, and leaves a vaporous trail across the park. I throw it a synaesthetic glance and see a slight petroleum rainbow that Carrie cannot resist.

I AM on my way to meet Kenneth. It was his idea. When I called him on behalf of the group to find out when or if he might be coming back he suggested we meet.

'Let's meet for a coffee. You can tell me what I missed.'

By the time I reach the Christian café the sun has paled and is slipping down, but the day feels new. Kenneth is already here, sitting where I wouldn't normally sit – in full display at a table by the window. His coat is draped over the back of his chair and he has brought his Elmer Fudd hat, which is hunching on the table like a dozy cat. When I approach he half stands, pushing back his chair but not quite straightening his knees.

'You made it then.'

'Yes, it's such a lovely walk. I took my time. I'm not late, am I?'

'No – I was early.'

He was early and he sat by the window and waited for me.
There is an openness here, a lightness brought about by a
refreshing lack of history, no old grudges and nothing yet
learned, no grooves to slip into – parallel conversations in a
world where convergence means pain. We both sit down and
I warm my hands on my cheeks.

'So, how's the tree?'

'The tree? Oh, the tree is excellent. It's far too early but
I wanted to have one while my sister was here with Morag.
I don't think it'll survive till Christmas. Morag has covered
it in her own homespun creations – huge baubles and things
she's cut out from white paper. Not sure what they're meant
to be, the whole thing is a complete mish-mash.'

'Lovely.'

'Yes. The fairy is mine, though. I've had her since I was
three.'

'Aw – is there lights?'

'Oh yes, lots and lots of lights. Three cables of lights.'

'Wow – what kind are they, LCD?'

'Afraid not, no. Nothing so sophisticated. They're so big
they hum.'

'Huh!'

A waitress comes and gives us each a menu before pulling
a cloth from her apron.

'Sorry, can you just move your hat?'

'Sorry.'

He puts his hat on the low window shelf and studies the
menu as she wipes the table. When she's finished she takes
out her pad and tells me there is no lemon drizzle cake today.

'Oh no! I'll just have a coffee then.' (A coffee – that's all
the detail they need here.)

'Make that two.'

We hand back our menus and smile at the waitress, sharing

the goodwill that laps around us like a warm sea, and I wonder if this is how it feels to be a Christian. When she goes I lean over the table and whisper.

'Did she just ask you to remove your cat?'

'No, I don't think so. Did she?'

'I'm sure she did.'

I stroke his hat. 'Poor pussy.' Then I clear my throat and dutifully tell him about the last group meeting, because that's why we're here. I give him an update on the Christmas plans – who's doing what, that kind of thing – then I ask him if he's coming back.

'Of course. I wouldn't stop coming without saying anything, I've just been rather caught up with things at home. There's a lot to sort out.'

'We just thought, you know – now that your dad is in hospital long term.'

'Do you think that means I should leave the group now?'

'God no, not at all – you have to come back! I have been sent as an emissary to find out where you've been and to make sure you haven't defected to the hospital group.'

He is pleased to hear this, I can tell; his left hand is lying on the table and it looks relaxed. I'd like to place my own hand over it and squeeze it.

Please come back.

'Don't think it's because we like you or anything, we just want you to be Santa.'

'Oh well, it won't be the first time.'

I don't know if I want to know any more. Unless it is your profession, 'being Santa' suggests many laudable things – popularity, community, belonging – but too much goodness is such a spoiler. I could never have coffee with Santa, never. He'd find me out.

The waitress brings coffee in a pot and when we lean back to let her through there is a sudden reticence; I don't think either of us wants it, but it's there. Kenneth turns his face to the window.

'What is it you do anyway, besides being Santa?'

'I'm a meteorologist.'

He's craning his neck to see through the glass, and then, with a brush of his sleeve, he changes the day, lifting the mist like a weather god.

'Really! My gran's a meteorologist, kind of. Where do you work?'

(I have raced ahead to a sunny room where Kenneth and Gran are discussing snow; when they look through the window their heads touch.)

His reply is dark. It gathers at the base of my mood centre, damping me down.

Kenneth is temporary. He lives and works in Southampton. (Southampton! Where the hell is Southampton? Hampton already sounds impossibly far.) There is a weather station there that has links with the satellite receiving station at the university here, so he managed to negotiate a kind of part transfer, part sabbatical – a year to be with his father.

'Ah. So when do you go back?'

'January.'

'But what if your dad is still—'

I stop to rephrase what I was about to say. We don't speak easily of the *fourth stage*; as members of the same group we speak of stage three with a certain eloquence – the nurturing retreat into pre-language movements and sounds, the working through of unfinished conflicts (thwarted love, infanticide, things like that); the resurrection of mother.

But *stage four* tends to stick in the throat.

'Still what – alive?'

'No. Still needs you. What will you do?'

'He doesn't need me. I need him.'

Then stay. I look at him, his eyes more blue than before.

He is wise, temporary, needs his father – who doesn't need him, perhaps because he is old-old and in *stage four*, where the struggle has passed, muscles have loosened and a new grace has begun.

'I know what you mean.'

'Yes, you do. How is she?'

'She's good. She's—'

I sigh and pull my hair back from my face, elbows on the table and my head down, taking my time. When I meet his direct gaze I hold it and puff out my cheeks. *If not him, who? Who else might understand?*

'I don't know. My family think I'm fixated. I tire them out wondering about Gran's past. The thing is I feel very confused because she's mentioning stuff I don't think she wants us to know. Well, I know she doesn't, otherwise she would have told us before, but I can't seem to let it go.'

'Difficult,' he says, drawing on the table with his finger, and this simple confirmation has a huge effect – a sense of reclaimed sanity.

'It is difficult, really difficult.'

And suddenly there is a freeing-up and all the yellow clues I have stuck above the fireplace – those arctic poppies in strange arrangement – finally cohere. I tell him about the magazines, and about the poem that so firmly locates her in the hospital, and, finally, in an implicit pact of complete confidence, I tell him that I think there was a baby – that I've kept her vague and ghostly for as long possible, but that now, I think I know exactly where she is.

That X marks the spot.

'She can't speak about it. I think there was a critical moment when she might have said more if I'd just stayed calm and gone with it there and then but we can't seem to get back to it. It's like she's moved beyond it – but I can't stop thinking about it.'

'Well, sounds to me like you just want to understand her life, but reminiscing about something as painful as that – I don't know. I just don't know, Aggie. I can't advise you.'

'No.'

'It's not like you can access her medical records unless you're her guardian, and even then you probably don't have the right.'

'I know. It's not what I want anyway, sorry—'

Covering my mouth I close my eyes against a sudden press of tears. He passes a napkin and leans in towards me.

'Come on, Aggie – don't buckle. We need you in one piece.'

And even now, with tracks down my face and a sense of aimless despair, I feel light. I don't know how he does it, this man from Southampton. What is it about his words? And who is *we*?

'I'll order more coffee,' he says.

Lighter still, I am rapt by his attentions. I go and wash my face in cold water, replenish myself under a wet compress of paper towels, then I peel off the mask.

By the time the waitress brings the bill she is *our* waitress, she will always be *our* waitress (that's how long we've been there). We thank her, our smiles more subtle now, as if we have become wise. I sense a mutual ambivalence, but we have to go. He promises to come to the next group meeting and when I say 'Oh thanks, Kenneth – mission accomplished', I blush, for so many reasons. He picks up his hat and drinks the last gritty dregs from his cup.

'I'll say this much for God – he makes a damn good coffee.'

'He does, and his lemon drizzle is to die for. You should try it.'

'Maybe I will. I like a cake.'

When he leaves – grizzly in his bear hat and openly sweet-toothed – I marvel at the things he has said, the various expressions of love (familial, coniferal, sugarial). The café is crammed with people who are in no hurry; they want to enjoy the nativity scene that has been set up near the till. Folk are peering into the crib; it is too big, huge beside the tiny plastic donkey, who looks suspiciously like a pony without its saddle (clearly not part of the original set). The baby Jesus is a painted wooden doll; he's swaddled in one of those cloths for cleaning spectacles.

'Aw, look – his wee face.'

It wouldn't matter how much of a rush you were in, and irrespective of beliefs – to not look would be odd, a kind of disrespect, and not to be moved by the peep eyes would be odder still. At the very least there is a disconcertion – the infant Jesus is usually asleep; one does not expect to meet his kewpie doll eye.

I weave my way towards the door, holding the bill and the cash Kenneth insisted on giving me.

'Was everything all right for you today?'

And normally I would have said something about the missing lemon cake (they quite often run out) but today, despite this, everything is all right.

'Yes, thanks.'

I have survived my first encounter with Flossie since the revelation and have shown forgiveness (at least about the dog); I have had coffee with a lovely man who has left me indebted; I have borne the news of Southampton with stoic dignity; and with relatively little discomfort, I have looked the baby Jesus in the eye.

Of course, I shall revisit the news that Kenneth will be leaving in January – I need to make sense of what I'm feeling about that – but for now it brings a kind of freedom. I can talk to him about more than I might have done, knowing that soon he will be gone.

Pennyland

Lᴀsᴛ ɴɪɢʜᴛ I told Alasdair I was going to Nithsdale to visit Gran's farm. I didn't say I was going to look for the spot where I think her baby is buried, I just said I was curious to see the place where she grew up, that it would help me reminisce with her if I could 'flesh out' her life story.

'What about our life story? When are you going to flesh that out?' he said.

I barely slept, and when I did I dreamt of Pennyland as if I knew it, as if I had already been. The arching moon was baying like a wolf. It was the same moon – here as there, then as now.

The same changing moon.

Aᴛ ʙʀᴇᴀᴋꜰᴀsᴛ I notice he has changed into his foxy cycling trousers – a long riding pant with front zip and double snap fly; they have inner-thigh ventilation too, and are supposed to be loose fit but I don't see it. I know these things because I bought the trousers, not as a gift but as a replacement for his padded bib tights, which I threw out (I would have given them to charity, but I was worried they might find their way back).

In sync, he leaves the table as I sit down. I ask him what's the best way onto the A74 because, despite everything, I want him to be a part of this.

'So you're going then?'

'Yes.'

'When?'

'Now – today. I've booked a B&B.'

Standing with his back to me he grips the edge of the draining board and his head drops, his shoulder blades sprouting like stunted wings.

'You did that?'

'Yes.'

I follow him into the hall. He's rummaging through a drawer and pulls out some ankle ties.

'Take the AA map – and check your tyres.'

'Is that it?'

'That's it. You know my thoughts.'

He looks at me, waits.

'Don't forget your hat,' I say.

'It's not a hat, it's a helmet.'

He goes, tight in his loose winter trousers, annoyed and looking silly in his teardrop hat. Winter sun slants through the window, heavy and pale. Like Alasdair, I can't wait to go. I stack the dishes and consider leaving a note but decide not to because I don't know what to say. 'Sorry' seems appropriate but I'm not sure why. To not leave a note is a message in itself, and as soon as I drive off I regret it. I can still see him standing in the hall, waiting for me to step towards him, and I am almost overwhelmed by it, but I don't turn back.

THE ROAD in front of me is a hundred miles long and edged with ice – a rimy crust that spreads out and into the brown scrub of heather. With Glasgow only just avoided and the landscape a sudden open moor, I feel intrepid. I am crossing land populated with elusive wildlife – weasels and black grouse, wild cats the size of pumas (creatures Gran has seen with her own eyes). As the sky clears I know what to look for – peregrine and raven, red kites at Durisdeer. She has been holding it all in her head and I realise that over the years she has told me more than I thought, although it was her speaking rather than telling, and me not so much listening as overhearing. And now, with the speaking almost done, I am beginning to sense another world here, a different life – Gran on a horse, her legs bare in all weathers, just as they were a few days ago when, looking out, I saw her at the foot of the orchard, burning leaves.

I don't know what has brought this back, the notion of eavesdropping perhaps, but as I drive further south I remember a moment from childhood with every sense, including the taste of liquorice in my mouth, and the ache of separateness, as if something is severed. I can hear the muffled tones of my parents' voices droning in the next room, and I am back there, listening at the door.

'She's too happy.'

'That's a terrible thing to say.'

'The truth is always terrible.'

'No it's not, you know it isn't. Sometimes you come out with these lines, Mary – I don't know where they come from.'

There is a kind of spoken laugh, then a deep sigh and a murmur of pleasure. I can hear the rustle of Dad's jacket. Mum has turned to him and put her head on his chest, he has wrapped his arms right round her and is squeezing her as tight as he dare, like he just can't draw her close enough.

I look through the crack where the door is slightly open, and what I see is love.

Twenty years on, such is the vividness of this scene it is

not the moment I am thinking of, it is the memory itself – the way sometimes, as soon as a thing happens, it sets, like a drop of boiling toffee on a cold, wet saucer. This firing and fixing is complex; sugars invert and molecules split; syrup boils until it cracks. There are a lot of factors involved, and many possible outcomes – toffee can be hard or soft, or not toffee at all. It might be caramel, or burnt sugar, or fudge. It's like that with memory; there is a physics to it, a science that is concerned with forces and energy, and relationships. It is a messy, motley thing, but a science nevertheless – with hidden laws and consequences. My gran is living proof. Her memories are in various stages of preservation, or disintegration, depending on how you look at it; pieces of her picked out and kept, guarded by whatever means, I don't know how – a pickling or freezing, something like that. Somebody somewhere is working it all out, conducting a kind of calculus on the bits of brain that store up the past – but I don't see it that way; what I see is a crowd gathering in Gran's head. Ghosts emerging from the glaze like true stars in her visible heaven; people I've never heard of before, and it turns out that all those times when I saw her looking up at the sky, when I looked too, because I wanted her eyes – all I saw was an imperfect expression, because it just isn't possible to see anything else.

Nithsdale. After only two hours I have arrived in a foreign place, an unexpectedly pretty village where the wide main street is lined with blazing trees, December and not yet bare. There is a straight boulevard of elegant Victorian villas and a crossroads with a stone column supporting a winged horse. My B&B is just as described on the website – superior, with high ceilings and tall windows – and despite the furnishings not quite living up to the grand dimensions of the room, I like the feel of it; there is an airiness to it that I wasn't expecting. What I was expecting was gloom.

I unpack my rucksack and put my things away properly, as if I'm moving in, then I spread myself out on the bed and browse the literature – Welcome, House Rules, Places To See. I contemplate relaxing for two days, as if on holiday. I could walk along the river to Drumlanrig Castle, visit the Queensberry Marbles perhaps, or enjoy the fine gargoyle waterspouts at Tynron Kirk. I can see myself now, wandering through the Nith valley, my thoughts about Gran and the baby and the asylum all following behind like ducklings. I could jump off a cliff and they'd still be there, their stubborn little feet splayed out, wings spreading like tiny fans.

Tomorrow is all planned out. In the morning I will go to Pennyland, then on to Dumfries (about seven miles away) to visit the grounds of the Crichton, followed by an hour or two in the town library, where I know they keep archive materials and articles about the old hospital.

I'm resting on the bed drinking water described as 'complimentary', when here it is again – my aniseed mouth.

'She's too happy.'

Mum voicing her worries about the spring in my step, not realising I had skipped back through the trees and into the kitchen because I'd forgotten the plum slice I was taking to Fiona's (an easy barter for a Lion Bar). *She's too happy.* And Dad was right – it may have been a terrible thing to say, but it was true. Now I feel ill equipped for what might be considered the normal amount of unhappiness a person can expect in life. I can't seem to accept it the way others do.

THE SOUND of a tractor trundling up the boulevard wakes me. I listen for another, and it comes. The room is cold, and without the glow of the evening lamps it has lost its charm. I check the time and realise I have slept through the alarm and have already lost a full hour. I wash and dress quickly, propelled by the touch of cold lino under my feet and a heated towel rail that doesn't work and doesn't even seem to have a switch. The map is on the bedside table together with my phone, a compass, keys and a set of L-shaped Allen keys, bunched together on a ring. I put these things in my jacket pockets and as I leave I take out my phone to switch it on, then change my mind and put it back on the table.

Descending the stairs without a sound, I place my hollow feet lightly on the steps, a shell in each boot. I am alert, and braced, and I know this crook-backed stealth is unnecessary, but there is a silence I don't want to break. This is a quiet, contemplative excursion – like a pilgrimage. I don't want to wake anyone. I just want to look.

When I was planning this trip all I pictured was the place, nothing else – just the land itself, and the sky above it, and the sound of the burn running down to the mill at Boghall. Beguiled by the cartographer's delicate hand, I would look at the pale blue thread of water on the map and I could hear it, the twist of blue growing in my head like an extra vein. The map drew me in; a flat sheet of hills and coniferous woods, with a key of naïve markings: tiny sprigs of reed and beds of osier, sketchy marsh, and the moors marked out in dots, like an aboriginal painting, becoming so familiar that now – driving the car as if the land is mined (and it *is* mined – there is an incendiary spot) – I don't really need it any more, I can follow my own inky imprint, the map in my head. When I roll down the window (it feels necessary, despite the cold) I can hear the burn, louder and keener than I remember, or should I say expected? – louder than I expected, swollen with rain and in a mad rush to join the brown waters of the Nith.

I follow the track to the abandoned farm at Pennyland, where I leave the car and walk through the gate and onto Fern Hill. Since the day we looked at the map together Gran has not said much more, despite my gentle probing, but she has mentioned a stone.

'Like that,' she said, raising her hands and drawing the shape of an arch.

There was a hill, with a farmhouse at the foot of it, and a long gate, and then, suddenly – there was a stone.

This is what I'm searching for – Eleanor's stone. Of course, I don't want to find it; I want to unearth a figment, but when I reach the first rise of the hill there it is – a solitary boulder that looks like it has fallen from the sky. I have barely begun and already I am practically upon it, the shape so tomb-like it would be an obvious choice. With a sudden scepticism (as if, despite the way everything fits, I am being duped) I approach the stone, close enough now to see that it is unmarked. Drawn downwards I put my hands on the ground and let my knees drop, but instead of leaning back I stay on all fours because this way I can't do anything else; I can't reach into my pocket and pull out the Allen keys to scratch her name on the stone, and I can't tear at the spoon of land dipping beneath me, foraging like an animal to expose her – the mottled greys and the creams of her un-fused skull, her dry bones clean in the dirt; less than a skeleton, now – tiny bits and pieces, ribs maybe, bones in disarray, rummaged by a fox that was disappointed because there wasn't a scrap left.

How long would that take?

The winds are bitter and blow in all directions. Cold clods of earth have penetrated my knees and a sudden bolt of pain makes me wince – *Christ!* I stand upright to dispel the shock and rub some heat back into my legs. The map did not convey the desolation, yet I recognise it – frantic jabs of scraggy gorse, and strange boulders strewn across the hillside. I see the old drove road she must have walked along, and looking north-east to where the moors open out, I know from the map that round the side of the hill a Roman fort rises like a submarine.

She's never mentioned it, not described any of it, and the familiarity frightens me. I'm still caught up in the terrible geography when I turn and look back towards Pennyland. And that's when I see her – Gran standing at the gate; her skin would have been smooth then, there would have been a plumpness; the moon face of a girl straining for the sound of her baby, even though she knew she was already dead.

I DON'T KNOW how long I was on the hill – not long (on account of the fear, and the cold), but long enough to numb all of my extremities. When I reached the car and took off my gloves my hands were bleeding, the pads of my fingers punctured by thorns, but I'd had no sense of it. Squeezing one hand with the other I watched the blood ooze from my fingertips, viscous globs of mercurial blood, darkening to a deep Rothko red. There is always, at Alasdair's insistence, a supply of kitchen roll in the glove compartment, and I wrapped several sheets round each hand then drove back down the track, leaning forward and peering ahead to avoid the worst of the boulders, some so big and so incongruous where they were surrounded by forest they challenged reason; there was a strangeness to the whole place, and I wanted out.

My progress was slow and exacting. When I reached the end of the forest road I was exhausted. I stopped at the junction, and like a character in a gothic tale I looked in the rear-view mirror, not from habit, but to see what was behind me.

There was nothing.

I AM almost asleep – but the darkness and swell of fatigue is not enough, not quite. Drinking water from a glass bottle that has been replenished by someone unseen, I wonder if

I'll ever sleep again – waking nights of *tell or not tell* stretch before me as my mind expands to fill the grand spaces of the asylum I had intended to visit today, but couldn't.

I did try. I came off the hill and I drove to Dumfries, where I visited a chemist to dress my punctured hands. Tending wounds felt exactly right; no matter how minor, the intense administration of treatment transcended everything in a sublime moment of care. With my fingers moving again I followed the river to a stone bridge, and from there I turned up to the church where Robert Burns was buried. Gran would have visited that, I'm sure (although again, she has never mentioned it); in her Burns anthology she keeps a postcard of the bard with Highland Mary. I have always loved it, the way he is holding Mary's arm, tenderly, as if she has just hurt it; he's wearing buckle shoes and stockings whereas she's in bare feet. It was this sudden recollection of Mary and the pale perfection of her feet that changed my mood. Everything was taking on a new significance where each small speculation was yet another concealment. This was not the journey of discovery I had imagined, it was a journey of duplicity – hers, not mine; a veiled place I had no right to enter.

Despite the Crichton campus being open to the public, as I approached it I felt a growing sense of trespass and uncertainty. It was not simply a loss of nerve, it was doubt, and a kind of weariness. I was no longer sure I wanted to know any more. I reached a junction of three roads. Unsure about which to follow, I pulled up and asked a passer-by, who told me to take the middle road, but I remembered Gran saying to me, more than once, *Never take the middle road.*

So I didn't.

Turning back at the crossroads I passed St Michael's Kirkyard and drove to the town library, where I stared at the building for a long time, as if sightseeing. I admired the red sandstone, there was a quiet grandeur to it, and the carved figures – personifications of Knowledge, Music, Art and Truth – fortified me.

Inside, I was glad to bury myself in books. I photocopied some articles that described the prevailing conditions in the Crichton during the 1930s. Everything I read about the hospital's reputation as a pioneering institution fitted the little I already knew. The Crichton made many claims: best farm, best gardens, best water in Scotland; and the climatological station was the best equipped in the whole of the British Isles (apart from the Government Observatories, of course, there was a limit to this excellence). I have no doubt that's where she first learned to measure rain so precisely, and there were other aspects that felt familiar – the departments, for instance, described here as an arrangement of wards, separated according to wealth, but all concerned with establishing a therapeutic community where artistic pursuits such as writing and painting were as much a part of the treatments as the more physical interventions: the leucotomy, the insulin therapy, the electroconvulsive shocks.

Those were the words – *as much a part of.* The sharp phrase flew like a dart, striking me just above the heart.

This is what is buried, deeper than any grave – the leucotomy, the insulin therapy, the ECT. Gran has a connection to it, but since she will not speak of it, I don't know what she endured. She has mentioned other aspects, has talked about the Turkish baths and something called a Scotch douche, and sometimes – when she sits at her window, bathed in winter sun – she says she's taking her 'heliotherapy'.

But she has never mentioned this – shock treatments, invented (not discovered) in the 1930s, and like her, I don't want to think of it. I prefer to picture her resting on one of the spacious verandas that were attached to the wards, enjoying the sunshine and a southerly view of Criffel Hill, with the Solway beyond.

I join her there and we sit together, fearless and completely still, waiting for ladybirds.

THE BREAKFAST room juts into what must have once been a pleasant back garden, spoiled now by this hexagonal assault of brick and PVC that is described, without any sense of irony, as the conservatory.

If you would like to order a cooked breakfast please ring the bell.

The sign is lodged in a poly-pocket that is anchored under a jar of raspberry jam, adjacent to the cereals. I am grateful for it. It means I don't have to talk to anyone (the owners of the B&B have a good understanding of Scottish hospitality and stay well out of sight). The other guest comes in and sits at the next table just as I'm finishing off a bowl of tinned peaches. I don't look up, and something keeps us completely apart, a sensibility, although whose I'm not sure. I leave just as he rings the bell. The sound is unexpectedly clunky, like a goat's bell, and it surprises me (as if I have a preconceived notion of how a breakfast bell should sound).

We hope you have enjoyed your stay and wish you a safe onward journey.
Best wishes from Ginny and Pat

I am grateful for this sign too. It is the final one in a long series; they are everywhere, like clues in a treasure hunt, finally leading you out — and because Ginny and Pat prefer it if you pay in advance, it means I can leave without speaking at all. I drive home in silence, stealing myself for whatever is next. My thoughts are small and spurious, as if my brain isn't up to the task, and I believe these vivid preoccupations – the goat meandering through my thoughts with his timeless bell, the slithery slices of tinned peach, these are the things that are getting me through this first day. It is all part of a settling that needs to occur before I can consider the dead baby who is already crowding at my window, fleshed out and plump as a grub.

Love Knots

T HE JOURNEY is over. I heard the rusty cry of a peregrine falcon, but did not look, and now I am back, struggling to squeeze past Alasdair's bike, which is taking up most of the hall, half stripped and with all its wee bits laid out on my eighteenth-century Scottish silver salver like a sacrificial offering to the God of Bikes. This is the kind of thing that makes Alasdair (with a *d*) so Alasdairesque. I used to find it endearing but now it just tires me out, or sends me into a rage.

I drop my bag and go into the kitchen, composed now, my mood flat as the sky. Alasdair is sitting at the table, descaling a fish. When he sees me he looks genuinely concerned. He stops and puts down the knife.

'Christ, what happened to you?'

'Nothing.

'But your hands – what happened?'

'I caught them on some broom when I was out walking.'

'What broom?'

'Broom. Just broom.'

'What do you mean broom?'

My voice rose.

'Broom! Broom!'

And I am about to laugh, we both are – but then something slips and I lock myself in the bathroom to cry. Not even time to say hello and already look at me – sobbing into the tattered tubigrips I've been wearing since yesterday.

Crying means nothing any more. Alasdair used to do what he could; he'd hover about, perch on the arm of my chair, or, if there were no arms (for example, when I sobbed standing up, or lying down, or when I was driving) he would place his hand on my shoulder like a priest, or like Jesus in those pictures where he is curing someone or forgiving them for being a complete wretch; but since the miscarriage he has become desensitised by a flooding that has left him completely washed out. One day he just turned away and did something else. He has been doing something else ever since, and who can blame him? It's not indifference, it's acceptance – and I have no issue with his liberal attitude; I *like* the permissiveness of home – it means I can cry whenever I want. It doesn't matter. Beckett tears streaming down my face.

Alasdair never cries at home, he only cries at the cinema, and this is one of the things I do love about him – the way his tears catch the light of imaginary lives, his shoulders quivering in the dark. We never mention it, we just blow into our tissues and pretend to read the credits, and then when the lights come on, we smile and give each other a shove. Films are a big thing for Alasdair, he's a huge Scorsese fan. His favourite is *Alice Doesn't Live Here Anymore* and I think what he loves most about it is the mother/son relationship; I believe that in his dreams Alice Hyatt is his mother (she certainly looks like I imagine his mother would look). Of course, Alasdair says that's all rubbish, but so many things point to it.

The gauze round my fingers smells of fish and my knees are cold, clad in the memory of wet moss. I run the bath and break the cellophane on a basket of Body Botanics that has been floating about since last Christmas. I wash myself with a bar of oatmeal soap and a net scrunch, exfoliate with a seaweed scrub, rub my thighs with a Brillo-pad glove, wash my hair in nettle shampoo, scour my back with what looks like a belt sander, use a rough towel to dry myself, and finally, I moisturise until I am all aglow and buttery – ready to grow a brand-new skin.

He calls from the kitchen.

'Aggie – it's on the plate.'

'Coming.'

I put on my white towelling robe and cross the hall, but I can't do it. I don't want to talk about my pilgrimage to Pennyland.

I'm not gong to tell anyone, ever.

I conjure up a sudden wave of nausea, a surge strong enough to carry me to the bedroom, disrobe me, and slide me into bed. Wrapped in a sticky cocoon, I can feel my skin growing, fresh cells pushing up to the epidermis – pearly and flat like the scales of a fish.

By morning I will be completely new.

UNTIL LAST year I was attracted to bad apples; any signs of canker drew my eye, the dark spot. Now all I long for is goodness. I look at Alasdair sleeping beside me, his pale skin grey against the sheet, and I want him to be good. When we got married I made him promise not to change; he swore on a copy of *The Giant Road Atlas of Europe* (because big promises require big books). But last September I changed, not suddenly, but starting from then – and now that I have, and because it's a change for the worse, I need him to be better than he is.

We don't always know what to look for, what questions to ask. I don't even know if I asked any questions. What did I ask? I know we reveal ourselves through the choices we make, but what happens when there's no choice? What about when things just happen and choice bleeds out of you, warming your thighs and pooling on the bathroom floor?

I should have asked some questions. Not *IF* questions, *WHEN* questions, such as:

What will you do when I have a miscarriage?

or

What will you do when I tell you I think my gran buried her own baby?

These are the things we need to know of one another. I know the answer to the first (although I never asked the question) but not to the second, and I don't think I can ask that one, which leads me to some tedious, corollary questions, such as:

Why can't I tell him?

and

What if I don't?

and

What do I think he would do if I did?

I am in a state of perpetual enquiry; my mind keeps contradicting itself, performing strange acrobatics and flexing its muscle − stretching bits that have been resting for a long time, probably dormant since the day I dropped out of university, or before that, definitely before that, but the date of my formal, in-writing withdrawal from the course was significant because that was the day I officially recognised that losing a baby was worth more than a few days' rest. It's not like in the movies where you cry your way through a sad song then move on. She (bound to be) merited something greater. With no name and no stone and nothing much to remember, there had to be a point. She had to change my life, the way babies do.

And anyway, let's be honest, leaving university was no great sacrifice since it was not what I expected. I knew from the moment I joined the matriculation queue that this wasn't going to be my route into white space. I liked my lecturers, and my tutor was kind and patient; I could tell she thought taking a year out was the right thing to do – unlike Mum, whose silence on the subject said something quite different. I have a number of modules under my belt – charms on a bracelet that she occasionally takes out and jangles under my nose like they're the keys to a magic kingdom – but otherwise all that remains is a rudimentary skill for enquiry; I have the tools to argue either way, always, no matter what, which does Alasdair's head in (he literally holds it in his hands and begs me to stop, but it's hard to stop when your mind is freewheeling its way towards stage six of Kohlberg's moral reasoning).

I am very drawn to theory as a way of thinking, but there is invariably a critical flaw, which is this: I never know where love fits in.

It's all half-baked anyway; when it comes to deciding whether or not to tell on Gran (and that's how it would feel, which says a lot right there) I'd be as well pulling petals from a daisy.

She killed her.
She killed her not.
She killed her.

I have no context for this, that's why I'm resorting to logic – pinning Post-its on a wall and ordering my thoughts through various binary functions (like the fault-finder chart for our new boiler). Ideas flash, then go, leaving the place I occupy darker than before.

And Eleanor is everywhere.

She is in the newspapers and on the television. She populates the Internet and features in magazines. She is fact and fiction; the subject of stories; history and social anthropology. She crosses boundaries and cultures and academic disciplines.

Forensic.

Poetic.

Dead babies everywhere.

Crushed buds pressed between the pages of a book. I'm reading those pages now. Wee dry bundles lying in the attic, or under the floorboards – wrapped in wallpaper and all trussed up with a knitting needle. The world is full of baby bones and the questions keep tripping over each other like a tongue twister.

Corollary. Corollary. Corollary.

TUFTY IS sitting on the floor, almost; not sitting *up* exactly, but definitely sitting, supported by nothing more than a few cushions and his mother's ardent admiration. Fiona and I are more propped, sitting on the sofa and looking at him, looking and looking until it starts to feel weird.

'Let's stop looking at him.'

'But what if he falls?'

He is staring at the concho studs on my moccasin boots. Whenever his head wobbles in another direction the studs jerk him back; to him, they are clearly astonishing, his eyes reflect their perfect round shape, and I know how he feels; I've never been too sure about my moccasins. They are black, ankle high, with a plaited top and silver buttons along the suede fringe. A favourite with Kate Moss, I'm not convinced they looked as good on me as they do on her, particularly given the fact that, unlike Kate, I have what Alasdair calls a 'shapely calf'. I've no idea why he always says it in the singular, and I didn't rise to it – yet the bovine analogy persisted, and now that I am reappraising everything that comes into my head about Alasdair I wonder if that calf was a mistake rather than a joke. Come to think of it there has been quite a lot of malapropisms from Alasdair, such as the saprophytic effect of my 'stodgy but proud' bread and butter pudding (he said once, yawning).

Still looking at Tufty rooted in his own special Danish shag pile, he appears to be in more danger of compressing downwards rather than toppling over, but then there is the McCubbin head to consider. He has inherited his father's precipitous forehead – all bone rather than brain (hence the weight); it judders and lolls in an almost perpetual ergonomic struggle, with just the occasional moment of perfect balance and what looks like enlightenment when his head sits briefly but squarely on what will eventually be his neck, and I can tell from the expression on his face, the sketchy little eyebrows already shooting up, that such moments come as a complete surprise to him, as if there has been a pause in gravitational forces – like a sea gone flat.

'I don't think he can fall, he's too—'

'What? He's too what?'

She's looking at him but the impatient frown is for me.

'Well, he's too . . .'

I'm looking for a neutral word.

'Squat.'

'Squat?'

Fiona looks at me now. She wants me to elucidate.

'Yes, dumpy.'

'Dumpy? Is that good or bad?'

'It's neither, it's just a description, not a judgement. Anyway, listen, I need to tell you something.'

Those were his exact words.

Listen, I need to tell you something.

When I say them they catch her full attention, just as they did mine.

'Alasdair has moved out.'

'What? You're joking! When?'

'Yesterday.'

'What happened?'

He stole my moment is what happened.

167

We were both pretending to read and I was about to say that maybe we should talk more, try to break the collusive silence, when suddenly he told me he was going. 'I need space to think,' he said, like it required a larger kitchen or a capacious hall. I wanted to point out that he'd just had space – two whole days of it, including one of his sly Sundays, but I couldn't speak. I was waiting for him to say Flossie's name but he just kept scratching his head and waffling on about feeling down and not knowing where he was going. *Scratch scratch* – scarifying his scalp; getting rid of all the old moss from the marital nest. The fluttering dandruff gave me a focus – minuscule pieces of skin falling away, making him less of a man than he used to be. Scratching like that – typical mousy behaviour, nibbling at the edges of the thing with his sharp little teeth, his flanks trembling, ready to run.

I didn't speak. I didn't ask the questions.

Are you moving in with her? Don't you love me?

Scratching and nibbling away, and me not so much speech-less as cautious – like anything I say might be taken down and used as evidence against me, making me share the guilt.

Then he said something about the baby.

What was he saying?

Something about when we lost the baby. How he can't seem to enjoy life any more.

'The whole thing feels completely pointless.'

He pushed away from the table and stood up. I followed him into the bedroom and watched him pack his stuff.

'We're not doing each other any good.'

My face assembled itself without any help from me, masking a confusion that was building with every unexpected phrase.

'I'm so pissed off, Aggie.'

But he didn't look pissed off – he looked rueful.

'Going off like that without even discussing it. All you ever do is look back – you probably can't help it, but you've been feeling sorry for yourself for a long time now and I just think you could at least try. You don't even try. You're so bloody – oh Christ, what's the point? You're not even here.'

My brain had turned to a thick soup, an inedible broth of regret and compassion and an obscure shame; uncomprehending because I didn't know. I didn't know he'd lost a baby too. *You never said.* I folded my arms to stop them reaching out. Tucked my sorry hands away from his.

'Have you got everything?'

Like he's going on holiday.

'Yeah, I think so.'

'What about the iPod?'

'What do you mean?'

'Aren't you going to take it?'

We'd bought it together last month, with the proper speakers and everything; such a lovely design, and the sound was amazing – clear and rich compared to the ugly great ghetto-blaster that we still use because he can't quite wean himself off his compilation tapes. The iPod is the best thing we have (not counting the bikes and my silver salver) – the rest is junk. Surely that was moving on, a start?

'Don't you want it?'

'Not really. You have it.'

'OK. Thanks.'

He looked genuinely grateful – relieved almost – as if with this he could make it through. I held the door open for him, and as he left he said, 'I'll call you.'

I didn't want him to go.

'How could you do that?' I said.

He turned round to face me, his arms full of things.

'Do what?'

'Take the iPod. I can't believe you did that.'

'But you said you didn't want it.'

I closed the door on him – quietly, so that he'd know I wasn't mad, I was disappointed.

I don't tell Fiona what he said about the baby. I tell her about his affair with Flossie.

'My God! What's he saying about it?'

'Nothing. We haven't discussed it.'

'What do you mean you haven't discussed it? He must have said something.'

'He didn't, he just went on about needing space and then he left.'

'Bloody hell. You mean he never mentioned her at all?'

'No.'

'Is it a fling?'

'No. He loves her,' is what I say, making it up as I go along because there is a poignancy to it all that I find unutterable.

When I told Mum that Alasdair had left she did the Copella Lip Press. This is a family manoeuvre, a tight compression of the mouth that shouldn't be confused with the apple presses of a certain famous fruit-juice company, even though those lips, when pressed, could probably squeeze more juice from a Cox's orange pippin than any industrial contraption. She was scrubbing potatoes at the sink, plunging each one into cold water several times, and I noticed that the hairs on her thin arms were standing straight up, like she was in shock.

The Copella Lip Press told me that my mum knew this would happen. All those unspoken words of warning squeezing her mouth shut.

Alasdair is the apple of his adoptive mother's eye, the result of a gruelling, interrogative procedure that lasted nine months and nearly drove her and her husband into a very different legal proceeding. Such was Di Thackeray's longing, and so determined was she to thwart the potential deprivation caused (she recounted to me in a cheerful way) by David's low sperm count, that she doubts the marriage would have survived without the securement of a child; she would have felt compelled to move on, leave her husband and find another mate.

'Isn't that right, David?'

And David nodding, smiling like it was the most confounded thing.

It was a lesson for me to witness Di Thackeray in full flow; it made me blush to hear her lamenting David's sperm as 'tadpoles that couldn't swim', not due to any coyness on my part, or concern for David's feelings, but because it reminded me of my own anxieties about Alasdair's spermatozoa. I wanted them to be robust – a speedy shoal with strong tails. I worried about anything and everything that might place his little fishes in jeopardy: certain medications; the fillings in his teeth; the squashing effect of that bone-hard saddle. Who knows what all that furious pedalling was doing to his scrotal temperatures?

But I would not have left him over it.

As it happened, little Alasdair was made available to Di and David Thackeray when he was ten months old. He was undernourished and (according to Di) unattractive, but had the red Thackeray hair that a real Thackeray baby would have, and she felt sure he'd fill out nicely over time (which he certainly did – a fat little carrot-top whose crowning indignity was a side parting, straight as a die and drawn in with a comb of the cruellest teeth). It was those framed photographs of Alasdair, podgy and miserable in a shirt and tie, aged four, the eyes unchanged from the baby pictures, frozen and watchful, two tiny crystal balls that held the untold story of those first ten months – those were the photographs that moved me. Squeaky-clean boy sitting on a plastic-covered pouffe (I can hear the squeak now, telling tales every time he failed to *sit still*). Di loved to recite the story of the baby they saved. She would pick the best mugs from the mug tree and get David to pull the cafetière down from the top cupboard, then she'd make coffee and we would all follow her and the tea tray into the lounge, where we sat on the G Plan and listened as she told us what it was like to bring up someone else's child. She'd been through a lot.

'But it was all worth it,' she'd say, looking at me, not Alasdair – and we'd wait to hear why, but she'd only smile in a rare act of reticence.

Sometimes she would speak directly to Alasdair, still using his name.

'We always thought Alasdair would be a doctor.'

'I know, Mum – you said.'

These are the things that are breaking my furious flow; the way Alasdair's mother talks to Alasdair about her adoptive son, Alasdair – his little crystal balls all clouded up with a short dark history that will never be revealed. The way he didn't tell me, then did tell me, that he'd lost a baby. The way he hasn't told me he's having an affair.

I want to hate him. I want to wish a bad case of caries upon him without feeling guilty. I leave his fetid cycling shorts hanging in the bathroom to remind me, and to help me appreciate how much nicer things are now that he's gone.

Light Changes

I'T'S ALMOST dark. She looks out of the window, her trees
moving gently, old and naked under a green sky; they
hush, calming her – the shush and sway from where they've
always stood. The older trees are at the top of the garden,
nearest to the house. The plum trees look close to death.
They sigh, leaning on their own gnarled, hollow trunks. Gran
never pruned them because she said the old ones couldn't
withstand it; she would just pull out the dead wood and
leave them be.

'Leaving them to die,' said Dad.

But the plums kept coming, and they still come; an abundance of fruit hanging heavy from trees that are rotten to
the core. These trees seem to live for ever, and I know there
is a lesson here, in the fact of their longevity – so I stare and
ponder, but I just don't get it.

There are over thirty of them in the orchard, not fancy
like some (except perhaps for the Guthrie's Taybank, a sweet
yellow plum that wets the chin and dribbles down the neck,
no matter how cautious and refined the bite). The crop is
predominately Victoria plums and Bramley apples, with a few
ancient pear trees.

You would think, given all those years of nurturing, that

the sight of those trees might draw Gran out, but in fact – they keep her in. It is enough to see their old limbs bending through the glass. She and Dad have different views about fruit growing. He's been tending the trees for a long time, but not in the way she would like. For instance, I remember watching him cut canker from bark. He was standing in the kitchen holding a knife I'd never seen before and when I asked him about it he said it was for pruning.

'Are you going to use it?'

'Yes. I thought I saw a bit of canker on one of the Bramleys down at the bottom end.'

'Can I watch?'

'Of course!' he said, picking up the cat and giving him a rare scratch under the chin, his back legs dangling like pelts from a hunter's belt. When we got down there he told me that canker wasn't terminal, it was a fungus that invaded wood that was already dead; he talked about symptoms – black rot and frog-eye leaf spot.

'Fog eyes? You mean like Gran's?'

She had cataracts back then, but now they're gone. I don't think she had them cut out, I think they just withered and fell off like bits of old bark.

'Frog – not fog.'

When I asked what caused canker he said wet, humid weather in the spring didn't help, and close pruning sometimes increased the chances of infection.

'So that must be why Gran never prunes the trees, she says she doesn't believe in it.'

'I know.'

That was all he said about it; I could see then that the trees furthest away from the house looked different, and I realised that he was pruning the ones Gran couldn't see from the house and not telling her.

'I don't think you should be doing that,' I said, and he knew what I meant.

GRAN HAS become lunar; she is receptive, but has no light of her own. It makes me think she probably shouldn't be alone, which presents yet another dilemma since I know she enjoys her own company best. She has developed a new laugh – no, that's not right (I don't think there is anything new under Gran's particular sun, just surprises about what has been there all along); she is using her old laugh in a new way; it bubbles up in a kind of soothing 'let's not fight it' gargle, and although it sounds just as it always has, it is abbreviated, and ends differently, coming to a full stop rather than trickling off, the savouring ellipsis gone.

'I made a new friend, Gran. He's called Kenneth.'

She raises her eyebrows and smiles as if we are conspiring, she and I.

'He's a meteorologist.'

She laughs, and when she stops I pick up one of her jotters and flick through it.

'Kenneth would know what all this means. He speaks your language. You should meet him.'

She smiles again and nods towards the jotter, like it's the funniest thing. There is an odd smell in the room that is no longer the result of any specific *event* – it has become its character, a native blend of pear juice and pee that is beginning to permeate through the rest of the house. This sweet acrid fall-out is settling on wood and wool, seeping through the chairs and curtains, spreading through the rooms of the mildewy interior. The house, with its fragrant fungus and bulging walls, is joining the orchard; we are dropping our fruit, our old branches unpruned, the rot in the high window frames slowed by a dry December wind that has wrung itself out.

Whilst I've got used to the smell, I'm still aware of it, whereas Mum has habituated; she doesn't notice it at all.

'What persistent smell?' she says when I mention it. I'm standing at the back door, filling my lungs with a cleansing blast of cold air, and when I close the door and come back into the kitchen I can see she is indignant; she's thrashing about, still with her coat on, having just brought in some sheets from the line. Mum heaving up the loaded pulley, straining like she's hoisting the mainsail of her own one-woman ship.

HE HAS been gone for three whole days. Allowing for work and sleep that leaves him with over twenty hours of thinking time – a whole spin of the earth and we're back where we started. On a good solar day there is about an hour of stunning winter light, the river turns blue and if I stretch my neck and turn my face to the sun it feels warm. I should be out there walking through banks of crunchy grass. Instead, I move the chair to the sunlight – follow it across the room, then into another room, soaking it up and craving more as I catch the last teasing drip from a tap that might not flow again for weeks.

When the light moves beyond the window, I call Fiona.

'I'm freezing.'

'Put the heating on.'

'I don't know how to re-set it.'

'Do you want to borrow Donald? I could send him round.'

'No. I'll call Alasdair.'

'Are you talking?'

'Yes. I suppose so. Boilers are higher order. They transcend broken hearts.'

'Oh, for goodness' sake, Aggie.'

'What?'

'Do you have to be so dramatic?'

'Sorry. Oh! That's the door. I'll call you back.'

I put the phone down and look for a sunspot to cry in, not because my heart is broken but because already I have exhausted the patience of my friend. She shouldn't speak to me like that – like I'm one of many competing siblings who can roll with the punches. I am an only child; she should be more careful with me.

No tears come. Fiona has not hurt me after all, she has annoyed me. She has interrupted my pathos, and I must either look for sympathy elsewhere or stop being so dramatic, one of the two. Still undecided, I call Alasdair.

'Hello. I'd like to speak to my husband please – Alasdair Thackeray?'

As if I'm not sure who I married.

'Hang on—'

The man who has known me up to now as 'some woman' is still holding the phone, but this time he has taken the trouble to muffle the microphone (with a wet palm – I can feel the clammy heat).

'He's not here at the moment.'

'Oh. Will he be long?'

'I don't know.'

'Well, can you tell him his wife called?'

'OK. Any message?'

'That is the message.'

Fiona does not believe Alasdair is in love with someone else. She says he loves me, that it's obvious to anyone with eyes in their head.

'Keep busy,' she said. 'He'll soon come to his senses.'

'How soon?'

'Sooner than you think. Just don't mope. He'll be back before you know it.'

I could tell from her answer that she'd misinterpreted my anxiety regarding the imprecision of *soon*. I'm not wishing for *soon*, but I do decide to follow her advice.

I empty a bucket that is full of crusty cloths and old cleaning products with strangely boyish names such as Flash, Vanish, Mr Muscle! – pronouncements that conjure up a world of comics and wizardry. I throw them all under the sink and clean the bucket, then fill it with hot soapy water, and with a new cloth I begin to wash the room, wiping the worktops, the walls, the wood around the window. It feels important to be gentle – like I'm soaping up the best bone china, cleaning the way Gran cleans her little Noritake cups and saucers. I wipe all the doors and handles then I spoon one chair into the other and get down on my hands and knees to wash the floor, crawling under the table and circling the square hole, careful to stay out of its immense gravitational pull, because once in, there is no way out.

When I'm done I look at the glossy squares and wonder again at the sheer pleasure they bring.

'Our own abstract,' Alasdair said, and our appreciation has never tired. That floor was our boldest thing – a shout. It gave us the confidence we needed to paint the room in primary colours – walls yellow, cupboards blue, a kitchen where mess is cheerful, and whilst there is no conscious theme it must all be following something because I have always felt the 'hint of barley' ceiling lets the whole room down.

'I like it.'

'I don't. It's cream.'

'It's not cream. It's white with a hint of yellow.'

It was the only thing about the room we disagreed on. I stare at the ceiling and it whispers something indecipherable.

'What is it?'

Nothing. A sigh comes out. I drop my chin to my chest to ease the knot in my neck. There is something wrong with my muscles; they keep knotting up like twisted ropes. I take more Panadol, wash them down with water from the bathroom tap, my hand as a cup – all expertly done to keep my chin dry. As I rub my neck I realise I'm still wearing my coat. It's the sort of thing Mum does, but I keep it on anyway.

Looking towards the kitchen I sense the vortex – the Malevich under the table, an insistent black square, assertive against the backdrop of my pale hesitancy; the greyness since Eleanor.

I stand in the doorway and survey the room as if it were someone else's – such a bold, happy space, and so clean! If it were my kitchen I'd make it taller.

Still in my coat, I prise open the lid on an old tin of white emulsion. I'm really just checking to see what we have but there seems no reason to delay, so I start to paint.

It's just as I thought – the 'hint of barley' is more than a hint, it is overcooked and creamy, with an emphatic sheen of pearl. The matt white rolls across the ceiling, chasing the buttery hue round the colour wheel. This milky whiteness is so pleasing I keep going until the job is done. To help Alasdair appreciate the full effect I leave a small patch of barley in the area above the window, but unfortunately it is the patch that draws the eye, its mealy paleness spoiling the look, so irritating that now I *am* wishing for *soon*.

I need him to come home so I can finish what I started.

Mum calls, and when she speaks I wonder if she is wearing her coat too, if we are both in our coats, talking on the phone.

'Your gran says it's going to snow.'

'Really?'

'Yes. She says it's going to lie and I should bring in the mats but I don't know what she means.'

'Did you ask her?'

I can hear Mum breathing the way Fiona did when she was on the phone. I have a knack for making others breathe in a hatha yogic kind of way, inflative questions – an almost soundless bellowing of the lungs caused by a simple 'did you?'

'Sorry, Mum. Ignore me.'

'I try to. Anyway, you said we shouldn't ask her questions.'

'I didn't say that.'

And you know it. She is being deliberately careless.

'I said to not ask intellectual "why" questions, but asking about the mats would be good. It would be more like reminiscence.'

There is a pause. I hope it is just a natural pause as she brushes flour from her apron or untangles the phone cord (they refuse to upgrade). I hope she isn't holding her breath.

'I fell asleep last night in the middle of *Little Dorrit*. I'm so annoyed with your dad. He didn't even wake me.'

'He was probably asleep too.'

But we both know that is unlikely; Dad has never mastered the art of taking a nap. He wouldn't sleep through *Little Dorrit* but what he might do is sit and look at Mum sleeping through *Little Dorrit*. Lulled by a distant background cadence of Dickensian eloquence, he might lean forward in his chair to gaze at her without risk of being caught. He loves to look at her; in his eyes the soft morning sunlight refracting from the river has never left her face.

Caught or not, it would be worth it.

'Did you watch it?'

'No. Haven't you taped it? You usually do.'

'No – the recorder thing isn't working. I was hoping you could tell me what happened.'

'Sorry, no.' (And it's true – that dust on my old leather-bound copy must be very old, or perhaps I never actually read it?)

'Damn. That's it then.'

'Isn't it repeated?'

'I don't think so. They never repeat anything that's worth watching.'

She sighs then yawns, a sudden sonic boom when she speaks.

'What did you do last night?'

'Nothing. I was reading those magazines that Gran keeps in the press.'

'I thought you'd already read them?'

'I'm reading them again, and I'm reading some articles about the Crichton, doing a bit of research.'

'And?'

This disjointed conjunction throws me; when I spoke to Mum before about *The New Moons* and what they meant – that it looked like Gran was hospitalised in 1937 – she listened intently then said, 'Please, Aggie – don't upset her.' I got the impression she didn't want to talk about. This is the first sign of curiosity she has shown about my research.

'Oh, well, it's just amazing. Sounds like it was a very pioneering place, completely ahead of its time. I think they treated some quite famous people there, including Arthur Conan Doyle's dad.'

'Really!'

Mum is a Sherlock Holmes fan. What she loves about him is his 'hidden tragedy', and since she often confuses the author with the character I know she is picturing Sherlock, or a strange mix of Sherlock and Arthur, an exotic detective/writer hybrid pulling on his pipe.

'Hey, do you think there's any chance he might have been there at around the same time as your gran?'

'I'm not sure, maybe. She might even have met Arthur on one of his visits.'

'Oh no – he didn't visit his father. Charles Doyle was an alcoholic and Arthur never forgave him for what that did to the family. He didn't even go to his funeral.'

This knowledge probably comes from a book she read last Christmas about Arthur Conan Doyle, but she says it in such an understated way it seems to spring from a closeness, like Arthur was a friend of hers. She is trying to work out if there is any possibility that Gran might have met the father, Charles Doyle, and even though she knows it is highly unlikely, I can see that she finds the prospect electrifying – that if it did happen, if Gran really did meet Sherlock Holmes's dad, it would change everything. Like me, she'd be hooked.

We worked it out together; by the time Gran was at the hospital Charles Doyle was probably long dead, but they may have sat in the same chair, since I know there was an excellent library at the Crichton that they both undoubtedly would have been drawn to. In fact, it is highly likely they did use the same chair, probably the most comfortable one in the room – high backed, and with wings to afford them some privacy.

This convergence got me thinking about DNA and the way experiences can pass into the genes of subsequent generations. It's a theory that might explain a lot of things, including Mum's affinity with Sherlock, which is baffling given her moral aversion to drugs and her intolerance of mystery, ambiguity and smoke.

SOMETHING ABOUT the light draws me back to the window. In the garden below someone has thrown a few tears of white bread onto the grass. The water in the birdbath has frozen and I can see wintry flecks sitting lightly on the ice, a signal of snow that would usually excite me but doesn't today, probably because I am still thinking about Mum.

The sky is greening, drawing my face close to the glass. I'm trying to look further into it, as if my stare might penetrate cloud. I imagine we are all staring through at this precise moment – each from our window, watching for snow:

the meteorologists – Kenneth and Gran – know what to look for; Dad just waits, and feels no need to anticipate; Mum expects whatever has been foretold; and in an unknown room, Alasdair rubs the glass with his hand then peers out, unable to surrender to the buttermilk sky for fear that a drench of grey mist might roll in from the sea, turning snow to sleet.

I am less sure of this, but further north – perhaps where it is already snowing – Edward forgets he is a retired psychiatrist. He forgets his dead wife and he doesn't know the people with grey hair who claim to be his children. When he looks out, the low sky fills him with loss. It is as if he has swallowed a cloud. But on days when the sky is clear and higher than usual he sees a woman in the hospital grounds. She's sitting on a bench by the banks of the river Nith. The woman is barely out of girlhood – and from this distance he can see how malleable she is. When she kicks off her shoes her feet are bare – she's not wearing stockings. There is a book in her lap, and although her head bends towards it as if she is reading, she never turns the page; every time the wind brushes against the sprawl of leaves above her she looks up from the book – not at the leaves, but to the side, where a narrow path of earth disappears into the woods. It upsets him to see her because he can't reach her. She waits and waits and eventually she puts on her shoes and goes, leaving him with nothing but the pale sustenance of despair.

As if she's the one. As if it is she that has abandoned him.

Terrible Trees

ALL THE weather bulletins predicted rain by late afternoon and the TV forecasters stood by their guns. 'It's raining,' they said, cheerful in their slightly passé outfits and swinging inwards towards the map – pointing to the rain without even looking, like they're showcasing the top prize.

But we are off the map. I step out of the shower and dry myself in a new light cast by snow. Here the snow is lying, just as Gran said it would, an unfading loveliness that might just shape the day into something other than another black cross on the calendar. (Five days since he left. Five thick, uneven crosses that I don't need to hide since to anyone looking they'll just think it's my countdown to Christmas – *Cross. CRoss. CROss. CROSs. CROSS.*)

The light marbles my skin. I put on my softest trousers – pale purple needle-cord (almost violet), a black cashmere jumper and cashmere socks; warm clothes for the snow, and, lastly, a light spray of my Gucci Eau de Parfum. The perfume was an unexpected present from Alasdair; such a tiny bottle from such a huge box! 'Is that even legal?' I'd asked, before saying thank you or telling him I loved it, that to a girl brought up in a perpetual Coty cloud it was the nicest present ever. I remember turning to him, bottle in hand, expecting a judicial opinion and getting a lame smile. All he said was, 'I'll make some tea.' Then he left the room. I knew there was something wrong but I was still too preoccupied with the size disparity between box and bottle to figure out what. I've only just worked it out now, ten months later and on the very last scoosh. *Damn!* I was saving that scoosh.

I don't want it to end just yet.

I nuzzle into my fragrant wrist, sniffing the spot and drawing back with my eyes closed, savouring the last sweet spill of vanilla sky.

The snow is making me drift. I'm trying to make a telephone call but the snow – it takes me from room to room, different views at each window, and each as pretty; even the view from the living room is pretty, the white street and crusted walls, and over their snowy tops a builders' yard where everything glistens, blocks of brick and concrete, stone flags and wooden pallets all stacked in high-rise clusters like a miniature city, and on the ground, a few long furrows of pan tiles, roughly ploughed. I take a picture and think about sending it to Alasdair; the picture is entitled *Jewson, in Wickes County, covered in snow, December 2008.* I would need to email it to his work since Alasdair hardly ever uses a home computer. He's not interested in world-wide-webby stuff, not since his scare when he tripped up on something he wasn't supposed to see, something really horrible that he won't talk about; he was looking where he shouldn't – an honest mistake, just a wrong turn – and suddenly he sees something that he says won't ever leave his head. He says if there was laser treatment available that could scorch it off he'd take it. He'd rather 'clean the wound' and do without that bit of brain.

'Even if it was something crucial, like your speech centre?'

He nodded.

I look for the connection lead that downloads pictures from the camera to the computer. This is the type of object that is either nesting in the fruit bowl or tucked up neat in a place so safe it will never be found. I scramble through the contents of the dresser drawer – string, tape, spoons, screw-drivers, curtain hooks, batteries (taken dead or alive, it doesn't matter), a compass, a map, bike lights, pens, screws, bulbs, a cheese grater, a whistle, the lost key to the press in the spare room – hooray! I stretch my hand to the back of the drawer and can feel the cable; I have to tug at it, and when I do it resists then springs free, bringing with it a scrunched-up ball of paper and a woven place mat. I throw the extra catch back into the mess, but before I shut the drawer I retrieve the paper and smooth it out on the table. It is a note written in pencil by Alasdair; the letters are all in capitals, the char-acters larger than usual and with more gaps between their component parts – but distinctly, irrefutably his.

THE ONLY REASON I AM HERE IS BECAUSE I MAY AS WELL BE.

I stare at the note for a long time. Does he mean here in the flat? Or on the earth? My chest tightens, constricted by the weight of it, and the terrible ambiguity, and then, when my breathing relaxes again, the sadness; Alasdair's grey mist rolling over me, so thick I can barely make him out.

I TIRE of Jewson city and drive out to Plum Town to look at the snowy orchard. I walk through the trees and up to the house. The kitchen is empty and smells of soup. From the stairs I can hear the television and I find Mum and Gran in the living room watching a children's programme; Gran is wearing a coat with a jacket underneath and is sitting on the edge of her seat, looking like she's about to go somewhere.

'Hello, Gran!'

'Hello.'

She looks at me and laughs (full stop).

'What are you watching? *Why* are you watching?'

Mum never watches TV in the afternoon and Gran stopped watching altogether during the summer; now she's staring at it like she's never seen a television before – mesmerised and slightly thrilled. I don't like it.

'It's the only thing that settles her. She was insisting on going out so I put on the TV really loud and shouted, *Quick, Mum, come and look at this!* And it worked!'

Gran is so compelled by what she's seeing it is impossible not to look, so I sit on the arm of Mum's chair and try to see more than meets the eye – but all I can see is people in brightly coloured puppet suits wiggling their bums and jumping about in a lurid landscape where the trees are a tree travesty.

Oh, Gran, look at your own trees – you are the keeper of the orchard and have so many trees, over thirty! You say the Bramleys are the best apples; you used to sell them to Beryls the fruit-seller and some went to Henderson's Temperance bakery, which was famous for its fruit pies. There are plums, too, and good bottling pears. You make jam and spicy chutneys crammed with plums. These are your trees. They brought you here and talk to you in the darkness. Today they are covered in snow. You always say the snow helps the fruit. Look!

I am close to despair.

There is snow, and the sun is dipping fast. I want Gran to notice; I want her to notice blue snow in the twilight, the tips of golden grass, and, flowing through her, the last light from the sun.

'You'll ruin those boots. They're soaked.'

Mum shakes her head; there is a salty tide-line forming on my moccasins and my shiny silver studs have turned grey – more button than jewel.

'How's the research going?'

'Yeah, it's good. I'm going to the library later. Where's Dad?'

'He's upstairs trying to sort out the draughts from her windows while she's down here.'

I let myself slide down into Mum's chair and when I put my arms around her she doesn't move, so I stay and watch the rest of the show.

Dad appears at the door and says 'What's this – *Watch With Mother*?' I smile, but right away I'm thinking about *not* being mother, classifying to see where we all fit and don't fit in relation to *being* a mother, thus – two watching with mother, two mothers watching, one mother watching with mother. Suddenly I wonder if this is the kind of thing Alasdair is referring to when he talks about not moving on.

'When's that going off?'

Dad is not willing to come into a room polluted by daytime TV; he throws the switch at the wall and we all recoil under the weak yellow light that dribbles from the long-life bulb.

'Dad!'

I can see he is no more comfortable with this than I am. He takes care to stay out of the 'deadly cathode rays' (his phrase, always uttered in demonic tones, with shoulders hunched); these TV rays are rendered invisible and therefore more dangerous during daylight hours.

'Put it off, Maurice – the dark keeps her calm.'

And there's another discomfort – Mum referring to Gran as 'her' when she is present, when we are all in the same room. At the exact moment when Dad switches off the light the phone rings and he goes to answer it, leaving us to soak up the rays.

'It's Alasdair for you.'

My sudden scramble out of the chair is aided by Mum,

whose enthusiasm falls just short of a shove. I bound down the stairs the way I used to, taking the last three with a sideways twist whilst keeping both hands on the banister.

'Hello?'

'Hi. It's me.'

The sheer contrast in pitch makes me realise I'm sounding too cheerful so I clench my face and teeth and screw up my eyes to dispel the kinetic energy I generated through that last swing on the banister.

'Hi.'

He doesn't say anything and I know if I just leave him to think he'll forget who phoned who. I want to ask him where he is but when I speak the 'where' turns to 'how' (which is a whole lot less intimate).

'How are you?'

'I'm fine. I'm at my parents.'

'Oh. How's that going?'

The only way I can imagine Alasdair surviving at the 'Thackeray residence' (a phrase his mother actually uses on the phone) is if he regresses by at least twenty years.

'Well, I'm not very happy about it.'

I don't know how to respond to that; I don't know what he's saying. There is music playing in the background so either he's in his old room or his parents are out.

'I need to collect some things from the flat and I was thinking of coming round tomorrow night. Is that OK?'

'Yeah, that's fine.'

Perhaps he is thrown too, stalled by ambiguity and uncertainty. There's another pause, longer and more comfortable. I can hear his tongue pop like he's eating magic dust; his mouth must be really dry. This is the closest we've been for a long time.

'Thanks for the email, by the way.'

'Did it work?'

'Yeah. It's a good shot. Did you take it with the camera?'

'Of course – what else would I take it with?'

'Oh yeah, sorry. I forgot.'

Forgot that my mobile doesn't have a camera. This slip into carelessness changes the whole thing; suddenly I'm interpreting the ambiguity in a completely different way.

'I found your note.'

'What note?'

'The one you left in the dresser that says you don't want to be here. It was at the back of the drawer.'

'Are you sure it's mine?'

'Yes.'

'I don't remember that. You shouldn't have read it.'

'I know. I didn't mean to. What do you want me to do with it?'

'Just chuck it. It isn't important.'

The next call was also for me. It was Fiona – checking up.

'I rang your flat twice but you weren't there.'

'I was there – but then I wanted to see the snow on the trees.'

'I was a bit worried. You OK?'

'I'm fine. Why are you so worried?'

'No reason. I heard your Dad saying "we're popular" when you came to the phone just now. What's that about?'

'Oh, he was just being sarcastic.'

'What are you doing, Aggie?'

'I'm watching the telly.'

'No. I *mean* – what are you doing?'

BACK HOME I switch off the lights and sit in my tall kitchen, embracing the dark – elbows on the table and my hands propping up my jaw. Sometimes I cradle my head. It feels expressive; it's saying, *I don't know what to do.* My husband has left me and I think my gran was in an asylum, maybe for killing her baby. They might have administered shocks – eighty volts coursing through her brain, then the amnesia.

Or there might have been love in there. Tenderness. Curative support.

I used to thrive on dilemma – *but this*. This is cracking me up, my face crazed like an old Vermeer. *Girl with a Grave Feeling*. Each morning I stare in the mirror, looking for changes because everything feels so different, I can't believe it doesn't show. I am full of regret. I regret the foraging, and I regret taking the magazines and the map with the blue cover the blue of the not-blue sky. I regret driving to Nithsdale, and I regret my collapse on that barren hill. It all feels reckless. I should have gone with the majority and accepted what Gran said as the ramblings of a confused old woman who can't tell fact from fiction any more (like it's a binary thing).

But it's too late. I have borne witness to something that was almost over, and now, having been disturbed, the baby just won't settle; glimpses of her everywhere, and at night, her pokey bones catching the moonlight, the waxy seams marbling the earth, filling my head with doubt.

I cannot speak to Gran about my visit to the farm; to mention it would feel like an act of cruelty. One thing I realise, though: Gran was lucky to have another baby given the fecundity of all those only-child mothers producing another only-child. Our spindle tree. There isn't even a collective name for us – the Kirkpatrick Brody Copella Thackeray women, a Teutonic line hanging by a thread.

And in these black comfortless rooms, my palsied mind jumping from one thought to the next, as if it were me on the shock machine, pinned to the bed with electrodes on my scalp, my temples washed and the conductors dampened with a bicarbonate solution, so my skin won't burn.

Apples From America

I AM in the public library, leafing through a book. I don't
want to read it but feel I need to at least look at it because
I ordered it, and then there was a complication, and now
the librarian is pleased to have tracked it down.

'It's been a small triumph,' she said, handing it to me as
if it were a rare first edition, long considered lost. I had
already changed my mind about it, but I couldn't bring myself
to tell her, so now I am thumbing through its pages, as if
searching for something specific.

Outside it is cold and already dark. I am enjoying being
here; I like the quality of sound, the way the shelves of
books affect the timbre of low voices, and I'm enjoying
the warmth, and the quiet proximity of others, there is
camaraderie in the way we nod and smile to each other –
but the book is wrong. Reading about infanticide in the
1930s is not helping. It's not as if I have to read about it,
there is a whole section on *Happiness* that I could be reading
instead; books on *How to Live*, written by people who know.
I wait for an opportunity to leave unseen, and as the librarian
heaves her over-loaded trolley towards the *Crime* section, I
slip out through *The Classics*.

By the time I reach the car park the mean glow from

the street lights has brightened, powered by the velvet dark and a white scattering of stars. There are only three cars left. They are gathered underneath a single lamp-post like creatures drawn by the light. A couple have just stepped into the illuminated circle of snow; the man is jangling his keys to accompany the woman's rendition of 'Jingle Bells'. They've been doing some late-night shopping; bags full of Christmas – both high as kites on the white stuff, like the snow has reached their brains and is gathering in the synaptic gaps.

When I step into the circle of light the woman looks up and waves.

'Hiya, Aggie! How are you?'

It's Louise from work. I like Louise – she's funny and has a good heart; she's always encouraging me to *train* because she thinks I've got what it takes to be a dental nurse (empathy and a strong back). She asks me about my ankle and whether or not I'll be back before Christmas and she tells me things are 'mental' and the bloody water jet on the speed drill has packed up and they fixed it briefly by sticking a plaster round the leaky tube but it didn't last and she has to use the manual spray in-between mixing the paste for the temporary crowns which means everything takes longer so there is the usual waiting-room pile-up not that anybody minds except you know who but we won't mention her and God isn't it cold and Flossie is acting very strange at the moment there's something funny about her she's gone all dreamy and secretive and our theory is she's in love and have I done my Christmas shopping and what a price everything is and when am I coming in for a mince pie?

It takes a long time to get back, car wheels creeping over snow like a hearse. Feeling nostalgic and homesick in my cortège of one, I read one-way street signs as orders, commanding routes that take me out of my way. I'm avoiding Alasdair, who will be at the flat now, collecting more things. The snow gives me the perfect cover for a slow crawl. I see parts of the town I've never seen before; low-rise blocks of flats called 'courts', untouched by Sirius, while derelict buildings loom and dip, their white roofs tipping at the moon. Towards the river there are rows of elegant Georgian terraces, and in front, open snowfields have been laid out like silk at a Turkish bazaar, lit by an arc of tall bright windows. And at some distance, well off to the side, trees watch and creak, ghostly at night. I lay down virgin tracks for others to follow, and when I finally reach home Alasdair has gone.

I call Fiona.

'He didn't wait.'

'He probably did wait. How long is he supposed to wait? You should have been there.'

'He didn't phone.'

'He probably did. You never have it on.'

I OPEN the curtains and check for Jupiter, then switch on a lamp and sit down, warming my feet on the radiator and drinking a large Baileys with ice. My phone – an old silver Nokia with no camera – is lying on the table like an unread letter. I would like to tear it up and burn it. I have decided not to open any messages, texts or emails until this is all over, because it's just too easy. I will take calls, however, and I would like to tell Alasdair about this decision but I don't want to talk to him, and leaving a message, text or email doesn't feel right.

Dear Alasdair, just wanted to let you know –

Hello Alasdair –

Hi Alasdair –

Alasdair –

Writing a simple notice of intent is beyond me; defeated, I go to bed and listen to the familiar tapping, an insistent chiselling across the inside of my cranium, the tiny hiero-glyphics of my life laid out in a herringbone skull that will never be read (unless my death is violent, or suspicious, or unexplained – only then will someone crack open my skull and lift out the pieces, palm-size plates of bone cupped in their hands.)

The room is blue with cold. Unable even to close my eyes, I get dressed again, pulling on trousers and a jumper, socks and boots. The kitchen is even colder because I left the window open to get rid of the paint fumes – not that paint fumes any more, but it can still give you a delayed kick in the head. There is enough light to read by, it is deflecting off the snow and again off the fresh white ceiling. I sit at the table and watch my breath in the moonlight as I smoke my pen, then I write the note quickly and put it in an envelope, hesitating over whether or not to add *c/o* to the address. Is Alasdair *c/o*? I have no idea how much care or lack of care there is in Di Thackeray's deeply puzzling behaviour; I've never been able to work that out. I decide to give her the benefit of the doubt.

Knowing I won't sleep until it is posted, I put on my coat and walk to the small post-box at the end of the road; it takes less than five minutes but by the time I get there my hands are freezing. I push my hand right into the mouth of the post-box and drop the letter, but it doesn't fall – it sits; the box is almost full with what I assume are Christmas cards. I thought when I let it go the thing would be on its way, but now I've been given the unexpected option of changing my mind.

I don't even need to think about it. I push the letter further down between the cards. I can't bend my wrist but I can press with my fingerstips and it crumples easily into an irretrievable place, that's how flimsy it is; barely a note at all –

Alasdair, we never even gave her a name.

THE SNOW melted without reply. A few cards appeared in the hall, some for Mr and Mrs Thackeray, some for Mr and Mrs A. Thackray, one for A & A Thackeray, another for Alasdair Thackray, two for A. Thackeray, and one for Aggie Copella, forwarded by Dad having been sent originally to the house, *c/o*.

I gather them into a neat, reassuring pile, then I make tea and pull out my musical Christmas mug, which plays 'Jingle Bells' every time I pick it up – my answer to Alasdair's wry, understated crockery. When I first drank from it, sitting opposite him and leaning forward with elbows on the table, cradling the huge mug with both hands and taking a long leisurely slurp, he put down his paper and stared, not at the mug (which would probably make his eyes water) but at me.

'Every sip is a symphony! It's a classic!'

I smiled and smiled at his narrowing stare, humming along as me and my mug went dashing through the snow.

'You're being provocative.'

I took another slurp. *Jingle bells, jingle bells* . . .

'What d'you mean?'

Jingle all the way . . .

'Put it down.'

'I'm thirsty.'

The Alasdair eyes now mere slits, like new button holes.

'Aggie.'

Oh, what fun it is to ride on a one-horse open . . .

I swallowed and put down my mug.

'Thank you.'

And he went back to his paper.

. . . . *sleigh.*

I'm surprised the mug still works after spending a whole year at the back of the cupboard. I welcome it back like a missing pet – 'Hello, ugly mug!' – and fill it with tea. The jingle is clearly struck and has lost none of its pace, but the tea tastes bitter. I put the mug on the table and in the obedient silence I pick up all the Christmas cards and place each one face down from left to right so they form a series of columns with one card in the first, two in the second, three in the third; then, with the slow deliberation of a fortune-teller I turn each top card over and deal out the remaining cards, face up. All those Alasdairs and Agathas, variously alone or together, joined, apart, indistinguishable. I move the cards around, looking for sequence and matching where I can until I am left with only one to play – a kind of wild card that I don't know where to place.

Aggie Copella, *c/o*.

I stare at my name. I've not seen that name in over two years, yet it's been there all the time – tucked up my sleeve like an ace. I can play it high or low, but patience has always eluded me. 'It's all about perseverance,' Gran said, but I never saw the point (although I loved to watch her play – her eyes at least one step ahead of her hands, and her head further on still). I look at the little tableau of our marriage and wonder if she was right. Maybe if I just persevere it will all become clear – the cards will just play themselves out, form a pattern. There will be a coherence.

A picture of Alasdair sitting in the back bedroom of his parents' deceptively spacious post-war bungalow forms in my mind. Di Thackeray is very defensive about her bungalow, as I discovered when I attempted a compliment (and a genuine one at that, since it really is rather nice, with a pretty front door and carved wooden eaves).

'What a lovely bangala. It's really cool.'

'Bangala?'

She was smiling, her eyebrows high with curiosity, but when I explained the origin of the bungalow – a comfy native hut originating in the Bengal region of India – there was a general tightening up. Despite the Thackerays' insistent interest in what they still referred to as 'the colonies', when it comes to cultural influences they prefer a one-way flow. Alasdair made a feeble attempt at 'digging me out of a hole', as he later put it – but as far as I was concerned it wasn't me that was in a hole, it was her, and when I told her that Alasdair was the one who called it 'the bangala' in the first place she practically fell off her chair (also Indian, with a woven seagrass seat).

'What a tight ass,' I said, when we got home.

'You have no idea,' he said, sounding so weary I threw my arms around him and gave him a longer than usual hug, then held his pasty back-bedroom bungalow face in my hands and kissed him.

Poor Alasdair.

'I FEEL like an old woman.'

Mum has moved her chair round to face the window. This small change throws the room out completely and everything looks wrong – the sofa is stranded, and the occasional chairs look bored. She has, in effect, turned her back on all of it, including us. Turning to look I see her pulling at her jumper, straightening the edge of it then gathering her cardigan round herself – a layer of brown wool across a layer of mossy green.

'Look at these colours, they're so dull.'

'They're not dull. I think you look lovely. You suit brown.'

She has always worn muted colours – earthy but not tweedy, blacks and nutty browns. I cannot picture her in any other palette; Mum in a pink dress, or a blue blouse, or a skirt splashed with poppies – it is unimaginable. I close my eyes and remember a birthday, a first of March that was everything you could hope of such a date (a warmth that turned our faces to the sun, our bodies uncoiling like tender shoots). We were in the garden, all four of us sitting on the wooden bench that leans against the wall of the back porch. Mum was holding a flat parcel wrapped in jazzy paper. It was from Dad, and eventually – when we realised the sun was going to stay for more than a snatch – we relaxed and lowered our faces, turning to watch as she opened her present. The unfolded paper revealed a cream jumper nesting on a bed of tissue. It had a scoop neck and an elaborate appliqué of Prussian blue pansies high up on the left-hand side. We all stared at the flowers; even Dad stared, as if the bold corsage had bloomed unexpectedly while the jumper was still wrapped. Mum touched the scattering of pearl-button anthers in a gesture of tender forgiveness.

'It's lovely, Maurice. Thank you.'

We all knew she would never wear it. Smiling, she carefully refolded the paper and placed the parcel on the bench beside her, resting her hand on it; then we all closed our eyes again and offered ourselves up.

DAD BRINGS in tea on a tray. It has taken him a long time to appreciate trays (men naturally resist them) but now that he does he has become a bit of a partisan, using one even when two hands will do. His favourite is the melamine sandwich tray because it is light; the tray is embellished with a whimsical design of flowers, butterflies and (strangely enough) a cuckoo, but this scene from paradise is covered by a plain tray linen that Gran never removes. She will engage with most objects, sometimes in novel ways – but those plain oblong tray linens always stay put.

Mum begins to turn her chair round but Dad tells her she's fine where she is.

'I'll be mother,' I say, lifting the pot. Usually we pour the teas in the kitchen and just put the mugs on the tray, but today Dad has laid things out differently, with mugs for us and a cup and saucer for Mum, and he's used one of Gran's tray linens. The sound of pouring tea catches her attention and she leans over the side of her chair to look – just a brief glance at the tray then straight talking to Dad, eye to eye.

'What's all this?'

'I thought it would be nice.'

I'm passing her the cup and saucer but she ignores it and stands up.

'I'm not an old woman.'

She says it defiantly, and waits, seeming to want a reply.

'I know, I just thought—'

'What? You just thought what – toss her a doily to cheer her up?'

'Mary, love—'

He speaks softly, and she hesitates, shaking her head to keep everything in, but then her mouth springs open and out it comes.

'Oh fuck off, Maurice!'

When she slams the door the china rattles in the tail wind – a slight tremor, like the very first shift of an earthquake.

Mum quite often speaks to Dad that way; I don't think she appreciates him as much as she should, but despite her frequent carelessness he is no tame snake. He is tall and attractive with eyes that change colour depending on the weather or what he is wearing. Fiona used to fancy him, said he was a real heart-throb.

'Your mum's a lucky woman,' she said, and I told her to

shut up because I knew she was thinking about sex. Of all of us, Dad is by far the easiest going; he appears impervious to change and seems to know what is important and what is not, perhaps because he lost everything once. He is complete – a finished piece, solid enough to lean on, and I suspect we just lean and lean.

I think he deserves more respect; for instance, a few years ago a man came to the house asking for 'the keeper of the orchard' and Mum came inside and fetched Gran, even though Dad was down amongst the apple trees assessing the crop. He is the one who can look at a whole tree and know how much fruit it will bear; that's something Gran could never do. When she first took on the orchard she was at the mercy of the hawkers; they would just look at a tree and make her an offer without even walking round it, then they'd crop it and take it away. Eventually she did her own cropping, but it was hard work; a lorry would come and take the fruit to Kirkcaldy, deal done.

This man, the one who asked if he could speak to the keeper of the orchard, was looking for a special tree called a *Lindorsii*. He said the tree was unique to this area – the sole survivor of its type, planted originally by the pioneering monks. As soon as the stranger, an ecologist from the Countryside Trust, described the tree (in so far as he imagined it, having examined a felled specimen back at the Abbey) we knew he was talking about 'Ginger', the old pear tree Mum named after Ginger Rogers on account of its womanly shape.

Ginger has a curvy trunk swathed in a crusted gown that swirls its way up to the branches above, and it is this evocation – the folds of bark, softened with algae that sparkles in moonlight – that reminds Mum of the dress Ginger Rogers wore in *Lady in the Dark* (that dress really stuck in her mind – it's the only example I can think of where Mum has gone dreamy over clothes).

The ecologist was very excited to meet Ginger, and the attention he lavished on her seemed fitting – but when he commented on her neglected state the visit was swiftly brought to a close and the stranger left not knowing that the tree still produces the most delicious pears; they have a strong aromatic flavour with a juice of such concentrated sweetness it should be stored in phials and measured in drops.

Unlike Ms Rogers, our Ginger thrives on neglect, and I think the Countryside Trust would be interested to know about the deliciousness of her pears and how all Dad's attempts at cultivating new trees have failed. When that man asked for the keeper of the orchard, Mum should have taken him to Dad. That's what I mean about not appreciating him.

With Mum brooding in the bedroom and the tea completely spoiled, Dad goes back down to the kitchen and I hear him go out into the garden. I move to the chair Mum was sitting on and watch him walking through the orchard; he has put on extra clothes – another fleece, a coat that gives him a barrel chest. Where the ground dips downwards at the far end I lose sight of him, but not before I see him pull a dead branch from another pear tree (not Ginger, who remains untouchable). Gran says these trees are self-pruning. She would have left that branch to run its course – let the birds use the lichen in the spring, leave the husk for spider eggs, grubs and weevils – but Dad doesn't like the trees to be so busy; he prefers to guide them, keep them on track, much as the monks would have done.

'The monks were very fond of a pear,' he said once, contemplating his half-eaten Ginger and using the stalk to dislodge the trapped flesh from between his teeth. He enjoys working with the fruit more than his work on the farm – but there is no living in it, hasn't been since the late-Victorian era when globalisation brought fruit from Europe and North America.

Out of sight, Dad will be pottering about down by the old stone byre, squeezing the onion sets or tidying up the winter flowers – enjoying the frosted beauty of the hydrangeas and the cold flesh of the elephant lugs. I consider joining him but decide to stay put until I've thought of some way to help Mum that isn't too obvious. Curling up on the nettled chair I push my boots off in that toe-on-heel way that you do when you've stopped caring (they couldn't look worse), then I tuck my feet in, and almost immediately an idea comes.

I'll find someone who has recorded that missed episode of *Little Dorrit* and take Mum out to watch it.

The most obvious candidate is Kenneth; I remember him telling the group all about BBC iPlayer, how it meant his dad could watch his favourite programmes whenever he wanted. There was a general glazing when, entirely unprompted, he explained the notion of an 'Internet television service', but we listened again, and afterwards Mima sidled up to me and spoke *sotto voce* from behind her hand, asking me, as a youngster, if her new Panasonic was actually a computer as well – she was no longer sure. I could see that this new iPlayer thing was beyond most of them, but despite the confusion they were very impressed, and now that they knew someone who actually had one there was a sense of shared advancement.

Assuming *Little Dorrit* is important enough to get into the iPlayer (not everything is, apparently), I'm sure Kenneth won't mind if Mum and I come to watch. Already I can see us gathering round the Christmas tree with the huge great baubles and the three cables of lights. I feel destined to touch that tree, to smell the lingering forest.

While Kenneth is setting up the iPlayer Mum and I will

sip on our Baileys and admire the fairy he has had since he was three – cardboard wings and a coif of nylon hair, a net frill sticking out from under her white dress, exposing her feet.

With only a quarter moon rising I decide to drive back to the flat and call Kenneth from there. I am stretching in the chair, legs out like pokers when the door creaks open and in walks Jack. He looks sleepy and annoyed, as if he has been discovered and thrown out. Automatically he heads for the chair. When he sees me he stops and closes up, hunching on the floor with his head low and his shoulders poking upwards to emphasise his discomfort (one hundred per cent pure wool thick pile Axminster is just not good enough). Stung by his flinty eye I vacate the chair and stand at the window.

Dad is walking back towards the house. He's holding some onions and when he stops to smell the eucalyptus I suddenly feel bereft, perhaps because I notice a slight rounding of his shoulders, the first bending of old age; or it might be the obscure sadness that comes when, from a distance, you watch someone you love doing ordinary things.

Accidental Hurt

I HAVE *0* unread messages.

This makes keeping my resolve not to read them easier than I expected. I dwell on this too long, remain completely still and listen to the hum of uninterrupted nothing.

'You have a lot going on,' Fiona said, but sitting here in the stillness all I can sense is the emptiness of this room; I can't make a dent in it, can't even interrupt the nothingness that was here while I was out. We do not usually coexist in the same room at the same time.

The main subtraction might be my missing dog. I have thought about Carrie a lot since that day in the park. It seemed obvious that she had no recollection of ever having been my dog, and that's what threw me, since I don't believe that dogs – even exceptionally clever dogs like mine – are capable of pretence. They are entirely without artifice, being wholly and consistently *dog* (greedy, grateful, happy and, above all, loyal). I think I have good radar for artifice; I don't look for it, but when I do bump into it I can feel the hammer of my own pulse bouncing back – an ironic discomfort, since the only response to artifice is to pretend it isn't there. Hence, chatting to Flossie on a cold December day, pretending I don't know.

Even allowing for my missing dog, the room still feels empty. Of course, the more obvious absence is Alasdair, but everyone seems to think this is a temporary state – otherwise surely people would rally. Make soup. Visit.

I would have *many* unread messages.

And there are other missings – answers, love, a child running stiffly through the room. She is fifteen months old and she can't sound her *s*'s at the beginning of a word but she can sound them at the end. She's very scared of 'nakes' and loves to play What's the time, Mr Wolf? – screaming when we chase her, her little hands rigid with shock.

It's funny, I always think of my baby's birthday as the day of the miscarriage. Actually, I don't do this, I don't chart a ghostly chronicle of my baby's life, but today – perhaps because I have been still for too long – she has jumped out at me from behind the curtain.

Boo!

THERE'S BEEN a development. Mum has declared that she needs a break from the constant battle. She doesn't want to spend Christmas trying to get Gran to wash and eat and occasionally change her clothes whilst at the same time wanting to just leave her alone and grant her the peace she craves, even if she does smell. Why should she be the one to ruin every remaining day of her mother's life?

The GP is sucking a cough drop, for which he apologises. He needn't, since we are all enjoying the slight sting of camphor, and anyway, there is something oddly reassuring about an ailing doctor. Gran is very taken with him. He is tall and thin with a twinkle in his eye, and when he pulls out his crisp white handkerchief she murmurs in approval. Content in his company, she sits like a toad watching fireflies. Perhaps this doctor reminds her of someone else? Maybe she's thinking of Edward?

We are here in the room together – Mum and I beside her, the doctor opposite. He's already packing up his stethoscope, preparing to go. Jack gets lifted and is unceremoniously dropped onto the floor; he twitches all over, his brain stuttering to catch up with his body. With galloping hearts we wait for the doctor to make his pronouncement.

'Fit as a flea.'

And he snaps his bag SHUT.

I watch him, keep a close eye on him because someone in the group said this one's different; this one can hear what's not being said. But when Mum smiles at the diagnosis, lips closed and her tired face white as a winter moon, he doesn't seem to hear anything.

He is practically through the door when he mentions his intention to refer Gran for respite. He thinks she will enjoy the company. When he says this, Mum swallows her scepticism and looks at him, grateful that he is the type who sugars the pill.

'I doubt very much if we'll get her in by Christmas, though.'

'That's all right. Any time is fine.'

And we all sigh, knowing we have avoided something terrible.

Mum sees the doctor out and goes to the kitchen to make more tea. I stay with Gran for a while, sensing a new kind of disorder. I can smell it too – a noxious mix of disinfectants and sprays, perhaps even some kind of room freshener, a thick odorous mask that fails to cover up the smell of condensed pee.

Gran is restless. She looks at me, uncertain. Her hair is flat on top, oily and rough and fraying on her shoulders like old rope. It's hair no one wants to touch, no more stroking or teasing (if ever there was), another element in the multiplicity of losses, the world creeping away like an outgoing tide. They call it *mutual disengagement* – but what's being given, and what is received?

I cross to the window, bang it and pull up the sash. The cold air hits our faces and we fill our lungs, swelling with the shock of wet air and the green smell of lichen creeping into wood. I pull a quilt from the bed and put it across her knees, then sit on the floor beside her and ask her to brush my hair.

'No,' she says, 'it's too cold.'

She shivers and pulls her cardigan tight across her chest.

'Do you want me to shut the window?'

'No.'

And with her hands still crossed at her neck she turns her face into the cold again and smiles, closing her eyes. There is a symphony playing – the notes falling across her mouth like the first flakes of a snowfall.

'Shhh—'

Shushing the creak of a naked bough.

'Don't tell them,' she says, her eyes still closed.

'I won't, Gran. I promise I won't.'

And at last things fall away, and we are still.

WHEN I contacted Kenneth to ask if I could bring Mum to watch episode thirteen of *Little Dorrit* he didn't hesitate.

'Yes, of course. I'd really like to meet her.'

'Fantastic. When can we come?'

'Any time, whatever suits. Come tomorrow if you like.'

The next stage was to convince Mum. I decided the best strategy was to present it as our Christmas outing together – just her and me (and Kenneth, of course, but the key was to play him down). Mum and me on a Christmas outing has no precedent, but tradition has to start somewhere. I could feel a slight festive stirring, a greening of the bone. *Good things will come of this.* I called Mum and extended the invitation, keeping it light, to sound as if I were acting on an impulse. 'Yes,' she said, so quickly it left me feeling like I'd just arm-wrestled a stick of celery. I took the warm prospect into my cold bed, and when I woke there was a dull ache in my jaw that suggested I had been smiling in my sleep; the phone was ringing and I just knew it was her. We began with the usual.

'Are you dressed?'

'Yes.'

'Aggie, are you even up?'

'Of course I'm up. I've been up for ages.'

Then she told me the good news – we didn't need to go to Kenneth's after all because Dad had been studying the listings, which are apparently a right guddle, and it turns out the missed episode is on again on Sunday, so she can watch it then. There have been lots of complaints about the seemingly erratic scheduling of *Little Dorrit*, which began (she says) with a double episode on a Sunday, then a repeat of episode two on the Thursday, episode three the following Monday but then no episode four until the next Wednesday!

'Ridiculous for a period drama.'

This detailed charting of the *HMS Little Dorrit*'s winter voyage across the BBC demanded careful listening if I was to follow it, and I did want to follow it, since it was the most I'd heard Mum say for weeks. It was lovely to hear her – not just her girlish voice (on the phone, you'd say she was twenty), but the varied pitch, her words bobbing up and down like a boat on choppy waters; and the surge, I realised, the undulating narrative that poured from the phone, was the gush and swell of relief.

I am so disappointed. Having pictured the evening, I am reluctant to let it go – Mum and me admiring Kenneth's fairy as we sip on our Baileys, sticking close together like girls at a dance. What is this grip anyway? The complete submersible power of costume drama, and in particular this early work of Dickens, its sprawling canvas ruthlessly trimmed back to just a small troupe of characters? I think she can see the parallels – the prisons within prisons. She is trammelled, caught in the fine mesh of hourly duties, a good daughter yearning for the parent who sits – reliant and careless, self-absorbed, presiding over their own absence like an unwanted chaperone. She would not thank me for saying it. She would suggest something more straight-forward – the sheer pleasure of a good story: the music; the dresses; the ridiculous hats. And, of course, escape – she would admit to that, but I know there is more to it, that when it comes to *Little Dorrit* she is watching an allegory of love.

I called him right away to cancel.

'Come anyway,' he said.

'Are you sure?'

'Of course I'm sure. I've already defrosted the sausage rolls.'

It's been almost a month since my accident and for most of that time I have been crutch free, my blood thin – awash with aspirin, ibuprofen, paracetamol. I reached a state of analgesia within hours and have developed a taste for it (actually, my taste was already well established, but it has grown keener). Armed with my little boxes of Panadol Ultra I feel calm and believe I could run a mile if only I could muster up the energy. I am amazed how willing the GP is to sign me off, in fact – it was her suggestion. She smarted each time she looked at me, like the sight of me was scratching her corneas.

'I don't think we're quite ready yet, are we, Aggie?'

Fiona says I'm losing weight, and I know from the way my jeans slide over my hips that she's right. I said it was probably because I'm no longer dishing up Alasdair's hearty 'man with bike' portions, but truth be told, I've lost my appetite.

'You mean you're not even trying?'

'No.'

'Lucky you.'

She's eyeing my unfinished Christmas slice.

'Help yourself.'

Fiona looks at me like the offer is unbelievable, or a trick.

'Don't you want it?'

'No – you have it.'

'My God. Thanks.'

Donald lit the fire before he left for work (it's part of the deal) and we're lounging on the sofas in bare feet. It feels decadent – a fire, a sleeping baby, enough fruit loaf to sink the *Bismark*.

'I'm going to have to put this back before I eat the whole lot.'

She presses the tin foil over the cake and takes it away. I go limp in front of Donald's fire, my feet basting, smothered in the foot cream we have just opened (a present stolen from under the tree – she always does it). Squeezing the plump tube, I check the long list of contents – fruits of various kinds, oils and butters; it reads like the recipe for Mrs McCubbin's Christmas cake and I wonder if it will make my feet fat. A magnifying glass reveals over twenty less palatable ingredients – *ethylhexylglycerin, sodium benzoate, alpha-isomethyl ionone*, a right mouthful, but in print too small to worry about.

'What are you doing?'

She's back, plumping a cushion and resuming her state of collapse (as if she has just hauled in a hundred weight of coal rather than the tiny scuttle she filled earlier).

'Nothing.'

I put down the cream and look at her through the magnifying glass. She is sore on the eye, a distant blur.

'My mother-in-law is always making cakes – it's a nightmare. I hate to think what she'll make for Thomas when he's bigger. Does yours bake?'

'Does my what bake?'

'Your mother-in-law.'

I snort unexpectedly, surprising us both.

'No, not that I'm aware of.'

Hard to even think that I have a mother-in-law, yet the title suits her so well. Perhaps if she did bake cakes, precise pink and yellow Battenberg to complement our kitchen colours, things might be different. Recumbent on the sofa, Fiona draws one of the throws over her legs and closes her eyes. She can't be cold.

'Are you tired?'

'Mmmm?'

When she looks at me I can see the tree lights reflected in her eyes. This year she has gone for red LDC with four settings – steady, fade, twinkle, random (all of which she demonstrated earlier). She must have left the switch on random because suddenly her eyes ignite and I'm conversing with the devil.

'I'll leave you to sleep.'

'Oh no! It's fine – I'm much too excited to sleep.'

'Oh? What's happened?'

'Christmas! It's Thomas's first Christmas! I just find that really exciting.'

'Do you think he's got any awareness?'

'I think he's picking up a bit. More than you anyway.'

Her eyes flash then dull to a deceptively normal Anglo-Saxon eye colour (a vague absorptive grey – like an undercoat).

'Ah, well, you might be right,' I say, too relaxed to argue.

Concealed behind closed lids, she moves around, seeking comfort between the sprung springs and the horsehair. The moment she finds a comfortable niche she falls into what I know will be a dreamless sleep. She says she hasn't dreamt since Tufty was born, too exhausted, I suppose, or too content. Submerged in cushions, she looks like a pre-Raphaelite muse, plumes of hair in lustrous disarray, and a wrist hanging loose, the jumble of cushions and throws appearing sumptuous against her milk-white skin; she even makes the old sofa look good, but six months without dreams must take its toll, a piece of her gone.

The first time Fiona brought Tufty to the house she let me carry him upstairs to show Gran. The room was very hot so I loosened one of his pure lamb's wool shawls and took off his hat. Gran peered into the cocoon, humming a note or two.

'Look at that, bald as a coot.'

She was smiling at Tufty, and he was lighting her up the same way he lit all of us up, there was no difference; the exquisite baby mouth, the baby ears, the distilled pleasure and sheer impossibility of baby pinkies. Then her expression changed.

'My baby wasn't right.'

'What do you mean? Do you mean Mum wasn't right?'

But she wasn't listening. She pointed to the soft spot on Tufty's head, turned his skull like she was checking an apple for scab; then she pressed his skin where the surface was flat.

'Look at that – she's not got any bone. Poor wee thing.'

Tufty began to cry. She sat back in her chair – a fast movement, as if recoiling. Done with the baby, she opened the drawer of the side table to look, scrambling the contents and dipping her head so she could see right to the back.

Tufty was yelling now, his red face fit to burst. Fiona rushed through the open door, cooing baby talk like she'd known it all her life (which she probably had, being the third of seven). In a kind of swoop she took Tufty from me and put him over her shoulder, shoogling him like a giant cocktail

'There there, that's it – ssshhhh. You were holding him wrong, he needs to be cradled. You're not even paying attention.'

'I am!'

'You weren't. When I came in you weren't even watching him. You've got to pay more attention, Aggie. Poor wee lamb.'

I probably wasn't, not at that moment; the baby was probably lying in my lap like a bag of old washing while I watched Gran ruffling through that drawer. She had stopped now, and was looking at Fiona, shaking her head.

'Aye, poor wee lamb. She's not right.'

Fiona assembled the smile she kept for old people and raised her brows.

'What's that, Mrs Brody?'

'This?'

She pulled something from the drawer and looked at it, giving it her full attention for a moment, then turned back to Fiona.

'It's a comb,' she said, happy to help.

FIONA IS still asleep and the fire has compressed into a hot, flameless bed. I press out 200mg of Panadol from its sealed tray and my thumbs look for another, pressing every blister, but they are empty, each one already burst and looking like a well-worn molar. My usual dosage is 400mg, enough to make me feel well, or, more accurately, enough to stop me feeling unwell. I have some ibuprofen in my bag, but it is the codeine in my Panadols that smoothes out the muscles, all my bodily rage dissolves: the ubiquitous aches and pains; the clamp on my head; the stick that pokes me right between the shoulders, just below that tricky juncture where the spine joins the skull. The thing about pain is you need to keep your nerve (so to speak) and stay one step ahead of it, weaken it before it sticks to the bone like a mollusc. The best approach is to 'mix and match', so I wash down a couple of ibuprofen with a mouthful of Fiona's Limoncello (a drop of which would easily loosen the grip of a limpet's foot).

Then I too close my eyes.

We all wake together, as if we have been sleeping in the same web. There is a slight chill in the room. Fiona scrambles out of her throw and goes to fetch the baby.

'Feed the fire,' she yells, with an urgency more associated with quenching a fire than building one up. I lift the scuttle and empty the contents onto the grate – a few meagre pieces of coal, just enough to catch the winking eye.

'Here he is!'

Tufty sprouts rigid from his Grobag, his strong arms locked straight against Fiona's chest. Brought into the room, robed and with his Shakespearian scowl, he is indeed kingly.

'Is your ankle bothering you?'

'No, it's fine. Why do you ask?'

Fiona points to the empty foil of painkillers on the table.

'Oh, those – I had a bit of a head. Probably that Limoncello.'

'It's made from all pure ingredients.'

'Oh, I'm not complaining. It's delicious, but you know, alcohol in the afternoon. Never good.'

'It's just an aperitif.'

'It's lovely. Listen, I have to go. What time is it?'

Tufty and I are slowly adjusting to the stark fact of no

longer being asleep. His arms have softened now, the scowl gone. I pull my socks out from the back of the chair and feel better as soon as I've put them on.

'It's quarter to four.'

'Oh God! I need to get a move on. How long did we sleep? This is your fault, Tufty.'

I wag my boot at him.

'Where are you going?'

They both watch me stuffing my (possibly fatter) feet into my boots. I gather up my things – coat, scarf, gloves, bag.

'Don't forget your pills.'

'Oh, that's OK. They're finished.'

'You seem to take a lot. Better watch you don't become addicted like that old comedian – what's his name? My dad really likes him.'

'Who?'

'I can't remember. Where are you going?'

'I'm going to Kenneth's.'

'Oh? *Oh.*'

'No – not *Oh.* I'm just going to look at his HD television.'

Her head retracts. I ignore the sceptical but forgiving smile. She's pulled her chin right in and it's not flattering.

'You can see them in Currys' front window.'

I tweak Tufty's foot and walk to the door, stopping in the hall to look in the mirror. I'm too pale – a wan, neglected face. I take a lipstick from my bag and lightly dab my cheekbones, smoothing it in, then apply some generous layers to my lips, pausing occasionally to speak, but staying close up to the glass, almost kissing it.

'Oh, by the way, Fiona . . .'

Pause for upper lip.

'I hate to say it, but . . .'

Pause for lower lip.

'I think you're getting a double chin. Maybe you should lay off the Christmas cake.'

Smack lips together, cap lipstick, put in bag, last pout, look up, smile.

'Bye now.'

Throw a kiss. Go.

SHE'S NOT the first to mention the pills. Last time I was at the house Dad came into the kitchen and put a small pile of Panadol empties on the table.

'Aggie?'

I didn't know what he was asking.

'What?'

'You left these.'

'Where?'

'Everywhere.'

'Sorry.'

I gathered them up like playing cards and put them in my bag.

'Thanks, Dad – my memory's shot. Must be catching!'

'There's no point in keeping them, they're all empty.'

'Oh, right.'

I took them out again and put them in the bin.

'You all right?'

'Yeah, I'm fine.'

'When are you going back to work?'

'Soon. I'm going to pop in before Christmas.'

'Good. Alasdair home yet?'

'No. Not yet.'

He lowered his head and rubbed the back of his neck, finishing with a rough scrub – fast and furious like he was shaking out the devil.

'I left once.'

'What do you mean?'

'I left your mother. It was before you were born. I—'

We were both standing with nothing to lean on, like we were in a public place. Dad stopped to clear his throat and that's when Mum barged in backwards carrying a laundry basket. She brought a gust of cold air in with her.

'That's the rain on. I've just this minute pegged these out.' *Why bother? It's December, for God's sake.* She hauled the basket onto the table and glanced at me.

'Aggie, close your mouth. You look like your gran.'

As she moved across the room the chilled air stayed with her, winter mist clinging to the wax of her jacket, her stone back clad in it. I wished she hadn't come in. Dad started to unwind the rope from the pulley and Mum opened the door to the hall and held her hand up to still us while she listened for Gran, then she put the kettle on and swished out the pot, squeezed the old teabags over the sink before taking them to the bin. When she opened the lid she noticed the empty foil trays and pulled some of them out.

'What's all this?'

'Oh, just my old Panadols. I've been clearing out my bag.'

She gave them a twist, moved them around in her hand as if she were charmed by them. The silver snapped like a blaze of dry wood, the sound of clean flames taking her elsewhere, to a beach at midnight, or a forest.

'I thought for a minute they were your old Christmas decorations, the ones you made at school. Do you remember?'

'Oh yeah – my silver stars.'

'But not very starry – they were all different shapes!'

'That's because I was trying to do proper stars. Gran told me that every one was different. Do we still have them?'

'Mmmm? Somewhere, I suppose.'

She took off her jacket and hung it over the chair. It had been a while since she'd laughed like that and suddenly hope rose like the Hallelujah Chorus.

'Oh, Mum – please get a tree! Maybe we can find the stars and hang them up, or if we can't we can make new ones.'

'Och, it's too late for that.'

'No it isn't, is it, Dad?'

'No, it's not too late.'

'I could make the decorations with Gran. She would love it – all that crackly tin foil and naming all the stars! Dad can easily get a tree, can't you, Dad? We can look out some of the old stuff too, or just keep it all silver – no lights, or loads of lights! I could bring ours over from the flat.'

It was exciting, an urgent, sudden prospect.

'Oh no, Aggie. I've too much to do.'

'But you wouldn't need to do anything. We'd do it, Dad and Gran and me.'

'It's too much, all those needles to hoover up. It would probably confuse Gran anyway to have a tree in the house. God knows what she might do if she saw it when she was wandering about at night. We'd have to lock the door.'

The suggestion appalled me.

'You couldn't do that!'

'Of course we could. We used to lock it when you were wee to stop you getting into the living room.'

Of course – it was a locking *out*, not a locking *in*. I took a deep breath and expelled the short shock that had winded me moments before. It was the briefest of misunderstandings.

'I thought you meant—'

I stopped, not wanting to say what I thought because it was too harsh. Mum had stopped too.

'You thought I meant what?'

'Nothing.'

It was something and nothing – a single grain of sand in the eye.

'What did you think I meant?'

'Nothing, it doesn't matter.'

But I couldn't undo the careless construct that had barely formed. I didn't look at her but I could tell from her voice that she was facing me, staring straight at me.

'I'm asking you – what did you think I meant?'

'Mary—'

I lifted my head and saw her holding an open palm to Dad, looking at nothing but cocking her head like a bird until she was satisfied he wasn't going to say any more, then she turned and shouted in my face.

'What is it you thought I meant, Aggie? Just say it!'

So close I felt her breath, and so sudden I burst into tears just with the shock of it, and because it was her. Dad put his arms right round her from behind, encasing her like a shell and gently turning her away from me. Bending and with a strange sideways gait, he walked her out. She didn't resist. At the door she spoke to him.

'Did you think that too, Maurice?'

'Think what, love?'

'That I'd lock Mum up?'

'Of course not – neither of us did.'

High Fidelity

T HE NISSAN is still there, frozen to the spot, its daisies faint against the frosted blue. There is a blurring – but no sign of wilt. I need to draw close to see it even though the security light is already on, triggered by him perhaps, or her – or by the ailing fog that seeps from the earth.

The sight of the Nissan cheers me, as any declaration of enduring love might. Keen not to be noticed, I walk past the end of the short driveway faster than I want to. When I glance at the front windscreen I fancy I see the dark shape of someone sitting in the car, motionless. It might be my imagination or a trick of the light, a shadow cast from a nearby tree, nevertheless I walk with greater urgency, striding down the hill towards Kenneth's house, imagining someone sitting in that car watching me disappear through the last gasp of fog.

I reach the low wall in front of Kenneth's house, and then the open gate, and then the door.

When I knock I'm still thinking about the shape, and when the door opens and the bright interior of Kenneth's house spills out and shoots up the path I realise that the dark shape in the car was on the passenger side – which feels like the wrong side, a shift into something much more desperate.

'Hi, Aggie – what is it?'

Kenneth's immediate concern prompts me to close my mouth and remember my expression.

'Oh, nothing. Sorry – I was miles away. How are you?'

'I'm fine. You look—'

'Deranged?'

His face remains set, other than a slight emphasis on his serious mouth.

'No, not deranged . . .'

There is a hesitation that gives me time to look at him. Pensive but easy in a charcoal sweater, his hair is sculpted in its usual way, a kind of considered mess that men much younger than him go to great efforts to achieve, only his is not considered – it is erratic and occasionally arresting; were I to run my fingers through it there would be a very slight springiness and lots of teasing out.

I am trying to disentangle my fingers from his hair when he speaks.

'You look different.'

'Do I?'

'Yes.'

'I've got lipstick on.'

'Ah, that's it.'

It feels like a confession and I think my mouth is beginning to form a tiny involuntary pout. We stand on the threshhold, not moving.

'I'd shake my can but I don't seem to have it with me.'

'What? Oh, sorry – come in, please.'

'Thanks.'

We do a bit of a shuffle, I think because I'm wiping my feet and he's trying to close the door. I'm in the way but it doesn't matter – as far as heat's concerned, it's gone.

We walk through the front porch and into the hall. Each door we pass is open, expanding the space. The generous stairway is carpeted with a threadbare runner and wooden stair rods; the wear is uneven, distinct pathways of different feet, and frayed edges where children have bumped themselves down. He leads me to a room at the back of the house, stooping slightly in a way I've not seen before, as if he thinks his head might hit the ceiling, yet the rooms are tall; a tall man might stretch his long arms upwards as high as they go and the rooms would still be tall, so Kenneth's bowed posture is puzzling. The stoop is not cringing in any way, it is not an obsequious stoop; it is polite and endearing, and nothing to do with deference – which makes me wonder about his house in Southampton. Perhaps the houses there have very low ceilings? Maybe he lives in one of those Elizabethan houses with interiors like an old ship – dark-timbered places that require stoops?

He steps below deck and shows me into a living room where a large state-of-the-art television sits on a treacle-black kist with leather straps. There is an open fire and the coals are stacked perilously high in the narrow grate, but with a bashed-up guard to catch any slaty sparks. The walls are lined with garish wallpaper – cream with geometric swirls of orange and yellow and brown, precise petals set out in such symmetry I tilt my head this way and that, willing them to shift and re-configure like shapes in a kaleidoscope. Directly in front of the television there is a sofa, and beside it a huge leather-ette chair with plump arms that seem to sit too high; the maroon colour reminds me of my old school blazer. Next to the chair is the swivel-top table I recognise as the one Kenneth mentions in his notebook. He has brought me to the control room of his father's ship. This is where he navigated his way through, counting coins and marking his pools, eventually abandoning the television – for what use is a television if it doesn't have any knobs?

The room confuses me. It holds an assembly of things that

are there solely for their functionality; there is no artifice
– and I do admire that kind of aesthetic, but I cannot decide
on the feel of it, whether I like it or dislike it.

'Dad pretty much lived in here. Believe it or not this is
the modern part of the house – done up in the sixties, I
think. Have a seat.'

'Thanks.'

I perch on the edge of the sofa and raise my hands to the
heat from the fire.

'Are you warm enough?'

'Yes, thanks – toasty.'

I rub my hands and smile.

'I love the wallpaper.'

'Do you?'

'Yes, it's warm.'

'Is it?'

He looks at the walls – each one in turn, twisting to look
behind him, then back, standing more upright now, more
tall. The walls seem to surprise him. He is standing in front
of me, his head facing the door to the kitchen.

'Would you like a sausage roll?'

I get the feeling he's forgotten why I'm here, what we're
about.

'I would!'

'Right. And what to drink? We have everything.'

When he says *we* I suddenly picture him curled up in the
big fat chair like a sleeping dog, missing his dad.

'Ummm – I'm not sure. Maybe just a tea?'

'OK. That's one tea, and I'm going to have a whisky mac.'

'Mmm – that sounds good but I'm just not sure if it goes
with the sausage rolls?'

'Why not have both, tea with a whisky chaser?'

'Go on, then – not too strong.'

'OK, I'll just wet the bag.'

I meant the chaser not the tea but he's in the kitchen now and even though the door is open and we can hear each other we don't talk. A clock chimes somewhere, then another – one of them slightly out; or both out, just one more than the other, but each telling us the same thing. Quarter past something. Plenty of time.

I rest my head on the back of the sofa and close my eyes. I'm in Southampton and Kenneth's tiny period house is the smallest in England; it's not much bigger than a shed and would easily fit in his dad's back garden. There is a lovely succulent tree growing at the front door – possibly a type of palm or banana, the leaves are slapping in the sea breeze like the snap of a sail, but there are bats in the attic, rats in the thatch, woodworm, termites. It sits on reclaimed land and is at high risk of flooding. The windows are rotting but because it is a listed building he can't afford to fix them; they let in very little light, and if he did fix them, they would still, at best – and on the brightest day – barely illuminate the dark. His lamps are always burning. He is shut in. A dark, gloomy place – not fit for a hobbit. It would be far better if he stayed here. He could stretch out, enjoy a proper yawn – his arms aloft and his back arched. If he moves back south he'll end up with rickets and a widow's stoop.

When I open my eyes there are two tumblers on the coffee table, pale whisky macs served in thick cut crystal. He's put them on beer mats, so I didn't hear anything; it was the smell that brought me back. Kenneth comes through with a platter of sausage rolls and two plates.

'Oh, I forgot the tea.'

The china is utilitarian too – chunky with a pattern of brown squares round the edge (they'd look good in our kitchen). The whisky smells of greenhouses, or is it tomatoes? I lean forward and breathe in the peaty aroma, trying to pick out the scent of ginger. Moving my hand towards the tumbler, I ping the crystal with my middle finger. On the first sweet note Kenneth reappears with the tea.

'I'm not checking – I just like the sound.'

He smiles and puts down a delicate cup and saucer painted with a mix of flowers. The cup has a fancy handle that is too small to accommodate my finger, I have to pick it up by my fingertips, my pinkie automatically forming a crook, just for balance; it's a matter of ergonomics rather than etiquette. When I put the cup down it is rimmed with lipstick – a bold stain that somehow completes my sense of misrepresentation. I look at the cup and saucer and wonder if he picked those flowers for me. *Who does he think I am?*

'I saw you in the library the other day.'

'Did you? Where were you?'

'I was just returning some books. I thought you saw me?'

'No. I would have said hello.'

Hopefully I say this without a trace of disappointment. I can't believe *he* didn't say hello, that after last time, and in the warm friendliness of the library, he didn't speak to me.

'I did wave, I thought you saw. Perhaps you were too wrapped up in your book – what were you reading?'

That bloody book.

'*Massacre of the Innocents*. It's a book about infanticide.'

I say it as plain fact and with the same intonation I'd give to a book about lawn care. He nods – just moves his head and bites into a sausage roll. My heart is racing like a bolting mare.

'It's really fascinating.'

He chews his food slowly. There is a slight sideways pull on the jaw that I find distracting; I'd like him to speak but all he does is chew, so I say a bit more about the book, paraphrasing a few sociological statements that distance us from the actual subject of women who kill their own babies. As I talk I'm aware that there is something else on my mind, something much more personal, but instead of working my way towards it, I veer off.

'What I find interesting is the way they talk about practising rather than committing infanticide, but I suppose that's just semantics.'

'No. Not *just* semantics – it's a crucial distinction.'

'Do you think so?'

'Of course.'

I expected him to say something else, something that would bring us back to the actual subject, but I don't think he wants to discuss the history of infanticide from 1800 to 1939. He would rather talk about shades of meaning. I take a sausage roll and rest it on my Christmas napkin, pausing before I speak.

'I find it hard to ignore things like that. That's why I'm such a slow reader.'

He looks surprised.

'Are you? Me too. I can skate through graphs and tables really quickly, but I find words imprecise, or possibly imprecise, I'm never sure. That's the problem. The only thing I understand anything about is maths.'

'That's not true. You understand lots of things.'

He looks up when he shouldn't, a fast glance that is immediately deflected onto something else by my own, more settled gaze. I can see he is thrown. I lift my napkin and begin to eat, catching the light spray of pastry that propels from my mouth as I speak.

'My problem is I ask too many questions. I can't get beyond them.'

'Yes, well – it's a curious world.'

'Ex*act*ly! Alasdair says I'm too dogged. What I call curiosity he calls ruthless probing. He says it's like living with Dostoevsky.'

'A compliment! Is he very well read?'

This is the last thing I want to talk about.

'I don't know. It's more that he reads well – he remembers stuff.'

The room is fat with heat. I'm beginning to sweat slightly, sticky under my arms and my mouth dry. I don't know what I expected, but it wasn't this.

'So, what kind of maths do you like?'

He looks at me, smiling but not answering.

'No, honestly – what kind? I'm really interested.'

'All kinds. I suppose I'm not so much concerned with the disciplines as the principles. I tend to see the world through a mathematical lens. Without it I wouldn't know where to start.'

'You could start with the senses.'

'Ah, the senses. Hardly the best guide if you're searching for truth.'

And to counter my intuitive argument that it may be the *only* guide, he picks up an envelope from a nearby pile of junk mail, finds a pen and sits down beside me on the sofa. Clearing some space on the table he starts to draw, first one illusion, then another, disproving my senses. I recognise the first one, the classic Ernst Mach illusion, where two lines of the same length can appear different depending on the direction of the intersecting lines at the end, but what follows is new – the bending effect of herringbone, curves that are actually straight, the distorting power of the oblique line. This man! When I think what he might tell me about the stars and the universe, that he might be able to explain the tides . . .

And as if he is reading my mind he pulls me up and takes me to the window, where he opens the heavy velvet curtains a little way, then stands behind me to direct my gaze precisely towards the North Star.

'See it?'

But the sky is ablaze with stars. They begin to dance. I lean against the cold glass and he puts his hand on mine – I think he does. He's telling me about Isaac Newton, how he compared his amazing achievements to that of a small boy playing on the seashore who finds a smoother pebble or a prettier shell than usual whilst the great ocean of truth lay undiscovered before him. Our hands are together, a clasp of fingers tracking the lifeline, the traces of sorrow, the skin, the heart – the simian crease. His heavenly body. His breath on the back of my neck.

And I know if he closed his eyes.

If we closed our eyes now.

In the urgent darkness.

I WAKE in a high bed. I wake *on* a high bed; somehow I sense the unusual elevation right away. I am lying under an old-fashioned quilt, the predecessor of what Gran used to call the 'continental quilt' (although even that has gone now, a whole geography lost as she zooms in like Google Earth – a continent, a country, a hillside, a clod in the shadow of a stone). The substance of the quilt is extraordinary – swollen pockets that weigh down my body in a pleasing way. I pull my arms out from under and press my hands on the quilting, following a wide arc (as if straightening my crinoline!). The pockets yield to the slightest touch, an incongruous paisley-patterned puffiness that keeps me intrigued. I am content just where I am – high off the ground and neatly arranged under a covering that stops at the edge of the bed, like a pie crust.

The door opens and Kenneth walks in.

'Oh, you're awake. Thank God.'

Behind him there is a woman wearing a flak jacket over a heavy jumper. She's carrying a kind of briefcase.

'This is my neighbour, Dr Desai. I asked her to come and check you over. You just seemed to collapse.'

'Really? I feel fine. I do remember feeling dizzy, but honestly, I'm fine. I really don't need to see a doctor.'

'Well, we're here now. Let's just take a look at you,' says Dr Desai.

'Thanks, Kati.'

He touches her arm and Kenneth leaves us to it.

Besides acute embarrassment I am perfectly fine, so fine I stop Kati before she has even begun. I apologise profusely for wasting her time, and give her an impromptu account of why I *might* have passed out: it was probably just a momentary malfunction due to a particular convergence of entirely innocuous things, a synergetic pool that included sitting in a hot, stuffy room then standing up too fast, a slight cold squeezing on my airways, plus I missed breakfast and then coated my empty stomach in sticky lemon liqueur, followed by—

'Aggie, can you just stay quiet for me and breathe in? That's it, nice and relaxed.'

And here I submit, surrendering to her doctor tones. I have spoken with my head but Kati is listening to my heart. She looks distant, weary.

'Sorry – my bag is like a small fridge,' she says, warming her stethoscope.

The old approach of the young doctor seems primitive and familiar – taking blood pressure, tracking the moving finger, the limp swing of the stethoscope. We chat for a bit, rule out the obvious and the serious, a blether about hypotension as she packs up her briefcase.

'Your blood pressure is certainly low. I suggest you visit your surgery in a day or two and have it taken again. Meantime the best thing is to rest.'

And as she walks to the door she turns and asks –
'Could you be pregnant?'

Spoiled Fruit

THERE IS something curious about Noreen – a dich-
otomous mix of coy and bold, both true. She is holding
herself in a different way, and seems taller.

'New shoes, Noreen?'

'Oh no, I've had them for ages but I don't usually wear
them.'

'Why not?'

'I don't know really.'

We all survey the shoes that Noreen has positioned neatly,
the toes lined up to the same gap in the floorboards. They
are light brown – a leather ankle boot with a brogue flourish
and a fringed tongue, rather like a golf shoe, but with a small
heel. Noreen has her hands on her thighs and is bending
towards her feet for a better view.

'I sometimes wonder if they're a bit fussy.'

'Not at all! They're lovely,' says Joyce.

'D'you think so?'

She sounds hopeful, and looks surprised – we all do, since
Joyce is not usually one for the compliments.

'Mother never approved of heels.'

'It's hardly a heel!'

'More of a court shoe,' I suggest.

'Mmm.'

Noreen bends down even further, catching her chiffon scarf and pressing it to her throat so she can see her shoes clearly, then she straightens up – rather abruptly, as if she is suddenly bored with them.

'Shall we do the box?'

We have congregated round the Christmas Lucky Dip and are all feeling cheerful.

'Oh no! I forgot! I've left my present at home.'

I hadn't given the secret Santa a single thought all week, and despite having lots of excuses (moral torpor, family rupture, bodily collapse) it feels like a careless omission, as if I don't care. Noreen can't hide her disappointment.

'Oh, Aggie.'

She tilts her head and pulls her mouth down in mild rebuke – and that's when I notice it. Lipstick! A pink shimmer, applied with an unpractised hand that has left a slight silting at the corners of her mouth, like she's been eating something with jam in it. The lipstick, despite its pale frosted subtlety, is so noticeable and strange on her usually naked lips that I suddenly realise how odd my own uncharacteristic layering of thick juicy plum must have looked the other day, so now, when Kenneth speaks to Noreen, we both blush.

'Christmas suits you, Noreen. You look lovely.'

He pulls a small parcel from his pocket, tugs the whole thing out so the pocket is left hanging from his coat like a dog's tongue.

'Here.'

He offers it to Noreen, causing more fluster.

'Oh no – don't give it to me! I'm not supposed to see who puts in what. Just hide it in the box.'

Kenneth puts the parcel in the box, pushing it deep down into the shredded paper so it is completely concealed. The rest follow, burying their gifts, and even though compliments are paid to Noreen for the way she has decorated the box (lined with Christmas wrapping and ablaze with tinsel), she is clearly frustrated at the way everyone is watching everyone else, clocking the parcels and noticing who has given what. And then there is the dilemma of being one short.

Naturally I try to help.

'Don't worry, I won't join in.'

There is a slight soothing as she strokes her chiffon, then Kenneth undoes her again.

'Nonsense. I'll duck out. It's my last meeting anyway.'

'No, you can't do that!'

Her reaction is fervent and strangulated, as if – with all the twisting and tweaking – the chiffon has tightened round her neck and is starting to choke her. She pulls at it, but the clawing makes it worse.

'Oh—'

Noreen drops her chin and lifts both hands to the back of her neck, where she tugs at the scarf, feeling for the crucial knot. Released at last, she gasps, her pitch still high.

'What I mean is – no. You can't duck out. One of the presents is for a man.'

Gladys, like the rest of us, is perplexed.

'But hang on, how do we know which one is Kenneth's?'

'Well, I know.'

'But we don't know, so what's the point of putting it in the box?'

Noreen sighs. Her lucky dip, so carefully and lovingly prepared – with all that shredded paper and a box of blazing gold – is slipping away from her.

'Oh, OK.' She sighs again. 'It's the one with the stencilled paper and the green ribbon.'

There is an appreciative murmur that causes a resurgent blush across Noreen's (now visible) neck, and someone then adds the *coup de grâce* by suggesting we should have just pulled numbers from a hat.

I am to blame. I look into Noreen's lambent eyes and try to catch them, but they are too fast; they have darkened to a cerulean blue and don't seem to care what they see, as if she has suddenly relinquished everything – the secret Santa, the crackers she has yet to pull from her bag, Christmas in general; as if suddenly it all has nothing to do with her.

'How about . . .?' I pause, because there must be something, a way to sort this out and restore Noreen to her winsome self.

'Look, it doesn't matter. Let's just get on with it.'

'No, hang on – how about if I—'

Kenneth's voice flows in, deep and sweet – 'If you be the master of ceremonies, which is more than you deserve.'

I raise my closed eyes and shake my clasped hands in thanks as he talks in mellifluous tones.

'We can blindfold Aggie and get her to pull out the presents. Each of us will have a number so we know what order we're in and Santa won't know who is getting what. OK?'

He rubs his hands together.

'Can you get some paper, Noreen? Oh, and you guys can keep your covetous eyes off the green ribbon because that one's mine.'

And with Kenneth as our saviour, Christmas resumes.

I am assiduously avoiding his eye, and he mine – skimming glances that land and lift, creating a tiny fissure, the thinnest crack, but noticed by some. Jessie fashions a blindfold from a chequered tea towel and I am willingly cast into darkness. Presents are distributed, crackers pulled – a sherry, a mince pie, Kenneth crowned in a paper hat, some singing, a quiz, women giggling to the point of tears. *Stop! Oh dear!* The stars in the bright sky look down from above. They see a party. Joy to the world. And we are joyous, for although we group according to our misfortune, gathered thus we are born anew; it says so in one of the articles Noreen keeps in the box file. We create energy – a birth, a life in every meeting. And for the next sweet hour there is no one back home fretting or searching or chewing their fingers, rocking or swaying up into a dance, muscles loose, graceful. Swinging their hands. Humming. Moaning. Crying. Every day a pantomime.

And then we close.

This would have been the ideal time to introduce Mum to the group. She could have brought her spiced apple cordial and warmed it up in the tiny kitchen while Gladys showed her where everything was kept and how things worked. Busy with the cordial, the cups and the napkins, some shortbread for dunking in the hot appley drink – she could have opted in or out of whatever she fancied. There is an apron she could wear – it hangs on a hook in the 'equipment' cupboard, or she could bring her own, her *chic noir* pinny. She wouldn't need to say anything other than her name, and maybe Gran's name and where they lived. *I am Mary Copella. I care for my mother, Peggy. We live at number eight the High Street.* That's absolutely the most she would have to say. She could just serve the cordial then go. No one would mind. Next time, after the long Christmas break, she might stay a bit longer – fill the empty chair left by Kenneth, who will be back in Southampton by then, his bones bending in the dark like moist willow.

But she didn't come to our little party because I didn't ask her; there would have been no point so soon after suggesting that she was capable of locking up her own mother, and now there is a melancholy creeping through the house that will spoil the fruit; the orchard seeped in slush apples despite all her work – every picked apple cupped in newspaper so there

236

would be no bruising; Mum singing out of season as she wraps them up for winter, something about Christmas and reindeer and cutting down trees.

Singing songs of love and peace, oh . . .

Her voice lapping through the house, pellucid notes dropping to the water's edge, and when Gran heard her she smiled and said, 'Someone's happy!'

'Yes,' I said, as the lament faltered, Mum's song breaking into tiny pieces. She's wishing for a river, wants to skate away and leave us.

Shards of sound so delicate they just . . .

floated . . .

off.

I SHOULD call Fiona. She knows there are things going on we haven't spoken about, important conversations that require a cleared room and at least one full bottle of red. But rooms are no longer clear – they are cluttered places, warm and sticky, the air moistened by the clean steam of nappies drying on a nearby horse. They usually house a baby, but even when they don't they are still dense jungle places that cause tiredness and compel Fiona to just put her feet up and sleep. Otherwise she'd know more than she does. She would ask, and if that didn't work she would pour more wine and ask again. As things are, and certainly until Tufty is weaned, very little is expected of me. I am off the hook, clean free and accountable to no one when it comes to things like worries, fears, dreams.

But there are some things that need to be told timeously, whether asked for or not, and spending the night – the whole night, including breakfast and use of shower – with a man who is not your husband is one of them (even though nothing happened other than a moment of light-headedness that I have no intention of mentioning to anyone, ever).

I'm not in the mood to call her, but I do, just to get it over with, and to protect myself from her intense scrutiny.

'Nothing happened.'

'Oh? Did he try it on?'

'Try what on?'

'Your knickers. Come on, Aggie, you know what I mean.'

'You're so common, Fiona.'

'Huh! I'm not the one staying out all night. Come round tomorrow and tell me all about it.'

'There's nothing to tell.'

Except this –

After Dr Desai left, Kenneth insisted I rest. 'Doctor's orders.'

I was content to slide under my crinoline and sleep. When I woke all the lights were off. I thought it was almost dawn, but then I noticed the soft glow under the door, a house light from the hall perhaps, or the porch, certainly from a distance, since it was only the dim fringes that reached into the room. Waking up in an unfamiliar room full of soft smudgy dark was lovely; why so lovely I don't know, but it was. I felt as a guest does – worthy of the crisp, laundered sheets that had been starched and pressed, and the quilt, and the matching water jug and glass on the bedside table. The two clocks chimed, first one, and then the other – still quarter past the hour. But what hour? I climbed from the bed and opened the door. The wooden knob was smooth as bone and rattled in my hand, as if the handle rod didn't fit. I flinched, worried that the noise would wake Kenneth.

'Hello. Feeling better?'

The door led straight into the room we had been in earlier, and the light I thought distant was right there, an old standard lamp glowing in the corner like a dying torch. He was sitting in the middle of the sofa watching television, but with the sound down. The fire was still burning, the air warm and smelling of oranges.

'What time is it?'

'Quarter past eleven.'

'Is that all! I thought it was nearly morning.'

I perched on the side of his dad's chair and looked at the screen. There was a caption running along the top – *A broken Mr Dorrit returns to Venice, and Arthur warns his mother she may be in danger.*

'I thought I'd watch *Little Dorrit* anyway, see what all the fuss is about. I quite like watching period drama with the sound down. It's restful.'

'Yes. I suppose.'

'Very visual.'

'Yes.'

I slid from the fat arm into the chair, and because we were in 1850s London just watching life go by without any need to listen, we talked.

'I see you're into the long-life bulbs – good for you.'

Everyone is complaining about these bulbs, their light is dim rather than soft, weakened no doubt by the sturdy white casing. Nobody really knows what these plasmic bulbs are made of; they are strangely primitive and sport the superfluous warning: *Ne pas utiliser avec gradateur.*

'Well, I wouldn't say we are into them exactly. I think Dad gets them free. Luckily his eyesight is quite good.'

'It would have to be.'

I pondered the light again, but with a growing sense of preamble, as if inching towards something else, something that needed just exactly this – a fragrant room, a fire, tangerine peelings lying on the hearth. Kenneth was kneeling in the semi-darkness, loading some coals onto the grate.

'We have one at home.'

He leaned back on his haunches and turned to look at me, his right hand poised in what looked like a welder's mitt.

'Have one what at home?'

'One of those bulbs. We keep it in the fruit bowl.'

He's still looking but doesn't speak.

'It's a Panasonic. Funnily enough, Mima was just talking about her Panasonic the other day. Is that a Panasonic?'

I nod at the television, my eyes still fixed on Dorrity things while I let him stare.

'I can't remember – yes, I think it is.'

A small coal fell from the fire and he struggled to retrieve it with his giant glove. We both laughed at his fat leather thumb, then he took off the glove and picked up the coal with his fingers, placing it on the fire with great precision, as if he were setting the last tiny bead in an elaborate pavé setting of perfectly cut diamonds.

'Can I get you a drink?'

I pressed my hand to my stomach.

'Uh, maybe just some ginger beer?'

He kept the door to the kitchen wide open, and with my eyes closed I followed his path across the room. When he opened the fridge his face lit up.

'Would you like ice?'

'Yes please.'

I opened my eyes and he disappeared. Scanning the room again, I decided I liked it – at least, I liked it late at night; the walls were quieter and everything had calmed down (including Kenneth and me). Sitting there in the old man's chair, I was beginning to sense a warm familiarity amidst the utility – the feeling of home, and with it, a terrible hurt. It was difficult to imagine what it was that could prove so impossible as to drive a person from their home for ever.

How hard can it be to accommodate an old man with a dying brain who wishes only to stay with the familiar?

But of course, it is not familiar, and it is not the man who has gone – it is the room. Each day it changes; he must check what is nearest to him and work his way out from the epicentre, looking for the next missing thing, for it is rarely obvious. It begins with a rearrangement, objects are moved about so they are either lost (in other words — gone from where they should be) or found (in places where they should not be) with their names removed, and during this time of searching and finding, people change too; they become indifferent, dismissing these strange arrangements and offering up platitudes — claiming it'll turn up, that they're always forgetting where they've put things. That they'd lose their head if it wasn't screwed on.

But he is not forgetting, he is noticing, seeing what others don't. Only he knows what's really going on — his home looted, things taken and replacements left (as if this will somehow trick him into thinking nothing has gone). As he struggles to save his house from complete decimation the only person he can rely on is himself. Everyone else is ignoring this insidious plundering. His son will not call the police. His daughter just weeps. And eventually, they all leave.

'Are you all right?'

'Oh!'

His voice startled me. I had to catch my breath to speak.

'Fine thanks. I was just dreaming about something.'

'Sounds good.'

He was holding out a tall glass of ginger beer. I was glad to see it, and when I began to drink I couldn't stop — multiple swallows as my lips stayed on the glass, then a sudden ginger rush at the back of my nose.

'No,' I gasped. 'Not good. I was thinking my way into your dad's head.'

'Ah, the power of the chair.'

He raised his hands up and waved them in a stagy gesture. 'You think?'

'Possibly. He did sit in it for a very long time.'

I crushed some ice with my teeth — an irreverent crunch that made us both laugh.

'Sorry.'

There was so much affection in that flickering room, I wanted to stay for ever. With a hand on each arm I stroked the worn-out chair.

'He doesn't miss it, you know. All this has gone. Did I tell you he wants to get married?'

'What! Who to?'

'Deborah Kerr.'

'Wow! That'll be some wedding.'

'I doubt it. She keeps refusing, not least because he keeps calling her Bunny. She enjoyed it when he called her *Mizz Carr* but she doesn't like Bunny.'

'Aw – I think it's sweet. Was Bunny your mum?'

'Huh! No. I think he met Bunny down Methil Docks. Possibly not one for the reminiscence group.'

The room felt very familiar now. I curled up and moved my head so I could watch the firelight on the ceiling. I was thinking about the brevity of strangeness – how the bed I woke in was only unknown for a moment, then the memory of it quickly retrieved, and I wondered if that brevity was reversed for Kenneth's dad, if, when he woke in this chair (having long since forgotten his way to the bedroom), there was a salient moment of recognition – a pinprick in the black canvas before the strangeness returned.

'You're off again.'

I shifted my head, widening the smile that seemed to have become the resting state of my mouth.

'I am. Sorry.'

'Do you always apologise this much?'

'Sorry.'

We were sharing a low table with acute-angle legs. It was positioned in the corner made by the sofa and chair, an arrangement so snug that sitting down on either required a sideways approach. There was a single candle burning in a small jar, and the coupling of the household candle and the jar (still with its black and white Gentleman's Relish label) was a pleasing, perfect match. I finished my drink and put the glass on the table. The movement stirred the already struggling flame, and it went out – releasing a waxy smell.

'I'll get matches.' And as he did so I pondered out loud and in a raised voice (since he was now in the kitchen again) about why candles smelt so delicious when the flame was extinguished, what causes the smell? He called through, something about either my furious or my curious nature, and when he came back into the room he said –

'All these imponderables, Aggie – you're worse than me.'

His choice of words unsettled me. Why worse? He wasn't exactly irritated, but I knew that at some point he would be, and our future – Kenneth's and mine, the one that had begun to strut and fret in my head – suddenly played itself out like a potted marriage.

Even during these sweet, intoxicating moments of our first night together I could see the way it would go.

With his eyes fixed on the candle I was free to watch, and it struck me how powerless he was – unable to prevent the stealing away of the one most dear to him. Suddenly I felt unsure about sitting in his dad's chair – perhaps it was insensitive? As he bent down towards the table, his cat eyes reflecting the narrow flame, I felt that we both lacked brilliance, that at best we would only ever be half illuminated, like the moon.

'You look exhausted,' I said.

He smiled and drew himself closer to the flame, as if for comfort, and I realised that of course he was exhausted – he had spent several hours with me, a woman so draining she drained herself, falling into a ridiculous faint.

'I exhaust my husband too.'

He picked up his whisky and lay back on the sofa, closing his eyes and resting his glass on his chest. By quarter past something I had told him all about Alasdair – how he is trapped, shackled to Mr and Mrs Thackeray by an enduring gratitude that he just can't shake, and how, when I asked him what he felt most when he thought of them (other than grateful), he considered this for a very long time, struggling to name it, and then said: compassion.

It was important to Alasdair that I understand this; he wanted me to see the source of it, take the generous view. He wanted me to get on with his parents. Be interested. Be nice.

'Pretend if you have to.'

And I did.

The first lunch with my prospective in-laws was pleasant enough. Served at the bangala on the fully extended oval dining table, the starter was hot vichyssoise, followed by cold turkey, then cheeses, crackers, grapes. The coffee was filtered, and there were mint chocolate twigs – thin and long enough to span the palate and prise both cheeks. It was then, my cheeks prised and Alasdair averting his gaze from my hamster face, that things started to fall away from us. If we had just kept the visit short, made an excuse to eat and run. Instead, the post-lunch conversation inevitably turned to our distinguished family names. The Copella story went the usual way – an unabashed no connection (despite the apples) that seemed to please them; but the Thackeray story was more substantial. Apparently there was a connection between David Thackeray and the late great William Makepeace Thackeray; I got the impression it was this that swung it when he proposed to Di. They could not quite trace a direct lineage, but there was a definite, albeit contorted, thread – frayed but nevertheless unbroken, despite a hundred and fifty years of twisting and tweeling.

'Amazing! Does that mean you're related to Al Murray?'

'Who?'

'The Pub Landlord. He's a comedian.'

And because I was scrutinising the large framed photograph of Thackeray that hung above the fireplace, I failed to see the look that might have stopped me from commenting on his markedly flat face.

'He's very pugnacious, isn't he? Do you think he had syphilis?'

It was a spectacular misfire. A certain darkness came down on the proceedings, just as it had in *Vanity Fair* when George Osborne fell flat in the mud at Waterloo with a bullet through his heart, but before I could muster an apology Alasdair had done it for me.

'Sorry,' he said, as if the faux pas had come from his own mouth, and on this occasion I said sorry too, I couldn't have said it more, but all too late according to Alasdair, who told me afterwards that I'd ruined that treasured portrait as surely as if I'd slashed it with a knife.

'There's no shame in venereal disease, you know. Anyway, it was only a print.'

'That's not the point, Aggie. You've spoiled the mood of it.'

BACK IN my own bed, I dreamed of dolphins. They were nesting in the branches of a tree, like slugs on a hosta, then the scale shifted and it wasn't the dolphins, it was the tree, the tree was huge. I think it may have been my first global warming dream. I'm not prone to topical dreams; my dreams are more visceral and probably bring balance to all the incessant reasoning that drives me mad when I'm awake. This feels more like one of Alasdair's dreams – I must have strayed onto his pillow. When I woke the dolphins were frolicking through the ripples of my corpus callosum, traversing hemispheres with ease. A strange exuberance in a gloomy place.

Re-established on my own pillow, I can hear the usual ghostly huddle knocking on the windowpane. The digital clock displays an intensely blue 4 a.m., and whilst the knocking is quiet, it is also insistent. I get up, put on Alasdair's Arthur Dent dressing gown and go into the living room. As I curl up on the sofa the generous folds of his robe work like soft mortar, bedding me in. This sofa was my dowry. Chosen by me and bought by the Copellas, it is our favourite thing. Bold green and with short sturdy legs, it is a mass of contradictions: plump *and* sleek; classic *and* trendy; Ikea *and* comfortable.

'You only married me for my Karlanda.'

'*Our* Karlanda.'

Lying here in my usual spot, I can see the moon through the gap at the top of the curtains. It gives the room a theatrical air, the promise of another world that will open out before me, and the exquisite feeling that I don't need to do anything.

Things will just happen.

I miss the heat of him; he is still trapped in the dressing gown and the unwashed sheets – skin cells and pheromones clumping at the base of each brushed thread; and his dream swimming in my head.

The room is a vague grey, suggesting a latent dawn. I pull the robe tight and gather the hood round my neck and shoulders, then shuffle towards the door, my feet arching slightly to grip the 'so-called slippers' I stole last year from a hotel in Lundin Links (only it wasn't theft, according to Alasdair, since these slippers – so called because they are impossibly flat and difficult to walk in – already belonged to us, paid for in full and providing small consolation for a breakfast of Wall's bacon and a sea-view that was marred by

246

the washed-up corpse of a seal). In the bathroom, I pee without switching on the light. My ankles are freezing. I rub them back to life then pull up my pyjamas (*his* pyjamas – *his* dressing gown, *his* pillow, *his* dream) and shuffle back to bed, sliding and flipping in my pitta-bread shoes.

Snake Road

I DIDN'T just go to her, I fled – an urgent escape.
Sitting in the flat, I sensed a touch of madness; it brushed
my cheek, but I saw it off – and now I am here, wrapping
her up in yet another layer because we are going out. We're
having a giggle about the buttons, but Mum is aghast.

'You can't!'

'Of course we can. It'll be fine. We're only going up to
the Cross.'

'The Cross!'

'I can take the car right up to the top. If it's too much
we'll just come home again. I could even carry her if I had
to – you're light as a feather, Gran!'

She echoed back to me as I fastened the buttons, her hands
flitting through a silent melodious phrase.

'Aggie, you can't, it's freezing – she'll catch her death.'

THE OLD road to Auchtermuchty is a steady climb that always
bears us up faster than expected, the vista sudden, and every
time surprising (less so in a car, but still a rush). This was
our Sunday-afternoon walk; almost every week Gran and I
would shove some sweets in our pockets and set out for the
Cross. I would race ahead, out of sight round blind corners,

248

waiting for Gran to catch up, then leaping from ditches, or I'd crouch in the grassy banks at the side of the road, shaking the long stalks and hissing like a snake when she passed. Dad told us there were adders in the ferns but I never saw any. He said he'd been bitten when he was a boy and now he was immune. He had a white V-shaped mark high up on his temple, just below the hairline – 'the mark of the snake,' he said, and I would trace it with my fingertip and wonder if maybe I had some of that snake venom in me. I thought the snakes would probably leave me alone because I was his daughter. I would stand on the banking and call out, 'I am the daughter of the snake boy. Begone!' But it was all just swagger; I never went into the ferns.

We called it Snake Road, not because of the adders but because of the way it twisted up the hill, and because of the view below – the serpentine river slithering back to the sea.

I was too flighty to learn much during our treks; sometimes Gran would point and my eyes would follow, but we rarely spoke. I knew every wild flower by sight but not by name (other than the obvious – dandelion and daisy, cow parsley, teasels and harebells). It was the same with birds, a lazy, nameless love, but still a love – their song more reliable than weather. My best love was the unruly screech of gathering crows in February, the sky peppered with sooty motes – a right menace.

'What's wrong with them?'

'Nothing. They're waiting for the plough.'

Then, geese with pink feet grazing in the flat stubble, and later, the impossible joy of the skylark. Gran's best was the redshanks calling from the wet grasslands down by the river – their far-off lament rising to the top of Ormiston Hill. The call of a redshank could make her cry.

'It's just the wind in my eyes,' she'd say – but I knew.

Every walk up Snake Road was different except for one

thing; when we got to the top Gran always sat on the same stone – a flat rock between two raised boulders, with another stone behind her. In grim posture and with her hands resting in her lap, she would sit in silence, completely still, even in a gale – cutting the skyline like a Henry Moore queen. These stones are steeped in legend; known as the Cross, the site is an ancient place of safety where, through certain rituals, atonement can be achieved, even for murder.

But I didn't know that then. The Cross wasn't even a cross – it was just a stone, with a few smaller stones surrounding it in a kind of protective circle. It wasn't a place to linger, particularly on a wild day, since the open aspect offered no shelter from the Nordic winds. I was always glad to leave it, and I think Gran was too. I asked her once why we kept going back to the same place, but she didn't reply, other than to hold me with an odd smile for longer than was pleasant.

The coming back was better than the going. We might dawdle on the way, stopping to pick rosehips or comfrey (leaves like spaniel's ears by the time we got home). Sometimes we'd link arms and sing 'She'll be Coming Round the Mountain' – marching with a tiny jump at the start of every line.

I can't remember when I stopped going, but for years and years Gran walked to the Cross alone, then one day she said she'd had enough of the Cross, and she never went back.

WE ARE on our way at last. Something about the varying hemlines takes her completely out of time, and yet – as she struggles across the cobbles that slope down from the front door – she seems more faithful to the old stones than any one else on the High Street. The wind almost lifts her off her feet. She is hooked into me, but quite loosely, her shoulder bumping against my arm as if she is moored in a rough sea; the uplift is wrapping the ends of her copious skirts round my left leg, which makes walking difficult. She is wearing a three-quarter-length duffel coat and the buttons, so funny just moments before, are bothering her. Crossing the few yards to the car is taking much longer than I anticipated, and I can see she is cold.

Already the excursion feels reckless, if not dangerous.

'Peggy! How lovely to see you! How are you doing?'

Gran is astonished. She smiles at the passer-by who knows her name; she seems dazzled by her, as if she is the most wondrous thing – a walking talking miracle. The woman smiles too, but looks concerned.

'Out on such a cold day? You're brave! Still, you've got Aggie here to take care of you.'

I don't know who she is, this woman in drip-dry trousers and a trim red anorak. Against the cobbled ground it is she who is anachronistic; her neatness throws Gran into chaotic relief and I want to offer an explanation for what might look like careless neglect (uncombed hair can mean many things) but I feel a sudden impatience to get Gran into the car.

'She won't keep her gloves on. Come on, Gran – before your hands drop off.'

Gran looks alarmed and tightens her grip. I move forward too fast, outpacing her; she stumbles, trying her best to move more quickly, head down and concentrating without any sense of resistance. The woman in red calls out.

'Bye then, Peggy! Have a good Christmas!'

And the dazzlement surges back, bringing with it a renewed tensile strength that belies Gran's fragility; she attempts a turn and a wave just as I try to prop her up against the car so I can open the door; I have to bend in and catch her mid-twist, which gives rise to what probably looks like a grapple. The woman – who is still watching us – puts her hand to her mouth, then holds her chin and glowers, really glowers (like one of those traditional Japanese dancers). Manoeuvring

Gran into the seat is like putting a Jack back in its box. When I push (gently) on her skull it strikes me how small it is, I can almost cup it in my hand. Fixing her seat belt is mercifully simple since her attention has now turned back to the cream buttons – which I can see might look like slugs crawling on her coat, but thankfully that particular horror has not occurred to her.

As the car pulls out the woman points to the bottom of the passenger door, jabbing her finger and shouting.

'Skirt! Her skirt!'

Gran laughs and throws her yet another wave, a very enthusiastic one, flat palmed and with her fingers closed, trim and fast like a metronome gone mad. Then at last we're away.

This outing is not planned as such, but having thought of it I couldn't delay. When I opened the window in her room I was aware of a sudden force, her face caressed all heavenly things and her skin drank the damp air in. There was a gasp, dusty eyelids I could smudge with my thumb, and it was then – when she turned towards the cold with her eyes closed and asked me not to tell – that I understood why the hill at Pennyland had seemed so familiar, and why, before I went there, I was able to dream of it so vividly.

Despite our inordinately slow pace (or perhaps because of it) Gran is sanguine, but her trust rattles me. If only she would cast a suspicious eye and say, 'What are you up to, Aggie?' If she could just see through my reassuring smile I could exaggerate it, stretch my Machiavellian grin into something we could laugh about. Whatever it is we are doing, we would be doing it together, me and Gran up to our old tricks.

But she has no idea.

As we climb higher I worry about the car sliding backwards on the ice and wonder if I should have taken the hill at speed. Too late now, and with my anxiety climbing more steeply than the road itself, it is a miserable ascent that can only lead to sorrow. What was I thinking?

This – a last shaking of the bones. An eye–brain shock that might bring Eleanor back one last time, because the whole thing feels unfinished. It is a final quest, not for sanctuary but for resolution – a task worth doing because it is never too late to put things right.

'I smell snow.'

'Do you?'

'Yes,' she says, sniffing the air like a perfumer.

'We're nearly there, Gran. We're going up to the Cross.'

'Up to the Cross.'

'Yes, I thought it would be nice to look at the view.'

She's twiddling her buttons, which is good, since as long as she keeps touching them they remain buttons and the world does not slip. She looks at me and her face tells me I am familiar, which is enough. At last the road flattens out, but I still don't trust it and the tight strain of driving on black ice leaves me aching for more Panadol. I can see the open gate now, and as we leave the road and drive into the field I accelerate towards the cattle grid, as if to jump it – hitting the bars too fast. The noise and thrum frighten her.

'Sorry, Gran – that was just the cattle grid.'

Tight-jawed and clutching her coat, she looks anxious. Her own movements catch her attention and she is near to tears, I think at the strange volition of her hands, the way they are grappling the neckline of her coat, pulling at the edges of a hood where there ought to be a collar. I have seen this dysphoria before, and it is always the hands, unrecognisable and with odd properties. 'Look!' she would say, pinching her skin into soft meringue peaks, and I would smile to reassure her, then smooth out her skin, dusting her bruises with *Je Reviens* in an act of miraculous healing.

We're in the field now and the track is throwing us about

as if we are rolling on dodgy springs, but I prefer this to being on ice. We lurch from side to side and then up. My head hits the roof and we laugh; we are laughing when we reach the Cross – a final lurch towards the dashboard, then a sudden synchronised thrust back into our seats when the car stops.

'Oops!'

'Oops!'

Gran burps, pleasantly winded, and we laugh again.

The first stage of our dangerous journey is over. I have positioned the car side-on to the view so the stones are in front of us and she can see the hillside beyond. Despite the cold, I open my window a few inches to keep the windscreen clear, then I wait like a wolf, my crafty snout pointing forwards so she will follow my gaze to the landscape ahead. Relaxed after all that laughing, and with her hands resting on her lap, she looks like a little old lady on an outing, enjoying the view.

'Do you know where we are, Gran?'

I can see she does not, but she knows she is sitting in a car.

'Don't you think it looks familiar?'

She keeps looking at me instead of the hill, and when I point she can't seem to follow any more; she just stares at my finger.

'Don't you think this place looks just like the hill at Pennyland?'

I have put my hand over hers, and I take care to speak gently, so the words don't obscure what I feel. At last she contemplates the field and hill, the trees.

This is why I have brought her here. I am coaxing her back to that other hill so we can be there together; so that when she remembers, she won't be alone. My idea is this: if I can be with her, if I can be with her at Pennyland and return the puma's stare, her exile will end. I want to break the trammel of time and walk beside her. I want us to bury Eleanor together, remember the babies, then leave. Show her that my love is transcendent – that I've loved her all her life.

But she will not be coaxed.

Her small eyes are drawn to the coal-black dashboard and the smooth shank of the gear stick, the slight concave shape arching inwards – like a sheep's leg bone. I'm still holding her hand and I don't want to let it go. I have to watch not to squeeze it – that's how much I miss her. There is a pain in my chest; salt tears stinging my eyes like a whip of sea water. She places a hand over mine, then lifts it and pushes my hair away from my face, teasing the strands free from my wet cheek.

'There, there – don't cry. Your mother will be here soon, don't worry.'

I look to her and she smiles.

She is beyond Eleanor now, beyond motherhood – she is the only surviving child of Jean and Robert Kirkpatrick. Her mother taught her poetry and took her on long walks; together they followed the banks of the river Nith, lingering where Rabbie Burns had lingered, lying in the grass where he had lain – a timeless fusion that turned her head. Her father taught her how to carry a dead lamb, and how to recognise a lamb with hypothermia, and what to do. When there was a sudden chill they would search on the hill for newborns, ridge after ridge in all weathers, two collies at their heels. She told me the sheep always stuck to their own hills, moving up and down the land rather than across, so it was always a hard climb. If the lambs were cold or malnourished she poured gin and linseed down their throats to warm them up, but if their heads were down and their mouths were too cold to suckle there was nothing she could do. The first dead one she found, she cried – but her father said not to because it was only nature. All that's happened is they've lain on the hill and gone to sleep.

STILL STROKING my hair she shakes her head, amazed.

'*Tch*! What a face!'

But she doesn't know my face; her lizard eyes are moving all over it, jumping in fits and starts. She is comforting a stranger. I smile and nod as I slip my hand from hers and press my mouth in a kind of stemming. When I bury my face in my hands a last sob catches my breath, my sorrow slaked – shaken out in one violent gasp

'Cold?'

She is solicitous, lucid – whereas I . . .

'No. Not cold. Have a tissue, Gran.'

I pull some from my pocket and she takes one, tucking it up her sleeve then fussing with it, twiddling with her cuffs as if they're the wrong ones. A bird comes down and catches our attention, pecking at the ground close to the car.

We look through the same window, and it is this that has haunted us both – the striking resemblance between Pennyland and the open terrain at the Cross, as if the whole of Fern Hill just upped and followed her north. This strange gusting has been pushing me all ways for days, and finally, it has pushed me here; pushed me up like a ram butting my back.

Look!

This is what drew her – this echo of land; for decades she has walked to the top of Snake Road in search of sanctuary, tracing the curves exactly, the rooted banks and the way the pale grasses twine together in clumps, like knotted hair. The most obvious mapping is the stones themselves – their foreign look amongst the thick grazing, with the same protuberance and relation to each other, and whilst here they have been placed and are the ruinous remains of an ancient monument, at Pennyland nobody knows how they got there. It is as if they fell from the sky, carried by a tornado perhaps, and dropped.

'I'm just going to stretch my legs, Gran.'

She touches her chin, worried.

'I'll just be a minute, you stay in the car and keep warm. You'll see me from the window.'

The air is ice cold. I can feel it against my cheeks as I cut through, keeping in her sights and waving as if I am happy. The stone is just a few yards away and when I reach it I bend down and stroke the marbly surface. It is remarkably similar to Eleanor's stone. I follow its edge until I am crouched on the ground and my palm is in the wet grass. Low down in the right-hand corner where I have pressed the cold blades flat, something has been scratched into the rock. The marks are slight and almost indecipherable, but I can just make them out.

E Stewart 26-2-1938

It can only be this – the birth and death of Eleanor on the twenty-sixth of February 1938. I can tell from the bloom of algae that the inscription was made in recent times – possibly when she last walked Snake Road. Perhaps she sensed the start of her illness and knew that ultimately she would reach the leaden hour, when nothing is recollected.

Of course, I have already put flesh on the bones of this ephemeral girl, this cold grub, her vapid face and eyes that never opened. She carries no shock.

But the date sets me reeling.

As the sole historian I am about to wipe the debris from the stone when a vital swelling pushes up from my stomach and threatens to drown me. I panic, turning to look for Gran because I'm suddenly worried that she might be gone.

She is there. I can see her through the windscreen. Her face is white with cold and oddly featureless, but she is there. I leave the stone and the inscription, tease up the flat grass, the brush of my fingers tricking the worm, and the little bird waiting – watching with his beady eye.

As I walk back towards the car her white face emerges, close to the window and moving in a strange way, one hand briefly splayed on the glass. She looks stricken. I get back into the car but fail to soothe her. She wants out. She's scrambling for a handle to turn, the back of her hand flapping against the door like a fish on the floor of a boat.

'Out!'

'It's too cold, Gran. We need to get back.'

'That's the snow. There'll be a good few up.'

I think she's talking about the lambs.

'They're fine, Gran. Let's go home.'

'Let me out now.'

She is growing agitated, held against her will and not allowed to work; not able to do what's expected of her.

'Out now!'

I think if I touch her she'll scream.

'It's all right, Peggy – they're in the pen. We can go home and check.'

'Get this off—'

'Get what off?'

I don't know what she wants but I lean across and roll down her window. The air catches her, gathers her up and calms her, the cold slap restoring her just as it did before. She tries to push her head through and out, twisting her neck and her hands curling round the top of the window as if she is clinging to rope. A few drops of sleet hit her face and I am astonished at how quickly she shifts – laughing and licking all round her mouth and chin in a way that she would never do, too much tongue and gum. For her, it is a moment of joy, an intensely physical delight, but I don't like this primitive joy, the way it cuts through layers and layers of life, discarding everything.

She is happy, punch-drunk on elemental bliss, her precious rain, the stuff she has cupped and measured all these years, wetting her eyelids and quenching the thirst she no longer recognises; but her happiness saddens me; worse – it embarrasses me, even here, where there is only us. I look away, not wholly to avoid the sight of her gaping mouth (although there is that – I don't want to see the small, dark hole in her colourless face), but to hide my shame.

Suddenly I feel flung over, cast into the ferns and forgotten as she moves on in a capricious world, leaving all of us.

'Let's go home and have some tea.'

We are both stiff with cold, our fingers white and set like birds' feet. She has pulled back from the window and is shivering now, intent on nothing but the hands that protrude from the sleeves of her coat. Eleanor has failed to appear. There has been no conjuring, no tiny evanescent ghost rising from the hillock like an arctic hare. The only constant is the earth itself – rain, sleet, sun, wind, snow.

I lean across her again and wind up the window.

'I want to go home,' she says, and we leave the hill for the last time.

Nothing matters. Back on the icy road I take my chances at every turn, driving at a tangent across each blind corner so I don't have to use the brakes. The road will take us back to the house, but no road will ever take her home. When we reach the village I keep to the left, accelerating because she is frantic, hands held out in terror and her head pressed against the back of her seat. She's been staring at the buttons without touching them and suddenly the slugs are on the march, grazing on her body as if she were dead.

Absent Love

W HAT A fuss. You'd think I'd kidnapped her and taken her on a joyride.

'There's no harm done, Mary.'

But anything Dad had to say could only make things worse. Mum was gently squeezing Gran's hands to get the blood flowing again, but you could tell she was furious; throwing daggers at me and yet massaging Gran's hands with impossible tenderness. It was odd, the way she could be angry and tender at the same time.

Me being there wasn't helping so when she accused me of reckless irresponsibility I grabbed my excuse and stormed out – like I was the wronged one.

THE FLAT is cold as a tomb. I take some Panadol to unlock my neck, then I build a fire and make a jug of strong coffee, which I drink black before gathering everything together – the *New Moon* magazines, the papers and articles I have collected, my notebook. When I spread them out on the table in front of the fire I'm surprised at how small the archive is, given the room it takes up in my head. On the wall the arctic poppies have faded to palest yellow and are past their best. I open the notebook and write down the name of the Second Assistant Physician, plus the name and date that was on the stone, and below this I add the dates of the magazines. I know they are connected, that a story binds these things together, but facts alone tell you nothing. They are knots on the lifeline, and when I trace round them the contours widen to form what looks like a slice of wood cut from the stump of a felled tree.

I pick up the last *New Moon* and look again, this time through a different lens. I ignore the poetry and go straight to the Staff Notices – the engagements, the happy marriages, the well-earned retirements. The items are either condolatory or congratulatory; warmest sympathy is extended to Miss Semple, the senior telephonist who, after twenty-five years of faithful service must give up her work permanently to nurse her ageing parents (there is no mention of a pension for Miss Semple, but she was given a beautiful mahogany china-display cabinet).

There is also a promotion – more warm sentiments, this time concerning the appointment of Second Assistant Physician Edward Stewart to the post of Senior Assistant Physician at the Murray Royal in Perthshire, where he will take up work at the beginning of September 1937.

```
Dr Stewart, originally from Den of Lindores in Fife,
leaves behind him an excellent record of five years'
devoted service as physician and psychiatrist, but
also the fragrant memory of a trusty colleague and
genial friend, greatly esteemed and liked by all. He
will be much missed, not least on the cricket field,
where he captained the XI for the last two seasons.
On the eve of his leaving he was presented with a hand-
some gold wristlet watch and a wallet of Treasury
notes. We all join in wishing Dr and Mrs Stewart and
```

Miss Lucy many, many years of health, happiness and
prosperity.

Fragrant memory indeed; I can smell the rot, the sickly scent
of those dark notes every time Gran opens that talc – overly
sweet to mask the stench of a terrible breach of trust. Edward
is Eleanor's father, and the fact that Gran moved to a place
less than two miles from Den of Lindores, tells me that for
her, something lingered, suggesting love.

But the betrayal reeks. I feel a sudden surge of bitterness,
a thwarted anger that makes me want to seek out Edward
Stewart and strike him down. These stark numbers – the
date on the stone, and the date here, in this intimation – tell
me it was not the baby that took her to the Crichton, it was
something else; illness, or crisis, or a nonconformity, the
insistent yellow eyes of a puma, perhaps, or a fondness for
long walks.

I read the intimation again. She has not marked the passage,
there is no need. Dr Stewart has gone, and Miss Margaret
Kirkpatrick is recovered and has been discharged back to
Pennyland, where, seven months later, she carries her newborn
from the unheated barn and leaves her on a hillside; a blue
baby, surely asleep, her heartbeat slowed by the inland drift
of cloud from the cold Atlantic fringe.

But I can't relate the tale because I promised not to, and
because she has never spoken of it, or rather – she has never
told it. This is not a story that has been 'passed down', prof-
fered in front of a roaring fire while the fag end of a North
Sea gale blows outside. There are no letters. No dusty old
photographs. There's just that picture of Gran in her bare
feet sitting on a horse; and now there is an inscription,
scratched rather than carved, still diffident and already
denuded by time's green creep.

She has carried her own memorial in her crumbling head,

but now the formal feelings have gone and what we have is this – fragments let loose by the falling away of a defensive life; the walls she has built denuded by disease, and where the brain shrinks, gaps appearing – glimpses of all that was hidden, and all that was not.

I can sense the isolation now, the shoring up that even Alasdair noticed, an insularity that contained a mourning so vague and so prolonged it became the life. And amongst the consequences, the unwitting neglect of a second child, a daughter with shorn hair, who, in the midst of unspoken grief, still waits to be noticed.

The Ghost of Christmas Past

I SAW Alasdair today. He was walking down the street carrying a small bouquet of winter flowers. They were wrapped in cellophane and tied with hessian string. My instinct was to follow him, but I managed to stop myself and now I'm back in Plum Town, wishing I could go home but feeling I can't because I'm still in the bad books, at least with Mum. I decide to go and see Noreen instead. She lives nearby and has had an accident, which gives me the perfect excuse to visit.

There's something about a neck brace that grips the heart. The monstrous collar is hunching her shoulders and locking her head. I notice the strange realignment even as I approach the house. The day after our Christmas party Noreen sustained a kind of whiplash injury at her yoga class. Her GP had recommended either yoga or salsa classes to help her body recover from all those years of helping Mother in and out of the bath. 'Why not do both!' someone said when she told the group, but Noreen had fixed on the *either/or* part of the recommendation and believed that doing both would be like mixing your drugs. She chose yoga for the meditative side, but as a novice whose muscles had been gripped in another, less visible brace for a long time, her neck had locked whilst doing the fish, leaving her gasping through an open throat. It had taken two people to prise her crown from the floor and roll her safely onto her side, where she lay like a stunned eel until a cold compress was applied (courtesy of the Spar across the street, who kindly donated a bag of party ice). Now she'll be braced up until January.

As I walk across her paved front garden I can see her through the window, sitting as if on display. She is illuminated by an already harsh overhead light even though it is not yet dark. The sight of her, the way she is holding herself – very upright on the edge of her seat and reading a thin paperback – makes me want to call out, tell her to take cover. She looks vulnerable in her neck brace, and strangely distorted, I think because the brace is flesh coloured rather than the traditional saintly white, and with a slight shine, so it looks like an actual neck. I wave, but with little hope of her seeing me out here in the blue shadows; she is holding the book higher than is usual and I can't see her eyes. I stop to look at the interior scene, its fine lines sharpening against the twilight. There is an empty companion chair beside the one Noreen is perched on, and next to it, a trolley with metal legs and two moulded plastic shelves with lipped edges. The trolley looks like something that would be 'issued' rather than bought, and is out of place in an otherwise pleasant room. *Oh, Noreen.* I'm itching to tell her to throw the thing out, and when she answers the door, turning the double lock twice then opening slightly and peeping through, I feel like barging in and disposing of it there and then – just to up the pace and convey a kind of urgency.

'Aggie!'

'Hello, Noreen. I heard about your accident and thought I'd pop round and see if you needed anything.'

It is an unconvincing gambit, we both know that, but effective enough. From inside the room the trolley looks even more ghastly, a relic that ensures the enduring presence of old Mrs Bryden; I fancy I see it tremble even before I get to it and plonk my bag on it. The companion chair stirs too, a slight slide of the feet in their little plastic castors – but I am used to ghosts. They don't scare me.

'When are you getting rid of this?'

'I can't. It belongs to the health service. I've asked them to come and collect it but they never do.'

'Noreen, it's been what – three years?'

'Two – such a waste! Someone could be using that. Mother loved it, she used to push it through from the kitchen even though they told her not to. I told her not to as well but she never listened. Very independent she was, knew what she wanted.'

'Mmmm.'

'Actually, since I got the neck brace it's been quite useful. I can't really look down so when I'm eating I have to place my food quite far away from my body. This is perfect!'

We both contemplate the trolley, which has fallen still now, playing possum like a giant insect engaged in an act of static predation, waiting for the moment when Noreen's hands gnarl their own way round the moulded grips, just as Mother's did. Not wishing to dwell on the invidious trolley any longer, I jump up, rather too energetically, so her eyes widen (startled rabbit eyes – set further round the head to compensate for the neck).

'How about some tea? Shall I put the kettle on?'

In the kitchen there are even more hauntings – a raised stool, non-slip mats and curious gadgets, a chopping board with a clamp; the kettle sits on a wire frame that looks like its own little zimmer, and the wall plug has a handle on it. The overall effect is a kind of strange inversion of Magritte, an enhanced functionality that exposes the real – the wrist as a tipping device, the hand as a grip. Noreen catches up with me, gliding through the doorway like she's on castors too. At the cupboard she takes down two cups, then moves to the tea caddy, insisting she can manage perfectly well.

'I'm not surprised with this lot! Funny how all your mum's old equipment has come into its own again.'

'Oh no, these aren't Mum's, they're mine. My hands are pretty useless now – well, not always useless, but when the joints flare up it does make things easier.'

She's talking to the wall in front of her, squeezing her fingers in that characteristic way that I have always interpreted as a kind of emotional wringing.

'Gosh, I didn't realise. Well, you do brilliantly. Is it painful?'

'Sometimes, but really, compared to Mum I'm lucky.'

I cannot see the luck in those tumescent pink-tinged knuckles. She insists on carrying the tray but when we sit down she lets me pour. Her book is lying on the table.

'What are you reading?'

She looks at the book cover, as if she's forgotten.

'Anita Brookner – have you read her?'

'Only the famous one. I borrowed it from Mum but I can't remember what it was called.'

'What was it about? No! Don't answer that, I think I can guess. I've read nearly all of them. I struggle with the words sometimes but they are so atmospheric.'

True. The one I read is coming back to me; not the story as such, that's the first thing to go, but I remember the book as an exquisite talisman, a melancholic buffer that brought eloquence and dignity to the solitary. I'm not convinced it is the best thing for Noreen to read.

She puts the book on her lap, and having manoeuvred herself round to pick up her tea, she balances the mug on it. I stretch out my legs and rest them on the lower bars of Mrs Bryden's trolley, then I tell her about taking Gran to the Cross; not the whole story, of course – but I tell her about how similar the landscape is to the place where she grew up, and I speak about her past and the time she spent helping her father with the sheep; the sudden death of her husband; the way she had to raise Mum on her own.

The more I talk the emptier the room becomes, spaces appearing where pieces of Gran's life have been omitted, removed like so many objects – a table gone, a chair, pictures taken from the wall; these artefacts are hidden, stored in another room, and it is from there that young Peggy Kirkpatrick is sent to the asylum, not because of a concealed pregnancy but because of an inclination towards poetry and moodiness (I saw it in that picture – the Scarlett O'Hara scowl); I believe this is what happened, having read in the archives of girls locked up for reasons of adolescence or grief, for babies or love affairs, for neurasthenia, for petulance.

And afterwards, Eleanor left to die on Fern Hill, abandoned for one reason or another, probably several; a terrible convergence that has clung like a canker to the meagre family tree.

But that is in another room.

In this room Noreen listens, sensing the weight of what is missing. She is oddly still, of course – but her eyes are very active; they flit about like blind eyes reading their own thoughts.

'What are you thinking?'

'Nothing,' she says, with an arcane smile, and I can't ask about her own missings because I'm not supposed to know. She has never mentioned her Irish love. I relax into the chair, accepting that there are so many things we can't talk about, despite the mutual trust, and the affection we share. She asks me if I'd like to stay for tea and I say no thank you, I need to get going.

'Of course,' she says, immediately assenting as if she has over-stepped the mark, 'you must be busy. Your husband will be wondering where you are.'

268

'No. It's not that. In fact, its quite the opposite.'

And I tell her about what happened earlier.

When I saw Alasdair walking down the street with those flowers I did follow him, but only until he turned into Kirk Close. I stopped then because the close is a narrow walkway with no place to hide, and because the whole thing was so bizarre. When I reached the mouth of the close I knew he'd be gone. With more courage and a different heart I could have stood at the crest and watched him dip down the alley, shrinking more with each step – a squat little man clutching a mean spray, on his way to Flossie's, I presume, his fat knees braced against the steep cobbled slope.

It is dark now, but inside the room is ablaze, lit up by Noreen's luminosity. I want to draw the vertical blinds but I'm not sure if I ought to in someone else's house.

'I don't know what to do next,' I say.

She takes a very deep breath and taps her book, as if thinking.

'I don't know either, Aggie – but do something. Get yourself unstuck, otherwise you'll suffer, and there is no merit in that.'

She speaks without bitterness, drawing from life.

'You know, it might not be what you think – there's lots of reasons why someone buys flowers. What kind were they?'

'I don't know. They looked very delicate, like mist.'

'Sounds like gypsophila. Most people call it baby's breath.'

I can feel an immediate, involuntary furrowing, eyebrows like a pulled stitch. Neither of us knows what it means. I stand up and button my coat. The interior light is so harsh now it casts out shadow, rendering us strangely flat.

'I really need to go, Noreen, but thanks – you're absolutely right. I need to stop being pathetic and just do something.'

'I don't think that's what I said.'

'No, but I'm saying it. I think we should both make some

real resolutions this year – proper ones that carry real consequences.'

'Yes – you're right!'

And as if already resolved, she pushes herself up from her chair and the book falls from her lap.

'Mind your book, it's gone under your chair.'

I bend down to pick it up but she raises her hand and keeps it there.

'Actually, don't bother, Aggie. I think I'm done with Brookner.'

I'M NOT sure which is worse – the empty flat or Christmas. I'm nearly home when I change my mind and decide to use the last shopping hour to resume my trawl of the charity shops, in search of presents. Buying second-hand is a family tradition that seems to satisfy a confusion of needs; a shared strategy that steers us through this impossible festival. Dad is easy to buy for, any old garden implement will do (the older the better, as long as it works), and Gran loves anything beautiful – a piece of lace or a silver compact, something to put in her rummage bag. Mum is more difficult; the last time I asked her what she wanted she said, 'How about a one-way ticket to Palookaville?'

Sometimes I don't even know when my own mother is joking.

There are blinking fairy-lights everywhere. I'm not in the mood for clutter, which rules out Save The Children and Shelter, and, unusually, there's a funny smell in Oxfam, so I go for the orderly themes of Barnardo's, who, according to Fiona, now have an evening-wear section that's 'perfect for cruises'.

The window display is attracting interest – people stopping to look at the plain wooden nativity corralled in holly. It is arresting, for reasons that are not immediately clear, and as

I jostle to maintain my view one shift triggers another, creating the impression of excitement; but it isn't that, it is more a kind of puzzlement. We settle as one, trapped in a collective frown. 'It's an allegory,' someone says, and the man next to her sighs and says, 'Oh, here we go.' And that seems to free us. Most move on, an exodus heading for Argos, leaving the few to browse peacefully in the warm scented interior, but it is useless; no matter how intently I stare at the bric-a-brac, all I can see is Alasdair clutching that small bouquet, his Rohan trousers flapping in the wind as he rounds the corner into Kirk Close. It reminds me of the time he brought me a bunch of foxglove for all the right reasons. He'd remembered my preference for wild flowers and his Belladonna eyes were wide with the happiness that comes from finding the perfect love token. He didn't know about the toxins and the bad luck. That's the thing about Alasdair, he really does try to get it right.

I am about to leave when I notice a book displayed in a glass cabinet – an unusually sized hardback, long and squat, like a picture book, and covered in a brown sleeve, with the title *The Doyle Diary – The Last Great Conan Doyle Mystery*. It is a reproduction of the sketchbook kept by Arthur Conan Doyle's father – the same Doyle Mum and I had talked about, the one who, loosely speaking, shared a favourite chair with Gran. I'm excited to find it, not due to any sense of pre-destiny or Jungian synchronicity (chance would be a fine thing), but because it will show Mum that I think about her. I'm sure she'll love it, despite the bizarre drawings, which even at their most whimsical, I can see are macabre.

Wrapping presents on Christmas Eve is another Copella tradition, so it is odd to wrap *The Doyle Diary* so early, and I can't think of a precedent; I just knew as soon as I got home that I didn't want to look at the book again, so I've covered it in red paper, taped on a plum pudding tag with the message, *Something Strange and Curious*, and put it in a drawer.

The book is out of sight, but there is a growing doubt – the suspicion that I've got things terribly wrong, a bit like Alasdair with the foxgloves.

A Sacred Geometry

WITH THE snow gone the towers of Jewson city have lost their beauty. I look at the dripping piles of blackish plank. Beyond the apocalyptic scene there are distant clouds that could be mountains, but then, as the wind picks up, glaciers floating towards spring. This is just the beginning. There is so much winter to come.

Last Christmas, Alasdair wanted us to go to Egypt but I refused, so he bought me a SAD Box. 'Kick January in the ass!' said his Christmas card, whereas mine said, 'Festive greetings.' (No pun intended, but nevertheless I have never cried more than I did last Christmas. It was my present to me.) This box – my Philips SAD lamp, came hot on the heels of my Philips Dawn Simulator alarm clock, a seemingly innocuous gadget that hollowed me out each morning as I watched the ritual trapping of a fake day heralded by birdsong, but without the birds. It was a sound that evoked a sense of desolation, as if birds were extinct.

The clock was my birthday present from Alasdair – a gift from a worried man. I was just two weeks into my new job at the surgery and had been late three times. He thought this was terrible; it bothered him much more than it bothered Flossie.

'She doesn't mind.'

'Of course she minds!'

And perhaps she did. I used the clock for about a week, and then I broke it.

'What happened?'

'I knocked it over.'

'How?'

'I don't know. I think I was stretching into a yawn, or maybe my morning smile just bumped into it – it's that wide.'

I shook my grin at him and told him that I didn't need the clock, I could simulate my own dawn; but then came the Box – my SAD lamp, even though my sadness was not an acronym.

'You're depressed.'

'But not seasonally.'

'I think you are.'

'I'm not – and anyway, even if I am, I'll be fine by the spring.'

I don't remember much more, just refusing the sorry lamp, and Alasdair taping it up again there and then, before he even opened his presents. And me telling him it'll be better next Christmas.

'This time next year we'll be sailing up the Nile. I promise.'

I'm deeply troubled by the baby's breath. If it had been a poinsettia, or a bunch of evergreen with a few seasonal berries (some deadly nightshade perhaps – such lovely shiny fruits), it would make more sense. Any florist would advise him – point him to the amaryllis, or some red anemones that have grown in Galilee under a desert winter sky; flowers are a sophisticated business now, and with such a wide range of exotic airfreight available no one is going to recommend a bunch of chickweed. He must have chosen it himself.

Louise has been on the phone insisting I pop in for that mince pie she mentioned, and so I can meet the new locum before the Christmas break. The locum is a *he* – the first man to be employed in the practice since 1977, and he'll be covering for Flossie while she's away. There is also the possibility that the new drill might be arriving, and the guy who broke all his front teeth on a concrete slab has brought in a Marks & Spencer Christmas hamper, so I need to be there to choose my share from the booty; there are wines and chocolates, chutneys, cherries in cassis, marinated olives, a comb of acacia honey! It was a frenzied list, reeled off from memory and reeking in spice. Really, it should all go to Flossie, and perhaps the technicians who built the crowns, people like Alasdair – the unsung heroes of dentistry whose anonymous art brings such bold in-your-face happiness.

I call Fiona, ostensibly to apologise for not going round to see her, but also to ask her what to do.

'Go. I bet Floosie or whatever she's called won't be there if she knows you're coming.'

'But what if she is there?'

'Then you can talk – have it out with her.'

'I can't. It's him I need to talk to.'

'Agreed. So do that, then. Go and talk to Alasdair.'

'I can't.'

'Why not?'

'I don't know what to say.'

'Say what you feel.'

'I'll try.'

'No – don't try, just do it!'

'I will.'

'And go to the work thing. I've seen one of those hampers – they're brilliant. Go grab yourself some champagne, or there might be a nice *Châteauneuf du Pape*.'

'You think?'

'Definitely. Oh and Bug – if there is any, get me some of their flavoured shortbread, it's bloody gorgeous.'

The flat no longer makes sense. There are living spaces that house the usual clutter, and there are other, non-living spaces of pronounced emptiness, with a neatness that doesn't change. It is as if the person living here has a complex visual disorder – some kind of hemianopsia (of the right side); I'm looking through a strange prism, covering one eye then the other with my hands, but the dichotomies persist – sofa, table, bed, all split by an invisible boundary, a force-field I find impossible to penetrate. When Alasdair left he traumatised my optic pathways.

I call the bangala.

'Hello, can I speak to Alasdair? It's Aggie.'

'Agatha! How are you?'

'Fine. Is he there?'

(And I know this omission – my failure to reciprocate with a polite enquiry of some kind – will irk Di, but I enjoy it; I like being the ascribed me.)

'No, he's not. Can I take a message?'

'When will he be back?'

'Oh, I couldn't say.'

I'm not sure what that means, whether she knows but can't say, or doesn't know. I resist asking her since it wouldn't change the facts, which are these: he's on holiday as from today (I know because he has it marked on the calendar – his big OFFs mucking up my big Xs); he's not out on the bike because that's still in the hall (the only place where I can find relief from my hemianopsia); and with Flossie at work and no declared friends living locally, he nevertheless has places to go. I decide to test something out.

'OK. No message. Love to David. Bye.'

I think I hear a plaintive, 'Wait!' But it's too late, I've hung up rather too quickly, cutting Di off with the press of a thumb. It is an ungracious act, like squashing an ant. I hadn't intended to cut her off, and wasn't even sure if that was her voice, since plaintive is not really one of Di's tones, but I couldn't face calling her back.

The strange calm I feel as I call work is rooted in an intuitive sense that Flossie will not be there – that if one cannot be found, neither can the other.

'She's not in today.'

'Of course she isn't.'

'Who's that? Is that you, Aggie?'

With the bright lure of chocolate-covered amaretti, and knowing now that the dentist will be out, I have agreed to pop in. I'm zipping myself into my warmest coat – a tight midi-length puffa, snug as a bug and almost perfect were it not for the pale taupe colour (Fiona says it makes me look like a maggot) – when a piece of old-fashioned mail is pushed through the letter box, a thin envelope landing face up on the mat, soundless and bearing Alasdair's handwriting, the letters tight and all joined up. When Alasdair writes his nose almost touches the paper and he holds the pen at the nib, scraping and scratching like a Dickensian clerk. He is my Guppy, and when he crouches at the table to scrape and scratch it is the small boy I see, his head bowed over a grubby jotter, turning the page back and forth like he has lost the memory of whatever has just been written. Preserving what little he has.

My heart races as I bend down and pick up the envelope. It feels empty, but inside there are four words engraved on a small piece of graph paper:

she is called Alice.

THE STAFF room is packed. There is room for me but not my wrap-around duvet, which I leave in the waiting room. We squeeze up, elbows tucked and keeping our polystyrene cups of Cairn O'Mhor elderberry wine close to our lips.

Foster, the new locum, is standing behind Louise; he seems shy, and is probably using her as a human shield. Louise has beckoned me in with great enthusiasm, relieved that we can now get on with it. The arrangements for a fair distribution of the hamper contents are quite complicated since someone needs to choose for Flossie, whose sweet tooth seems more deserving than ours. Eventually the spoils are shared and the last remaining item − a box of salted caramel biscuits − is foisted on Foster, despite him having no claim to the crowns. Although our number is unchanged we begin to swell, spilling out into the waiting room where the old 'Time and Tide' poster on dentistry provides a welcome subject for polite conversation with our new, very male colleague. The poster is a revered object, a fitting remembrance to the pioneering work of Flossie's mother, who never expected anything less from her daughter than full succession.

'Funny to think if Flossie had inherited her mother's rebellious nature she might not have been a dentist. She might have just left school and got married like the rest of us and had her 2.4 or 1.7 or whatever it is now. Being a mum with a wee part-time job would be quite radical in her family.'

'Yeah.'

'Eh, excuse me, but what do you mean "just"? And anyway, you're the only one who actually fits that category.'

I let the chat flow round me, lamenting my loss because I know this will be the last time I'll be a part of this, knowing that when the news breaks about Flossie and Alasdair my illicit career as a dental nurse will be over and these women (my nearly but not quite friends) will speak with care whenever we come across each other − solicitous chats about the weather, wondering what happened to the summer, and when, if ever, we'll be out of our socks.

I shall miss them.

In the background the switchboard is switching; calls are

being transferred to the answer machine – a range of voices playing out words that are indecipherable, even for us *denticians*, who are very good at deciphering the mutterings of our open, vowel-mouthed patients. No one is listening yet things can be heard, and with a sudden lunge Louise throws herself over the desk and grabs the phone, intercepting a call.

We all pause, just long enough to ascertain that the call is not an emergency. The hygienist rolls her eyes at the locum.

'Ha! You're off the hook, Foster. For a minute there I thought you might have had to snap on the gloves! I doubt if we could track Flossie down just now even if we needed her. She's probably braising in a seaweed wrap as we speak, lucky thing.'

This image of Flossie as fajita catches my attention and pulls me from my own sorrowful world.

'What? Where is she?'

'She's at that Yu Spa having the full package – deep-tissue massage, ocean wrap, the lot.'

'Very nice.'

'Yeah – it was a surprise engagement present.'

'Engagement present!'

'Yes.'

She looks at me, reading my face.

'Oh. My. God. You don't know.'

Then she turns to the others.

'Aggie doesn't know about Daniel,' she announces, as if translating the message from one language to another.

'Flossie's getting married! No date yet, and very sudden, but she's known him for years. He's an old flame from her student days.'

There is a burning sensation, and a roar – like swimmer's ear; hot bone scalding the sides of my neck. I know my mouth is open but there is nothing I can do about it. Dazed by the flashing heat, and with a surging in my Eustachian tubes, I can only just hear Louise, who — having just come off the phone again — appears breathless with excitement.

'You'll never guess who's back!'

We all freeze and wait (even Foster is completely caught up, showing great promise).

'Sylvia!'

And now it's not just me — we are all open mouthed.

'What about the roof guy?'

'Dumped, apparently.'

'What a nerve!'

With no grasp of the facts surrounding the errant receptionist, Foster can nevertheless feel the effects of them, and shakes his head in shared disapproval before sitting down to open his salted biscuits.

THERE IS *no merit in suffering.*

I think that's what Noreen said. It's the last thing I would have expected her to say, which shows how much I know when it comes to understanding people. I've been so busy thinking about 'how to listen' I may have missed something. The weather is grey and unforgiving. I am completely sober, but after three glasses of wine I would not be able to prove this scientifically, so I leave the car and walk, hands in my pockets and all the time holding Alasdair's note, the carrier bag of Christmas treats hanging from my wrist. My swimmer's ear has cleared and I have regained my balance. New possibilities are emerging through the mist, scented with rain and altogether sweeter — tolerable mysteries that I may never solve, but I can live with that.

I walk quickly, matching the pace of everyone else, all of us bent on avoiding the slow freeze. But there is an added urgency. I need to get home so I can think clearly. With the collapse of all my carefully constructed assumptions there is a new doubt, a scepticism regarding the appearance of things, and I do wonder. I wonder if the patterns of reality are just a means of strapping in chaos because we prefer it that way, and I wonder how much I actually know and how much I don't know, how much has been drawn from my own science of rationalised fiction – coincidence as a kind of sacred geometry.

And I wonder too, where he is, and what he is doing.

THE CHEMIST looks like Dr Alfred Prunesquallor. On my first trawl of the charity shops I bought the *Gormenghast* DVD for Dad, and now here is Dr Prunesquallor – just as I recall him from the books (thin and pointy, with hair like an abandoned nest and magnified eyes that fill his glasses to the rim). He has appeared from behind his screen following a muffled exchange with the woman who was serving me, his cartoon eyes so big I assume he must be practically blind. Too late, my eyes have widened in sympathy. I try to relax my lids and let them fall but suspect I now look sleepy – or drugged, which is not the desired effect when trying to bulk buy painkillers at the chemist's. His eyes are constantly moving in an odd, orbital way, probably just an exaggeration of the norm, the exposition of a ubiquitous tremor that's usually invisible, to the naked eye at least.

But these eyes are beyond naked. They are stark, and surely sore, and I want to take his glasses off and bring him immediate relief.

'Mrs Thackeray?'

'Yes.'

'How are you?'

In pain, obviously.

'Fine.'

'Can I have a word?'

He draws me to one side, cupping me in the arc of his bony arm without actually touching me, moving me like a magician's floating ball. He is smiling, so I smile too, then I see he is holding three packets of Panadol Ultra – and I know what he is about to say.

'We have noticed you've been buying these painkillers in quite large quantities for a while now. Are they for your own use?'

'Yes.'

He pauses (except for the eyes) and seems to be waiting, as if giving me a chance to expand on my answer, or change it, or maybe just reflect on it – let it hang in the air for dramatic effect. I do not have to say anything. I am not going to say anything. This is intrusive and irritating. *Who does he think he is?*

'I get headaches.'

'I see. Have you spoken to your GP?'

'Yes.'

We pause again, but this time I won't tell him anything else because it's none of his business (except, of course, it is his business – I suspect it is exactly his business, that he has taken a Hippocratic oath, but I'm still not going to speak to him).

'She said just to use the Panadol.'

He nods, his head pivoting round the cup of his eyes.

'Right. Are you on any other medication?'

'No.'

'Do you have a headache now?'

'No.'

'Good. What I think we'll do is give you a small packet of these today, just to tide you over – but you need to go and see your GP again and explain that the headaches are persistent. How does that sound?'

It sounds really patronising.

He swivels round on one heel and brakes with the ball of his other foot – nifty, as only the thin can be, his white coat stiff as an Eton collar.

'Just a small size for Mrs Thackeray, Gillian.'

He's holding out his hand, waiting for Gillian to deliver and checking his wristwatch as if he is timing her. I expect he'll snap his fingers any moment now, and I'd love to see those cartilaginous digits strike a spark, but I just can't stay.

The Blue Orchard

D AVID IS in the front garden salting the path. I watch from the gate, intrigued by the careless way he's throwing the salt down, with little attempt at an even spread (other than the occasional scuff of his boot). It looks strange because he is usually so methodical – in fact, it is one of his faults, a perplexing slowness that drives everyone mad.

'Are you expecting a frost, David?'

He jars upright as if he's been stabbed in the back. A handful of salt is thrown sideways, landing in the tilled border where he will plant a neat row of polyanthus mix in February.

'Christ! Aggie – I didn't see you there.'

'Sorry.'

'I was just salting the path again – just a top-up, you know. Di likes to keep it salted all winter in case the frosts undermine the slabs.'

'Ah.'

He has joined me at the gate now and is chatting as if I am a passer-by – he on one side, me on the other.

'We've had so much rain this winter I think when the frost does come it will be a particularly hard one. Just got a feeling about it.'

He looks at the ground with solicitude, and I look where

he looks and nod, trying to share his concern, but it only takes seconds for a normal look at the ground to become something else – a losing of some kind, or a trance, and I've been nodding for too long; it's beginning to feel weird.

'David?'

He suddenly draws a loud breath through flared nostrils and straightens up again, dispelling whatever was silting up.

'I was wondering if Alasdair was in?'

'No, he's gone for a walk, I think.'

'Do you know where?'

'No, he didn't say. He might have gone to the cemetery in town.'

'Why would he go there?'

The question had obviously never arisen before, so he had to think about it.

'I don't really know, I just know he goes there sometimes – says it clears his head. Bit morbid if you ask me, but that's Alasdair for you.'

'Oh—'

I am about to ask which cemetery when David quickly turns and looks towards the front window. I look too, and although there is nothing to see there is a sudden awkwardness, as if something is wrong, as if we should not be standing here chatting at the gate. With a craven apology for not inviting me in, he suggests Di is not feeling too well, and I end his discomfort by absolutely insisting I must go. His relief is palpable, and when, after a few steps, I stop to wave, I see him scuttling off, probably in search of an implement that might even out those messy piles of salt.

It saddened me to be told something I didn't know about Alasdair. More specifically – it saddened me to be told this particular thing by that particular person. Visiting cemeteries sounds like quite an important aspect of an individual's life; it makes me wonder what else I don't know, not that I need to know everything, but I would have liked to have known this.

When we met, Alasdair intrigued me. I couldn't figure him out.

'He's fascinating,' I told Fiona.

'No – you are fascinated,' Fiona told me. 'Big difference.'

'He's an impervious drifter.'

'Sorry?'

'A rolling stone.'

'No he's not. He's a nine-to-five technician. He makes false teeth.'

'Love looks not with the eyes, Fiona, but with the mind.' But no matter what I said about him, she wasn't convinced.

'He's working on an invention that'll make him famous.'

'Oh yeah? What?'

'I'm not supposed to say.'

And she laughed in her explosive way – a belly laugh that caught me by surprise and exposed the extent of my earnestness. So I told her.

'What?'

She calmed herself down so she could hear.

'What did you say?'

'Inflatable scaffolding.'

And we managed a respectful pause – a dignified moment when we tried, we really did – then she exploded again, only this time it set me off too and we fell about, mouths gaping as we wiped our eyes.

After two years, she changed her mind. Now she's telling me I should hang on to him, but I have to find him first.

I don't know how many graveyards there are, one for every church, I suppose. I decide to start at St John's Kirk because that's the prettiest and it has provided me with shelter in the past (during a spectacular summer deluge when the brown river gorged on the land in a wild and ruinous rush). The old graves at the back of the church are in a state of disarray, silvered with lichen, their writings indecipherable except for the occasional symbol – a skull, or what looks like crossed bones. Some lean at precarious angles and will eventually fall or sink, buckling under centuries of wind and rain; others are flat and feel more protective, closer to the dead. There are no trees or plants – just the neatly clipped Presbyterian grass, and a perimeter of ancient wall, nothing to distract the soul from its journey, and yet, the austerity brings peace and the desire to linger. In this walled garden of bones there is a sense of the living sharing with the dead, all beyond harm.

Alasdair is not here. I follow a narrow path that leads to a gate, and it's when I am through and out and turning to close it that I see the gypsophila bunched in an old milk bottle and centred in front of an ancient stone. I go back through the gate and read the inscriptions. The family goes back several generations to 1848 – deaths by sickness, accident, drowning and war; men, women and children alike, including several infants below the age of five, and a baby called Alice who died on the 22nd of September, the day she was born.

THERE IS a gap between Dad and the table. He is reading the paper, holding it in mid-air. I pull up a chair and slump, arms folded, legs out straight and crossed at the ankles, rubbing my chin against the zip on my coat.

'Why are you away over there?'

'The table's wet. Your mother doesn't want newsprint all over it.'

He lowers his paper and lets it crumple in his lap. Giving me his blank look, he yawns and bunches the paper onto one knee so he can scratch the back of his head. I smile, because I know *exactly* what he is going to do next – *smooth the back of his head, scratch, smooth, lift his chin and draw his hand down his throat, like he's checking for lumps* – and I watch as he brings his hand to a slow, predictable conclusion. The vague look is gone and he is curious, brighter.

'What's happened?'

I laugh.

'Nothing. Why d'you ask?'

'Because you look happy.'

'Well, it's Christmas!'

'Don't tell your mother, then – she thinks it's next week.'

He is wearing his creamy jumper – an Aran knit that needs a whole drawer to itself. He must have had it for over ten years because I remember he wore it on my eighteenth birthday when it was still being kept for best. I have always loved it.

'You're wearing my favourite jumper.'

'I know – but it looks better on me.'

He winks and begins to sort out his paper, flicking it back into shape.

'Have you spoken to your mum yet?'

'No. I wanted to ask you something.'

'Oh?'

He straightens in his chair, steeling himself. This guardedness is familiar too, as warming to see as his saggy jumper (even Aran wool sags, eventually).

'Yes. It's about what you said the other day, or started to say – when you told me you left.'

'What do you mean?'

'You said you left once – but then Mum came in and you didn't say any more.'

Suddenly, and so unexpectedly, he looks as if he might cry.

'Oh! I'm sorry, Dad – it doesn't matter.'

But he says no, it does matter, and as he speaks I move out of my slump and straighten up, so now it is my back pressed against the chair – a solid stance that fails to still my heart when I hear that he and Mum lost a baby, that he still feels guilty about going off and leaving her four months after the miscarriage, that he can't say why he did it – he was just driven out. Which is no excuse. When he did come back (six days later) she wouldn't talk about the way he left other than to say he should do whatever feels right, not in the moral sense, but emotionally; she said he should do whatever feels right for him. As far as she was concerned he could go or stay. It made no difference. That was the hardest part – the way she turned cold on him.

As I listen my discomfort builds.

'Do you think Mum would really want me to know this?'

'It's fine. We spoke about it and she said I could tell you.'

'Oh? You spoke about telling me?'

'Yes. She said I could tell you anything if I thought it might help.'

'What do you mean help? Help who?'

'Help you, Aggie. We don't really know what else to do.'

THERE IS shouting. Someone – a woman in a black apron – has stripped her, pulled down her skirts and yanked her sleeves from her arms. She is washing her down with a hot flannel, not caring that the water is spilling, soaking her underwear; this woman is lifting her wrists up high so she can scrub under her arms. It is an assault, but no one stops it. When she struggles the woman just tightens her grip, squeezing her upper arm where the flesh is soft, her fingers pressing the bone. She yields to the pain and finally gives way.

But she can still shout.

'Stop it! Leave me alone!'

I have not witnessed this before; Gran shouting blue murder as Mum struggles to wash her, terrified she might bruise her, fingertip bruising peppered across her upper arms in a lacy tattoo – or worse, a fracture where the thin bone cracks. What would the GP make of that?

We all worry about bruises. Purple patches have started to appear on the backs of her hands – spontaneous flowerings that (according to the district nurse) are not bruises.

'How did I do that?' Gran asks, over and over until you offer a lie.

'You probably banged it on the bedside table.'

But a fracture – that would never heal. I believe it would break Mum for ever.

Biologically, I cannot say that Gran has aged well; her joints still work, as do her kidneys and bladder, but her cells and tissues are wearing out, and her brain is a mess – thistle-head fragments of protein stuck between the neurons like burrs, the cells filling with fibrous twists of insoluble tau. These plaques and tangles are spreading like ground elder, choking the freshest shoots first. They block the pathways she spent a lifetime creating, forcing her off track. This is what Ruth called the 'dialectics of dementia' – where aspects of personality and biography are slowly incorporated into the actual brain structure. *Brain as self.* It is a concept that does my head in. I think of it this way: Gran walking through an altered landscape until at last she heads for the drover's road. It is the only place she still recognises, the place she has known the longest.

She has stopped shouting. Less frightened now, she lets Mum wrap her in a towel and pat her dry. Their eyes do not meet, but if they did, it would be as a mirror – each exhausted by the struggle of trying (and failing) to be understood.

'Can we talk, Mum – when you're finished?'

She looks at me and gives me a flat answer.

'When I'm finished.'

I leave the room because I cannot help, and because there are days (and today is one) when Gran does not like having more than one person with her at a time; when there are two, she thinks she is being moved.

'Am I being moved?' she asks, querulous but sometimes willing, other times not.

I go downstairs and sit in the living room with the light off, staring at the fire. Mum did tell me about this; she asked me to ask the group about washing.

'Ask them how you wash them when they don't want you to.'

But I forgot, I think because that was the time we had the dietician in to talk about nutrition. She told us about the importance of a balanced diet, how constipation can lead to acute confusion, and the way some 'elderly pensioners' are not very good at absorbing vitamin B12, which can make them anaemic. I remember feeling disappointed because the dietician (who looked malnourished to me) didn't have any suggestions about what to do when a confused 'elderly pensioner' hides her food, or spits out her teeth, or tries to eat her own faeces. Unimpressed by her enthusiasm for purées and baby foods, I became very caught up in her tautologies, and the way she failed to roll her r's – *woobarb, wice, wusks.*

I don't know when persuasion becomes coercion, when keeping a firm hold becomes violence – but I know if Gran doesn't wash she could be 'removed' against her will. People would come for her, ready or not.

'Aggie?'

She gently shakes my arm and when I wake it is her I want to see more than anyone else in the world.

'Aggie, wake up. I've made coffee.'

She smells like stale bread, and in the firelight the skin below her eyes is shaded in – two sweeps of a charcoal thumb, her cheeks flat and without shadow, her face thinner than before.

'Oh, Mum – I'm sorry.'

'For what?'

'For everything.'

She smiles and shakes her head.

'It's fine.'

And we could have settled for that, my unspoken mistakes and her implicit forgiveness, but I want to be sure that we are talking about the same everything, so I tell her it's not fine, and when she rests back with her coffee and closes her eyes I believe she is mustering the strength, making the effort for my sake when all she wants to do is sleep.

'I want to talk to you, Mum.'

'Fire away.'

'It's not about Gran, or Alasdair, or me. It's about you.'

'Oh?'

'Dad told me about your miscarriage.'

Eyes still closed, she smiles – which I didn't expect, a genuine smile that doesn't seem to be masking anything else.

'It must have been awful.'

'It was – but you get over these things.'

She is still smiling, her coffee cup back on the table now and her hands relaxing in the lap of her apron. I move to the Bose and put on *Blue* – her favourite Joni Mitchell, keeping it low. When I sit back in my chair I wonder if she is asleep, and since I'm not sure what I want to say, or at least how to compose it, I hope she is asleep. Napping together in front of the fire would be nice.

And because her eyes are still closed, I jump when she talks.

'I always feel so guilty.'

She looks peaceful, and despite what she's saying it is not incongruous.

'I just can't shake it. It has become a part of me.'

Her words are intermittent and softly spoken. They mingle with the music until I'm not sure who is saying what.

I am born with the moon in Cancer but she feels blue.

Blue because her first baby took two full days to go.

The sickness suddenly stopped and when she woke the tenderness had gone from her breasts and she just knew. Gran prepared the bed but lying down made the pain unbearable so she moved around the room, tracing the walls the way that woman did in that story – *The Yellow Wallpaper*. She remembers the room and the paper, the hideous colour and the florid arabesque pattern, like a fungus. She was lost in the ghastly shades of yellow, bags of blood sliding into the washbowl, and then the fever and the smell, a fungus smell coming from the walls, and when she got to hospital they scraped her clean – all the bits of placenta scooped out. 'Good as new,' the doctor said, and she rested for a day before stripping the bedroom walls, bit by bit, until every scrap of paper was gone.

There had always been an emptiness (like a hole in the heart, she said). It lifted during the pregnancy, but after the miscarriage it came back, and it didn't go, not even when I was born two years later. Whatever it was, she couldn't get to it, and eventually she stopped trying.

Then one day, when I was about four, something happened. She was sitting in the garden on the bench by the back door. There was a smell of green wood smoke, someone burning branches that were still in leaf. When she crouched down to look through the fruit trees she saw Gran directing my gaze to a coil of smoke that was rising in a straight column from somewhere further off, away from the orchard; Gran was telling me something, pointing to the silky filaments of cloud that were high up beyond the blue, like there was a connection between the cloud and the column of smoke, and as Mum watched the two of us

– thick as thieves and framed in apple blossom – she saw what she had missed.

Everything she'd ever wanted was there in abundance, a hurtful plenty, and all of it given to me.

She opens her eyes and drinks the cold coffee, then looks at the sludge, tipping the cup.

'I don't know why I told you that – I don't dwell on it.'

'I know you don't, Mum. I understand.'

My words make her frown. She's looking at me now and I think she is about to ask me something but she changes her mind, closing her mouth on the subject but still perplexed, realising that I do understand, that I know love can become too presumptuous, the object invisible.

Stretching towards me she tucks my hair behind my ears. Her touch is brief. We can hear movement upstairs – the soft noise of a drawer closing, then the same drawer closing again. Gran has woken up. Mum leans back, closes her eyes and tilts her face up to the ceiling, smiling.

'I'm sorry, Aggie.'

'Me too.'

She is wearing her apron and still has a huge towel tied round her waist. The knot at the back arches her spine but she looks comfortable, as if she is enjoying the flex. When she leaves the room I move quickly onto the chair and curl up in her body heat, pondering all she has said.

I'm feeling less troubled, even though I know I shouldn't, not considering what has happened, but the fact is the spindly tree survives; that meagre, self-pruning line of Kirkpatrick Brody Copella Thackeray women is stronger than I thought and I can see the lesson in those gnarled trees now, the ones that look finished but still produce fruit.

The voices above me are singing. *My bonnie lies over the ocean, my bonnie lies over the sea . . .*

In a book, this would be their time – a daughter bathing her aged mother, washing her hair. It would be a period of intimacy and forgiveness, of letting go.

But that's not how it is.

THE NOISE of my keys landing on the sideboard in the hall is too sharp, as if the wooden surface has turned to glass. I am suddenly alert and ready to soften my tread. All the doors in the hall are closed, which is very unusual and probably explains the echoing keys, the chopping and bouncing back. I prefer to keep doors open, even at night, I think because when I moved into my own room at home – made with love and housing brand-new in-scale plumbing – I felt cut off, buried in the basement like an unwanted relative, but unable to say because it would sound ungrateful and might hurt Dad's feelings. Out of sight and probably out of mind, at least with the door open I could hear the noises from the kitchen. Alasdair, on the other hand, prefers doors to do their job. He likes to keep certain things in and certain things out, and won't loosen up about it. To him an open door is 'an architectural ache' (his own ponderous phrase) – a kind of functional neglect that probably bothers him because of his early experience of abandonment (I remember his impassive look when I suggested this – the way he didn't move other than to push the door with his foot so it closed quietly, shutting me out).

'Alasdair?'

'In here.'

The kitchen window is open as wide as it will go. He is tipping old vegetables onto a newspaper that he has spread on the table – soft velvety cabbage and sprouting potatoes, half a turnip, a dull onion whose purple skin has puckered like a crushed clove. He's wearing a tartan fleece that makes my heart flip because I don't recognise it. *How can he buy clothes at a time like this?* I still have my coat on and I pull my collar up, folding my arms.

'It's freezing – what are you doing?'

'Letting out the smell.'

I watch him parcel up the debris and drop it into the bin. He stands at the sink and pulls up the sleeves of his Macbeth fleece.

'That's new.'

'It's an old one. I ran out of clothes.'

'It's nice – you suit blue.'

'Thanks.'

At last he looks up from his hands and I try to catch his eye but he's looking at the ceiling now.

'You've done a good job.'

When he pushes his hands into his trouser pockets I lean back against the worktop and try to relax, keep my breathing regular. He leans back too, so we both know that more will be said. Our gaze falls naturally onto the table, where I notice he has propped up the mail between the salt and the pepper. To the front, facing out, is a letter from Kenneth – his writing as lovely as the entries I tried to read whenever he opened that fancy moleskin notebook of his.

Looking at this letter, I picture the wild message within.

Dear Aggie, come with me to Southampton. I will raise high the roof beam and bring home jars of weather. You can open them whenever you want. I will never tire of your questions. Bring your tree lights and a pair of Wellingtons. Love, Kenneth x

We both stare at the envelope. *Aggie Brody Copella* has never looked more beautiful. He bends from the waist, torso straight and checking his feet – shifting them into a single black square.

'How's the ankle?'

'It's fine. Only hurts when I laugh.'

'That's good. And how's your gran?'

'Mad as a skunk.'

He's quizzed by something, but lets it go. Despite the ceiling, the kitchen has turned gloomy, the day shrinking under an intense cold. I shiver and move towards the window but Alasdair is closer and intercepts, closing it and turning the snib.

'Thanks.'

We're on the same side of the room now. I'm just three squares along, an ivory pillar of strength – ready to talk or not talk, whatever works best.

Then he speaks.

'Dad said you were round at the house. Sorry I wasn't there.'

So where were you? I want to ask, but I am tight as a clam – reticent because until he *really* speaks, until he gets beyond the platitudes, he is a stranger: a man in the kitchen wearing jeans and a tartan fleece, possibly just passing through. Here to collect.

He looks at me.

'I was out.'

'I know.'

'No – you don't know.'

'I know I don't . . .' And I am nodding because he must understand this; he must appreciate that I don't *know* anything. He needs to tell me what he means.

And he does.

He tells me he has been seeing a counsellor every Sunday for months. He's been talking about his life and the fact that he isn't worth a damn, that he has been a disappointment to everyone, for which he apologises. Not that he gives a toss; that's the problem. He wants to feel something. He wants to join in with the misery, break out from his frozen watchfulness.

297

Stop the perpetual pedalling and come home.

'Where is home?' I ask (because I am done assuming), and he tells me he doesn't know, so I move three squares along and one up, then I unzip my coat and draw him into the trapped heat.

Lady in the Dark

IT HAPPENED while Mum watched Mr Merdle's death and the collapse of Merdle's Bank send shockwaves through London for the second time. That's what she found so unforgivable, the fact that she had already seen the very last episode of *Little Dorrit* and had enjoyed it so much that two days later she set the alarm for ten to two in the morning and got up to watch the repeat.

If she'd had an iPlayer it would never have happened. Gran would not have squeezed her feet – fat with socks – into a pair of rediscovered size-five satin shoes and descended the four heavenly steps, attracted by the light shining under her door and the sound of her father calling from the room below. She could not make him out, but could hear the urgency, and knew he was calling her, and that he had probably found a lamb stiff with cold and had brought it in to thaw.

When Mum found her lying in the hallway she was chalk white and completely still – seemingly dead, or nearly dead, buried in her own swaddling and approaching the final amnesia with the same pathos as old Mr Dorritt.

'I READ somewhere that good dementia care is like an alpine meadow, whereas poor care is like a plantation of conifers.'

'What.'

Alasdair's question lacked the usual inflexion, which should have been a warning.

'It all comes down to interactions, there's an ecology to it – lots and lots of wee conversations flourishing here and there, where the staff understand the power of subjective truth.'

'Here's a subjective truth – I don't want to hear it. You promised to drop the dialectics when we were in social situations, Aggie, and I consider this a social situation.'

We had come to Lidl to buy Gran a box of individually wrapped amaretti biscuits because I thought she would enjoy the Christmassy smell and rustle and colour of each glitzy parcel, the bright papers twisted at each end in traditional sweetie style so all you had to do was pull.

Gran is lost in the vast conifer plantation that is Ninewells Hospital. She should have been admitted to the local hospital – but that's gone. In her local hospital, someone on the staff would know her or have heard of her; someone would know she's the old woman who keeps the orchard at number eight, which has the oldest pear tree in the burgh, maybe even in Scotland; they'd know she has a daughter who keeps herself to herself, just like she does – an elusive beauty (even now) whose husband is from that wealthy family who own part of the estate surrounding the old monastery. They used to lease Mugdrum Island to graze their sheep, and word is the son-in-law was cut off without a penny by his mother (that's how much he loved his wife). They might even know there's a granddaughter who visits every week (though probably not).

In the local hospital there would have been hooks for Gran to hold on to, an occasional glimmer of light suggesting a familiar place not too far off, even if she has forgotten it. But Ninewells is miles and miles away, and it is huge – one of the biggest teaching hospitals in Europe, someone said. Its corridors are longer than the High Street; its walls are festooned with garish paintings and do not bulge. Nobody knows her there. It is a forest of dead space where the trees are in rows and nothing grows between them. I want to take her out and lead her to an alpine meadow where there is grace and beauty, and where, in-between the trees, wild flowers sway in the long grass.

When we visit, she doesn't know who we are. She is wearing a nightie that does not belong to her but Mum says don't bother the nurses, they have more important things to worry about, and anyway, her blue nightdress should have been flung out long ago. Dad is telling her who's who, going at her pace, starting over whenever she gets distracted by the bump on her right thumbnail.

'How did that happen?' she says, and when he has named us all again she asks him who she is, then she falls asleep, suddenly, as if she's been drugged.

WE ARE still raw, Alasdair and me. Tender with each other and taking care to listen, we apply our brains to it when we'd rather not. He is wrapping David and Di's presents – an olivewood cheeseboard and a case of lip-smacking cheeses delivered from a Highland dairy near Inverness (including Scottish brie and gouda, 'perfectly legal' he said as soon as my eyebrow started to climb). I am making a mushroom and sweetcorn bake with ingredients that are 'on the turn' – stale bread and rubber button caps, milk (slightly sour), some bad cheddar. It is the kind of survival cooking I enjoy – tearing bread into lumps and cramming the blender, grabbing the machine when it's on and strangling it. With only one thing going on at a time (tearing, cramming, strangling), and nothing that needs much attention, there is room to talk – and because this isn't a social situation I'm talking about the malignant social psychology of hospital care, and how wrong it is to think that Gran's deterioration is the result of a neurological process that has its own autonomous dynamic.

'Eh?'

Alasdair is not aware of the malignant culture, or that we are all complicit; he doesn't know, for instance, that sending Gran to a hospital miles away from anything familiar is a kind of banishment. I can see from the look on his face that he thinks I'm crazy, so I let it go. It's my first attempt at keeping the promise I made when we agreed to change something about ourselves (without having to say what); I pulled out the *Giant Road Atlas of Europe* and with the solemn placing of hands over Bologna we made silent pledges. Mine was to practise 'letting go' and these cheeses are my first opportunity. I don't resent them, but I am suspicious of them. There is something fishy about the fact that Alasdair came back on the very day they were delivered.

'Lucky you were here or I would have sent them back.'

But I'm letting it go – the 'heaven on a spoon' curd, the brie and the gouda, the waxy one that has been smoked with the shavings of an oak whisky barrel. I'm giving them all the benefit of the doubt and settling for luck.

I AM worried about Mum. She is lost and can't relax. The sense of relief that she longed for hasn't come, and at night, with moonlight falling on the trees, she doesn't sleep. She has turned the chair to the window in the living room again and sometimes she just sits there in the dark drinking Barleycup. When Dad asks her what she is thinking about she says, 'Nothing – I'm just waiting.'

'Come to bed – wait there.'

We crave her attention, Dad and me. 'Rest!' we say, and we want her to, but not like this – drifting up river like the Lady of Shalott. You'd think, all things considered, we could just leave her to it, it's not like she wouldn't come back.

Would she come back?

There has been another pretty shake of snow. I have brought my Christmas lights and put them in the back porch, hidden under a pile of empty fruit crates. As Mum and I leave for the hospital I give Dad the nod – that's all I can do, the rest is down to him, and I know from the single tremor in his left eye that everything will be ready by the time we get back.

She sleeps during the drive, her face lit by the passing headlights – looming like a mask suspended above a ghost train. I adjust my mirror to look at her, so we can talk if she wakes, but she sleeps all the way.

The biscuits go down well, even though Gran has forgotten how to untwist the wrappers, forgotten the way a pull causes spin.

'Silver,' she says, smiling as she explores the pretty thing. I stretch over the bed to help her. 'Careful,' says Mum, 'I'll do it.'

She takes off her coat and drapes it over the chair. I'm astonished to see she is wearing the cream jumper with Prussian blue pansies that Dad gave her all those years ago.

'Wow!'

'You think?'

'Definitely!'

She looks awkward but pleased, pulling at the waistband to straighten the folds.

'You look different. What is it?'

'It's the jumper.'

'No. It's not that.'

She opens her bag and takes out a bottle of *Je Reviens*.

'Actually, hang on, Mum – I've got something here.'

I've brought an early Christmas present, wrapped in thin paper, and loosely taped so it will open easily.

'Merry Christmas, Gran.'

She thanks me very formally and opens the gift, slipping her thumb along the seams of Sellotape to preserve the paper. There is a new tremor, something more pronounced than the static charge that typically builds in her unearthed hands; I suspect it is drug-related, the involuntary kick of a medicinal cocktail, and despite all the care she takes to unwrap the parcel, the paper tears again and again, tattered by the sudden jerks of a prescribed palsy.

She is upset, horrified by the destructive impulse of these old hands. I quickly gather up the paper and push it into my pocket. When she discovers the talc she smiles. It is a wondrous thing, pleasing in every way; the golden container has the look of an ancient Egyptian treasure, a phial from Nefertiti's chamber, still imbued with the faint smell of water lilies floating on the Nile.

'Ooo – look, Mum, Lily of the Valley.'

'Mum,' says Gran, laughing (something about the word, or its application).

Holding the talc between them, Mum reads out the label. 'Powdery notes – that sounds lovely, Aggie. How come?'

'Well, she deserves a treat, don't you, Gran? It's much finer than that other stuff, better for your skin.'

I take the *Je Reviens* to the sink area and drop it in the bin.

Mum sits on the bed and clasps Gran's hands for a moment to still them.

'Let me help you, Mum.'

As her daughter powders and smoothes each glassy hand, Gran notices the strange blooms on Mum's jumper.

'Flowers – you suit the blue,' she says, gazing at Venus and seemingly transfixed, as if this woman has just emerged from the sea. We sit, wordless and content amongst the lilies, just the powder and the smoothing – nothing else. This is where love flows best, lapping at the foot of a hospital bed, a whole sea of it meandering in on a low tide.

When she is finished, Mum closes the top on the talc and puts it on the bedside locker.

'You can keep that one here until you get home.'

Taking Gran's right hand, she strokes it, running her thumb over the bump in the nail, then she guides Gran's fingers over the dent in her own thumbnail.

'Look – I've got one too. We must be related!'

'I hope so,' says Gran, and I add my hand to the loving pile, our lifelines fusing under the same skin.

THE DOCTOR describes Gran's X-rays as 'very interesting'. He peers at the screen with what looks like admiration, not because her bones are reasonably dense for her age, or because there are no breaks (thanks to the multiple skirts that cushioned her fall), but because of the shadowy trace of previous fractures that must have happened a very long time ago, probably when she was young. Beckoning us closer, he points a few of them out; some we see and some we don't – ghostly lines, faint as bird tracks.

He tells us there have been one or two thoracic compression fractures, which are usually asymptomatic, so she probably didn't know; but there is a long-bone injury too, and an old crack in her pelvis that would have been very painful when she walked. She has never mentioned them, and we have no explanation. In strange shock we speculate – Mum mentions her work on the farm, the physical demands of it and the risk of injury; and I recount the picture of Gran on a horse, cantering through the Nithsdale hills without saddle or shoes.

I have another view, an explanation I cannot share – a dark paragraph from a book about women and something called 'psychiatric modernism'; when I read it the words stuck, and now they are memory. Those fine cracks in her bones look like the morbid skeletal injuries associated with ECT. In those days, before the advent of muscle-relaxant drugs, the spasms were so powerful that patients had to be held down, and fractures were not uncommon.

Bones did crack.

'Ah well,' the doctor says, turning away from the screen at last (we had long since drawn back, our hearts heavy), 'I suppose we shall never know now.'

When we get home Mum tells Dad what the nurses told her – that Gran will be transferred to either ward 18 or 22, they're not sure which.

'They said it depends on what the psychiatrist says, but what does she know – she's never there.'

He brings out a bottle of Baileys and won't take no for an answer.

'Take your coat off, Mary – you and Aggie go upstairs and sit down. I'll get some ice.'

'Go on, Mum. I'll bring up a tray.'

When she leaves I pull out some glasses and Dad fiddles about with an ice-tray.

'Hurry up, Dad.'

Eventually a few snowy balls are released into each glass.

'OK. Is everything set?'

'Everything's set.'

And with a thumbs-up from Dad I carry the tray of drinks to the living room, where I find Mum sitting in the dark with her coat on and her back to the room, gazing out into the night.

'What do you think happened to her, Aggie?'

And here, I am glad of the dark.

'I don't know, Mum, but whatever it was she recovered.'

'Do you think so?'

My reply is silence – but we will not be swallowed up.

'Here – this is for you.'

I push the glass into her hand and she cradles it, sipping from the rim. Suddenly there is burst of light in the garden and there she is – Ginger Rogers all lit up in a crusted bodice of silver stars, her skirt flaming under the red glow of the lanterns that hang from her outstretched arms, and where the bark has fallen away, the smooth curve of a leg flashing in the moonlight, modest and daring all at once.

There is a flush on Mum's cheeks, a blush, or the sudden warmth of the liqueur, or maybe just the glow from the lanterns catching her lovely face. I am looking at her, rapt and still puzzling over the difference I noticed earlier, when suddenly, as she leans forward to look at the tattered hem of Ginger's dress, I see what it is – smoky wisps of hair curling onto her shoulders, longer than ever.

She must be growing it.

FLOSSIE'S WEDDING invitation arrived on the same day as her Christmas card. She will marry on the 23rd of January – a humanist ceremony, followed by a celebratory knees-up in the McKendrick Guildhall. There is no gift list, and children and dogs are welcome. The proximate date, whenever mentioned, elicits a range of looks, and normally I would throw in my own – but I'm keen to make up for things and remain aloof. Alasdair remembers the groom from his student days and 'can't believe it' but won't say why. After a long and futile argument I have to accept his refusal to tell as an expression of his moral rectitude, and of course, I'm not in any position to object given the scale of my own undisclosed truths, discretions I can never share (although they will undoubtedly surface when my own cuckoo comes).

Alasdair thinks I should go back to university. He says I

need to channel my relentless logic into something less personal, explore duality without dragging the family into it. He compared me to Dostoevsky again, pronounced it with a smugness that made him out to be the clever one – so I compared him to T.C. from *Top Cat* (and not just because of his colouring). I think Alasdair has a Freudian understanding of women; we are a dark continent that he finds hard to navigate, and when I say this he agrees, closing his eyes and fumbling across my body – kissing my elbow and tonguing the back of my knee.

'It's not about logic,' I say. 'It's about love.'

He groans and slips from the darkness, sliding out from the bottom of the bed and disappearing into the shower.

I wrap myself in his dressing gown and go into the living room. The fire looks cold in the grate, but if I hold my hands close to the ash there is life, the warmth of a breath on my skin. The arctic poppies have dropped like petals from a dead rose and are strewn along the mantelpiece. I gather them up and throw them on the fire.

In the kitchen Kenneth's letter is still on the table, still sealed and lying face down amongst the rest of the unopened mail. I take it to the bedroom and slip it into the canvas bag I keep in the wardrobe. The bag is crammed with course books and folders – almost too heavy to lift. I've not looked at them since the day I left university. I manage to inch the bag out slightly then try to push it back with what I still refer to as my sore foot – but it doesn't budge, and because it's blocking the doors I grasp the handles and pull it free, dragging it over to where it used to sit between the table and the bookshelves.

Curling up on the bed, I look at it from across the room as if it is a dog, as if Carrie has come home and I am testing her obedience. She doesn't move.

I am almost asleep when the phone rings.

'Guess what!'

'What.'

'Guess!'

'I've no idea.'

'Thomas is sitting on his own!'

'He's alone?'

'No! Not alone – by himself. He's sitting up by himself looking at the fairy-lights!'

I picture his wonder, his miraculous brain exploding like a firecracker under the random explosions of light. Fiona's joy unbends me, despite the ache in my stomach.

I tell her I'm sore.

'Is it your period?'

'No – I think it might be withdrawal pains, or—'

But before I can say any more there is a dull thud that I assume to be Tufty's head hitting the floor, and she is gone.

As I lie back with my head on the pillow, the room no longer tilts like a sinking ship; my optic pathways have fully recovered and are now surveying the mess. I look again at the bag full of books, the unopened letter crushed inside and beating like a heart.

Soon I will get up. I will dress, brush my hair, try to get into the spirit – inject some sparkle, despite having no lights (they are elsewhere, blazing in the orchard every night, the Baileys replaced now with something more sophisticated – a cocktail made with lime juice and ginger syrup and proper Plymouth gin). Alasdair hasn't said anything about getting a tree, but he has painted over the small patch of barley on the kitchen ceiling, and I have pegged out the Christmas cards – a single string of bunting smiling blindly above the fireplace.

It is enough for now.

I close my eyes and surrender at last to the heavy yearning that has pulled me down for so long. There is a girl in the distance. I call her name but she can't hear me, she's too far off, tending to a horse. She presses her face against his cheek, her head tilting upwards as if she is talking to him. His back burns without flame in the cold air. Sliding her hand down his neck, she steps clear. The horse gallops away and at last she descends from the familiar hill. I want her to look up and wave. I call and call but it is the wrong name. Only the landscape listens. She is disappearing, walking along the old drove road that snakes towards the moors, her bare feet slapping on the stones.